D1016930

# Reapers

## Books by Frederick Ramsay

The Ike Schwartz Mysteries
*Artscape*
*Secrets*
*Stranger Room*
*Choker*

The Botswana Mysteries
*Predators*
*Reapers*

Other Novels
*Impulse*
*Judas*

# Reapers

Frederick Ramsay

Poisoned Pen Press

Poisoned Pen Press
6962 E. First Ave., Ste. 103
Scottsdale, AZ 85251
www.poisonedpenpress.com
info@poisonedpenpress.com

Printed in the United States of America

*To Raymond Strait, author and friend, who, after reading a few pages of my first attempt at novel writing, insisted I had produced a Best Seller, an estimate which I heartily endorsed. As it turned out, we were dead wrong about that, but it was enough encouragement to keep me trying until I learned how to write properly. For that, many thanks.*

# Acknowledgments

As always, a shout-out to the folks at Poisoned Pen Press who labor mightily to make these little stories come to life. To them, and to Robert my publisher, and Barbara my editor, go special thanks for moving this project forward. Not every book falls out of the sky, alas. Some we struggle with and these good folk help us muddle through. Thanks also to my line editors, Glenda and Connie, for chasing down and rectifying my somewhat erratic and original notions of the rules of grammar. They know better than most that I never met a comma I didn't like. Thanks also to my son, Dr. Jeff Ramsay, a resident of Botswana, who vetted this book, helped with many of its themes and, hopefully, kept us both out of trouble. And last but not least, to Susan, who puts up with this year after year. It can't be the money and it certainly is not the fame.

Some necessary caveats: The persons, events, and institutions described in the book, particularly as they relate to Botswana, are necessarily of my own invention and any resemblance they might bear to persons living or dead is, as we say, pure coincidence. That said, the circumstances fictionalized as occurring in the Congo and the nascent presence in Africa of the Russian Mafia are drawn from the news. With respect to the former Belgian Congo, it is a sad fact that our Western preoccupation with the events in the Middle East has led us to overlook the tragedies ongoing in Central Africa. The facile but inaccurate assumption that the civil war that has raged in the area is somehow caused by diamonds creates an unfortunate disconnect to the facts. The sad truth is that the slaughter occurring there, its numbers allegedly approaching those attributed to the Holocaust, is fueled by the industrialized nations' covetous, and one might say historic, exploitation of the area's mineral wealth, not the least of which being coltan, the admixture of niobium and tantalum. Our insatiable lust for all things electronic, from smart phones to gaming devices and all the miniature capacitors they require, has created a Frankenstein's monster of epic proportions. One which may soon come to haunt the very appetites that spawned it in the first place.

And with that bright and cheerful bit said, enjoy *Reapers* and *Patriarche*, a survivor from whom we could and should learn many things.

*Even as I have seen, they that plow iniquity,*
*and sow wickedness, reap the same.*
— Job 4:8 KJV.

# Chapter One

The silver back *Patriarche*, the Old One, raised his massive head and peered down the hillside through the underbrush where he'd been grazing. He'd heard the sound trucks made before. It meant something bad would happen soon. He looked to his left and right at the fifteen mountain gorillas that now constituted his troop. There used to be more, nearly twenty. One or two had drifted away to form new groupings, but most had fallen to the ravages of the creatures who now drove up in their noisy, smelly machines. He would have to move again. When his bipedal cousins arrived, the ones who dug in the earth and hunted his kind, it would be unwise to linger. Now he must make his third move in as many months. The area he could comfortably control had become smaller with each of these moves and he would soon be crowding the neighboring troop and that could lead to a different sort of conflict.

He took inventory of his family. The young male who would someday pose a threat to his leadership was not in sight. He called out. Heads jerked up, some from dozing. No response from the male. *Patriarche* lumbered off his haunches and shuffled toward the sound of the engines. Then he heard the crack of the rifle and the scream of the missing male. He turned and signaled for the others to follow him. They would go higher and deeper into the forest.

The coltan miners had arrived.

◇◇◇

It had taken more money in bribes than he'd planned to spend to cross the borders from the Congo into Zambia and thence into Botswana. His cash supply had dwindled. Border guards wanted stable currencies—Euros, Pounds, or Dollars— always in short supply in these parts. Money changers charged exorbitant fees for them. And then, Botlhokwa's man had been especially greedy. Somehow he'd imagined with the connection to the ranger that there would be free, or at least cheap, access to the park. He wouldn't worry about that now. He'd pass the costs along to his sponsors in any case. It just angered him that this person had taken advantage of the cause. Different arrangements must be made before the next run.

He'd managed to slip through the fence where he'd been told without incident, and now bounced along in the dark with only night vision goggles to show him the way. He wondered what he'd allowed himself to commit to, how many more times he'd have to make this or a similar trip to some other river, some other alien outback. Fanaticism was one thing, practicality quite another. He steered through the bush with caution. Jungles he knew. The bush might be similar, but in the challenges it presented it was different, or so it seemed to him.

He kept his eyes on the GPS device he'd been provided, steering toward the coordinates set earlier. When the device emitted a gentle beep he braked and shut down the engine. With the motor off, he lowered the windows to allow air to circulate. It was hot and humid in the Chobe National Park. Perhaps there would be rain. He'd heard of the drought in the country. Everyone had. It constituted one of the reasons he sat alone in the middle of the game park in the early morning hours. He adjusted his night vision goggles and surveyed his surroundings. His view was defined by the infra-red signatures, the glowing shades of green that merged into form from the darkness and then passed by him as if underwater. A few gazelle drifted by in the dark, grazing with a larger herd of kudu. Bright emerald points marked their eyes. They seemed skittish. A predator must be close by. As if on cue, a pack of hyenas, ghost-like in the green glow, drifted into view. The kudu wheeled and faced them, heads lowered, horns shining in the dim light. The pack hesitated. Should they risk a slashing and possibly lethal foray against those horns, or not?

The crack of the rifle scattered the animals in all directions. The driver of the Land Rover never heard it. By the time the sound of the report would have reached his ears the projectile, traveling at something like fifteen hundred feet per second, had reduced the left side of his skull to wet confetti. The right side, that facing the shooter, bore only a small but very ugly entry wound. The impact knocked him sideways. His arm pressed the horn button and it continued to wail until a late model Toyota Land Cruiser pulled along side. Its driver alit and looked in the truck, staggered back with a curse, and waved his companion out of the second vehicle. He shoved the body away from the steering wheel. The arm fell away and the horn went silent. The second man stepped from the passenger side, glanced into the truck, and saw the body. He too, cursed. Then he walked to the rear of the Land Rover, removed four large bundles which he transferred to the Toyota, and slammed the rear closed. His partner released the hand brake on the Land Rover and the two of them shoved it forward. It gained momentum and rolled down the gentle grade toward the water. Satisfied it would go far enough—hopefully into the river itself—they brushed their footsteps away with a frond from a nearby bush, backed, turned, and drove away.

The Land Rover with its corpse came to rest in a shallow wash several hundred meters down the track.

Andrew Takeda had the Hi-Lux in gear and had started toward his contact when he heard the shot. He froze, foot pressed against the clutch and brake pedals, and still positioned behind the stand of acacia where he'd parked while he waited for the delivery from the Congo. He watched as the new Toyota SUV drove up and two men alit, watched as they unloaded the Land Rover, watched as they drove away. Who? No, not who. What sort of person disliked this particular mission so much they would kill an innocent man and destroy material that could heal and restore the planet? He waited until they were well away, reversed and drove off in a different direction.

This was not good.

Yuri Greshenko had never struck Leo Painter as one to gush. His checkered past had taught him caution in his speaking. Caution with a capital C—taciturn hardly covered it. Yet he waxed ecstatic on this bit of sporting news.

"Why? Because it's the biggest sports event in the world, Mr. Painter. Bigger than the Super Bowl and your World Series combined. Bigger even than the summer Olympics. That's why. It's an opportunity for us that will not come again in years, maybe ever. The bookings are pouring in."

"Which means what, exactly?"

"Money. There will be millions of people flooding into South Africa for the football—"

"You mean soccer."

"Everywhere in the world, it's called football except in the USA, Australia, and maybe New Zealand, but that's not the point. If we can finish the hotel and the casino in time, you could have a very big payday. The hotel at least."

"The event is in South Africa and it involves soccer fans—"

"Football fans."

"Okay, football fans. I've seen some of those fans on television. I'm not sure I want a gang of drunken thugs from Manchester or Spain piling into my casino and wrecking the place."

"Those are not the only people who are attending, I do not think, and if they do, they will not be the ones interested in flying north to the Chobe for relaxation at a high-end hotel and casino. Think about this instead—Sheiks from Dubai, oil men from

Saudi Arabia and Venezuela, capitalists, autocrats, communists even, all with a great deal of money to spend. There is a rumor that some Koreans will be in the Okavango, plus movie stars, celebrities, and the beautiful people."

"The what? You read too many magazines, Yuri. Beautiful People? I have yet to discover anything beyond the physical that could fairly be described as beautiful about any of them, and even the physical bit is a stretch for some."

"Nevertheless, these people will attend the matches. There is a limit to how much time the super rich will rub shoulders with the *hoi polloi*. Then they will be interested in our Chobe International Lodge and Casino. We can put large screen televisions in the gaming room and make book on the matches."

"If you say so. It's not exactly a sport that plays well in the States."

"Your USA team is in the mix. They could be a sleeper. They very nearly defeated Brazil earlier. Think of the possibilities."

"Brazil? I should be impressed by that? What is significant about *nearly* defeating Brazil?"

"Brazil is consistently the top team in the world, or nearly so. Yes, to give them such a close match is an important measure of the quality of a team."

Leo Painter sighed. He'd fixed his plans for the hotel and casino firmly in his mind. He had established a time line and saw no reason to alter it. Responding to this business meant changing things. He had stepped down as the president and CEO of Earth Global precisely because he wished to avoid this sort of hurry-up pressure. He no longer trusted his health, his heart in particular, to manage the stress of running the second largest mining and energy company in the world. He was content to serve as its chairman of the board, draw down an obscenely large compensation and benefits package, and dabble in projects like the hotel he was building on the Chobe River in northern Botswana. Putting himself into another high stress situation did not hold any appeal for him what-so-ever. Money, as his wife reminded him almost daily, was not everything. She was wrong, of course, but one recent near death experience convinced him that he might, in fact, have accumulated enough. Still as they say, money is money.

Yuri Greshenko was seven years younger, and had a concomitant energy reserve. Leo no longer tried to keep up with him. He thought it must have something to do with Yuri's being born and raised in Siberia. Leo had visions of that vast land, youths trudging to school through waist deep snow, fighting off large bears or wolves, and being disciplined by steely eyed school masters in uniforms with billed caps and looking remarkably like Tom Courtney in *Dr. Zhivago*. Greshenko had tried to disabuse him of this picturesque but hopelessly romantic notion, but Leo clung to it. He preferred his history to be colorful and Hollywood, thank you. The real stuff was too depressing. Charlton Heston *was* Moses and if Oliver Stone wanted to give Jack Kennedy a pass, what was the harm in that?

"I think we should get more crews on the job. At the rate we're going there will not be enough rooms. The labor market is very good here. We can do it."

"Can they pour concrete, set footings? We need experienced people."

"Our problem is not with the locals, Leo. Of course we can get that kind of labor. The problem is whether our Finnish module suppliers can manufacture and ship the rooms faster."

The hotel and casino had been designed to allow a quick and efficient build. Greshenko, calling on one of his myriad and, Leo thought, suspect connections, had discovered a firm in Finland that prefabricated rooms and suites for cruise ships. The modules were delivered completely furnished with *en suite* bath and were slipped into a steel framework. Plumbing and wiring were modular and accessible through a single back panel. They could just as easily be bolted into place on a permanent framework on land. The design/build team had easily reconfigured the ship modules to accommodate single and two room units. They arrived weekly at the Cape Town Container

Terminal to be off-loaded and carried by truck to Kasane and thence to the Lodge.

"You think?"

"Absolutely. And also investors, Leo, new, foreign investors. We can make money and we can acquire partners. The government will be happy to see new and diversified investment in the country. If a nation has its foot in the door, so to speak…"

"Okay, okay, I get it. You talk to the Finns, I'll talk to the construction crew. We'll explain all this to the Board and Travis Parizzi after the fact. Send him the bill. What's he going to do, fire me?"

# Chapter Two

Strong Turkish coffee and the scent of cinnamon filled the room. Only a single desk lamp provided light, save for the small Sterno can that sent blue-pink flame flickering against the underside of an urn placed on a scarred teak sideboard. Two men slouched in leather chairs while a third, behind the desk, spooned sugar into a teacup. Outside the sun eased over the horizon painting the eastern sky brilliant orange and gold.

"The goods were intact I assume?" he said.

"Have you gone crackers? There's nothing but rubbish in those parcels."

"What? I thought you told me—"

"Never mind what I told you. You heard me right, rubbish, small cone-like things that look like some toddler's kindergarten clay project. What are we supposed to do with them, hey? We were lied to. That Botlhokwa's man as much as said there would be rhinoceros horns shipped in from the north. He said the people paid them money to cross the border."

"Did he, or did he not say horns?"

The man paused and thought. "Okay, maybe I didn't understand him right. He definitely said priceless and we'd been talking of horns earlier. Either way, there should have been something worth going after out there."

"Then Botlhokwa's man took you for whatever you paid him."

The second man held the sniper rifle across his lap and rubbed the barrel with an oily rag. He smiled, remembering. "Nice piece you give me here. Very fine shot too, if I do say it. One hundred meters in the dark and spot on."

"You should have seen," the other man said, nodding. He high-fived the first, an Americanism they'd picked up in Cape Town.

"That man will pay for this. He said this person would be bringing goods to the Chobe Game Park. You paid him for that information, for value received you could say, and he'll deliver or…" His voice trailed off.

The rifle bearer opened the weapon's breach and applied the rag to its inner workings. "And you're going to mess with the big man's muscle? I don't think so, *Bas*. There are too many of them to tangle with and who have you got?"

The remark was greeted with a dry laugh. "At the moment, only you two."

"Oh, no you don't, Sczepanski. You haven't paid us for the last dance. You don't get another until you do."

The man identified as Sczepanski paused, tea cup in mid-transit to his mouth. "You forget who you work for. There are things that happen to people who refuse to follow orders. The police might be interested in how that dead man in the park got that way, for example."

"You are not that stupid, *Bas*. You cannot go to the police and you know it."

"An anonymous tip on the telephone?"

"That leads to us, but also to you. We do not go down but you go with us."

The man holding the rifle slapped the bolt closed, raised the piece to his shoulder, and swung it around so that it pointed at the man behind the desk. He pulled the trigger and there was a soft double click. "Bang, you're dead, oops."

"A hundred meters," His friend said and smiled. "You should have seen it."

"If killing is what you are thinking about, do not press your luck. You will cross me and end up that way yourself. We do not play silly games here. You two dolts forget two things, one, who you are in the big scheme of things, and two, why we came north in the first place. One, Lenka sends us here to be the thin edge of the wedge. We are to test this Botlhokwa and his operation. Shooting someone, anyone, is not on the list. From now on, you check with me before you go hunting. And two, remember you are easily replaced."

The man's voice had turned icy. At the mention of Lenka the other two shut up and looked uneasily at each other.

Sanderson, recently promoted to the supervisor's position in her sector of the Chobe National Park, had taken a run into a portion of the park nearest to Kasane. It was a thing she did at least once a week. Other areas she assigned to other days. She rounded a large clump of acacia and saw the SUV, a Land Rover, the same as she was driving, but older and definitely dirtier. Its number plate indicated it had come from the Democratic Republic of the Congo, but she couldn't be sure about that. It looked as if it had been driven hard for many kilometers, so perhaps it had. The sun had been up for two hours and this open area of the bush had begun to heat up. She saw no sign of wildlife. That didn't mean there were none nearby. The bush was dangerous precisely because it concealed so many things. A pride of lions could be sleeping off their last feed behind any large clump of vegetation. Hyenas could be lurking, hoping for an easy kill. At night the leopard prowled. She circled the stranded vehicle. There did not seem to be either a driver or signs of life. The circuit complete, she braked, removed the rifle from the rack behind her and cautiously stepped out. Thumb on the safety, she approached the truck. That's when she caught the scent of death; a scent she was all too familiar with lately. She looked skyward. Yes, vultures had caught it and were circling.

"*Manong*," she muttered. "You must always be the first on the scene. I do no not like you, you death announcers."

She stepped up to the window and peered in. The man's body lay slumped across the front seat. That's when she saw the blood spatter and the rest of the detritus on the passenger side window and door. She stepped back. This was not for her. She returned to her truck and thumbed on her radio, switched to the police band and waited a moment. This meant she must deal with Superintendant Mwambe. She did not care for this man. The locals called him *Tshwene*, Baboon. It was not fair. He was not a baboon, but he certainly did try her patience. Perhaps he would assign someone else to this case. She engaged the talk button and called in the shooting.

The dispatcher answered. She recognized Derek Kgasa's voice. Apparently Superintendent Mwambe had finally found a task his nephew could actually do without endangering the populace of Kasane.

"Derek. Is that you?"

"Sanderson? Yes, what are you doing on the official police band?"

"I must report what appears to be a murder in the park. Here is a Land Rover sitting three kilometers from the main gate. A man—he looks Congolese but who can say—is in the front seat and dead with a hole in his head."

"Oh, my. That is very serious, isn't it?"

"A large hole in the head would be."

Silence.

"Derek? Are you there?"

"Yes, I am considering what I must do next. The man is definitely dead, you say?"

"Derek, listen to me. The man is being shot in the head some hours ago. You must send a car and investigators. The sun is up, the park is filled with scavengers. Even now the *manong* are circling. You must remove this body immediately." Sanderson knew Derek was not the brightest man on the force. They had gone to school together and he had become a policeman by default. By his own admission he lacked the necessary brain power to function as an officer of the law. He needed help. "Derek, is there an investigator available?"

"Yes, I think so."

"Can you put him into this conversation?"

"Wait." A minute passed and a male voice spoke.

"Who is this I am speaking to?"

"I am Sanderson, the game ranger. Are you an investigator?"

He was. Sanderson repeated the details to him. He acknowledged and said he would be there in twenty minutes. He would not need her to stay.

"But you do not know where this dead man is."

"You said three kilometers from the gate."

"That covers a great deal of territory, you know." Why, Sanderson wondered, were the police so thick when it came to dealing with their colleagues in the other services? "I will give you the precise coordinates. You can enter them in your GPS and you will come right to me. And I must stay in this place at least 'til you arrive. There are too many animals that would have your dead man for their breakfast if I don't."

She disconnected before the inspector thought to give her more orders. Foolish man, the park was her responsibility. She would tell *him* what to do.

It was more like half an hour before the police made their way to her. Superintendent Mwambe accompanied a young man who didn't look much older than her daughter, Mpitle. The two men alit and approached her.

"So, Sanderson. You have created another fine mess, I see."

"Superintendent Mwambe, I don't think this is my mess, but yours. There is a very dead man in this vehicle and you will have an investigation on your hands for certain."

This was not going to be a pleasant day.

# Chapter Three

Mwambe and the constable whose name, as it happened, was Carl Kgobela, Constable Carl Kgobela in fact, strolled to the vehicle and peered in.

"You seem to have a murder on your hands," Sanderson said as she prepared to leave.

"It is not a murder until the evidence says it is," the Superintendent said and cut her a look. Mwambe had little or no use for women in positions of authority and the sight of Sanderson had become a chronic source of annoyance for him.

Sanderson knew she shouldn't reply. She knew Mwambe's penchant for officiousness and that he would give her some hard words and looks, but she couldn't resist. "This man has a very large bullet wound in his head. There is blood and gore all over the interior of the truck. I am but a simple game ranger, but I would think that points to murder, Superintendent."

Mwambe scowled and looked in at the body. "It could be suicide, you know," he said. His petulant tone was the sort that always set Sanderson's teeth on edge.

"That seems to be a very large wound for a suicide and besides, if this man is shooting himself, where is the gun he is doing it with and why would he drive unknown into my park in the dark of the night to do this thing?"

"Those are questions the police are trained to answer, not women game rangers. You did not pick up a pistol?"

"I did not."

"It may have fallen on the ground or under the seat. Constable, look under this Land Rover and see if there is a gun."

The young man did as he'd been asked. He fell to his knees, leaned over and peered under the car. He shook his head and stood. Unbidden, he opened the door and searched under the seats. No gun. He shook his head once more.

"It will turn up, you will see. Ah, Sanderson, before you make me a gift of your amazing detective skills, I will point out to you that there are no other foot prints here but mine, yours, and Kgobela's. If someone shot this man, where is the evidence?" He offered her a smug smile and waved his hand toward the Land Rover. "Ah, you see that is the way police work is done."

Sanderson suppressed the temptation to scream and merely nodded. Mwambe was the most exasperating man she knew. She climbed into her SUV and left, following the track the dead man's Land Rover had made on its way in. She wished to know how this vehicle had managed to intrude into the park. A hundred meters up the track she stopped. Here, the ground had obviously been disturbed. She scanned the area with the eyes of someone used to studying the ground for tracks and evidence of recent movements by animals in her park. Someone had swept the area with a tree branch, it seemed. She thought she saw a partial foot print. She stepped out and circled the area. She found the tire tracks of another vehicle. She didn't relish another round with Mwambe, but he needed to know about this. He would not be happy with it, but he needed to know. Mwambe, she knew from past experience, preferred the quick and easy answer. Suicide would be the way to close this case—quick and easy. And there seemed to be something else attached to his eagerness to move away from the obvious but Sanderson could not think what it might be.

She turned and drove back to the murder scene. Kgobela looked up as she braked.

"Constable, can you tell me if the hand brake is set on this vehicle?"

The constable peered into the truck. "No, it is not."

"What is this, Sanderson?" Mwambe's stout figure loomed up behind the murder vehicle. "You are interfering in matters that do not concern you again."

"Superintendent, there is something you must see up the hill."

Exasperated, Mwambe looked at her for several seconds. "Go with her, Kgobela, and see this important thing."

Sanderson returned to the place where she'd found the tire marks and explained her conclusions.

"You see, he was met by at least one person, probably more. They shoot him and then release the brake. A little shove and the truck, it rolls down the hill to where we found it."

"Yes, that will fit. The superintendent will not be so happy with you, Sanderson."

"Oh yes? Well, he never is."

She returned the constable back to the scene. He stepped out and Sanderson left. She still had to find out how the man or men got into her park.

The rifle seemed particularly menacing in the half light. If the person at whom it was pointed had any fear, however, it did not show in either his demeanor or voice. He stood and stepped around the desk.

"Put that thing down, you idiot."

The man hesitated and lowered the sniper rifle's barrel, then he placed it butt down to the floor with near military precision. "What will you do?"

"I will find and then talk to this man of Botlhokwa, and if necessary to Mr. Big himself, and I will find out what he is doing with his lies. Lenka will want to know of this. Let me see the rubbish you took from the man in the park."

The three men exited the gloomy warehouse out into the morning sun. Kasane seemed cooler than normal for this time of year. They squinted against the bright light. The Land Cruiser sat a few meters from the door in the warehouse's parking lot. The years of oil leakage on its surface managed to override the scent of the blooming mango tree next to the door. The first man opened the boot. One of the parcels was open. The man with the rifle smashed at the contents with its butt.

"There, you see? The people here would say, *matlhakala,* trash."

They studied the debris. "It looks like someone rolled iron filings, pebbles, and powder of some sort and stuck it all together with what looks like the compound panel beaters use to smooth out the deeper dents in body work."

"Why would anyone transport this all the way from the north?"

One man shrugged. The other scratched his beard.

"Perhaps they wanted to test the route." The beard scratcher said. "They roll up this tripe to look vaguely like a parcel of rhino horns, you know, and bring it in to see if Botlhokwa's people could be trusted. If he failed them and they are caught, there would be nothing in the boot to incriminate them."

"Test the route for what?"

"What were we expecting to find?"

"*Ditshukudu…dinaka.*"

"Rhinoceros horns, exactly. Or any number of things, you see? They know the World Cup comes soon to South Africa. The place will be crawling with Arabs and Asians. They will have their national teams competing and reasons to be here with their private jets. You can be sure that there will be much smuggling done. All sorts of things will bring a big price. They will fly up here to stay at the big lodges, perhaps gamble at the new one the Americans are building. But, you see, before you sneak the things in, you must have a safe and sure entry. This man is doing what you could call a dry run."

"I guess Mr. Big has failed his test."

"What shall we do with this mess?"

"Get rid of it."

"Where?"

"I don't care. Think of something. There is that new lodge, the American one I just mentioned, going up on the river. They have a huge bin for their rubbish. Throw it in there. A little more shouldn't bother them."

The men nodded and closed the boot.

# Chapter Four

Sanderson settled herself in behind the wheel and, eyes focused on the unfamiliar set of tire tracks, followed them south, back the way they had come. She paused at the short bit of graded road that led to the park's main entrance and stared down its length. She could make out the building and archway that faced the main road. Had they come through there? The gate should have been locked but people, she knew, were susceptible to bribes. It was not a common thing but certainly a possibility. Her gaze shifted forward and she saw that the tire marks she'd been following continued on the other side of the road, still heading south into the forested area of the park. She dropped the Rover back in gear and crept on. The tracks twisted and turned through the bush, around trees and across small clearings. She stopped and looked back the way she'd come. She saw the fresh marks on the trees. Someone had blazed a trail with white painted arrows that could be easily followed at night. This was not a one-time thing.

After another three hundred meters she drew up short. The high fence that separated the paved road and the park blocked her way. There was no gate. She inspected the area for wildlife. One must always use care when walking through the bush and especially here in the forest. Who knew what might be sleeping behind a bit of shrubbery or lurking in a tree? She leaned on the horn. A Thompson's gazelle and its mate darted out into view and bounded down the track and into the trees where they turned to watch her.

She climbed down from her truck and walked to the fence, She saw where the vehicle had crossed into the park, seemingly straight through the fence. It seemed to be a well used crossing. The area was worn down by what appeared to be many tire marks. So, there had been more than one vehicle coming through here in the past. A large shrub grew in front of one of the fence's posts. She craned her neck to look behind it. The fence had been cut and was now held in place by a series of zip ties. There was a camo cloth bag filled with them tucked under the shrub and several, no, many cut and discarded ones lay on the ground nearby. This entrance had been the one the vehicle used to enter the park, certainly, but not it alone. Many vehicles had breached this fence in the past.

"Who?" she murmured under her breath, "Who is using my park this way and what are they doing that keeps them from coming through the main gate?" She knew of the poachers, of course, but they were mostly outsiders from Zimbabwe hard up for money, and speculators from the south who had a bustling market in restricted goods. They could do better in the north where the surveillance was not so intense. But where there was game, there were those who would kill it. That was an historical fact in these parts. She jerked at the fence. It seemed solid. If you did not know about the opening, you would never guess what it was possible to do here. She debated returning to Mwambe to tell him about the gap, but decided against it. He would simply tell her the police were not in the business of securing the park. It was her problem to deal with.

"I must find a way to watch this place at night. If I repair this fence, whoever is using it will simply cut a new way in somewhere else and it might take too long to find it. If they do not know that I know about it, perhaps I can find out who they are."

The gazelles, which had been watching her and presumably listening to her as well, seemed satisfied she had no bad intentions toward them. They lowered their heads and began to graze.

Sanderson climbed back into the truck and drove away. She had some thinking to do.

◇◇◇

Leo Painter left Greshenko working the phones to the manufacturing plant in Finland. He had partially succeeded, it seemed. Whether the delivery date for new modules could be advanced would depend on another contract the manufacturer had with a shipyard, they'd advised him. With the current slump in the world economy, the possibility that they might switch their production line over to Leo's project was viewed as both a certainty and a blessing. Blessings were not usually something ascribable to business undertakings with Leo, but in this case he guessed they were. He sometimes wondered about the presence of the Almighty in the sorts of transactions he'd engaged in, in his day. The shipyard was happy to postpone their build and the payments that would fall due for a few months and that would help them ride out the slump as well. It would be a win-win for all concerned. Leo left before Greshenko could fill him in on all the details. He'd heard all he needed to hear.

He paced to the perimeter of the building site, pausing from time to time to look at the stark skeletal framework the builders had erected from different points of view. In his mind's eye, however, he saw the finished structure, not the skeleton; glass and steel, thatch and wood trim, a combination of traditional and modern. He turned to walk back toward the workmen and noticed an unfamiliar SUV parked by his dumpster. Two men were hauling material from the rear of their truck and tossing it into the waste container.

"Hey," he yelled, "what the hell are you doing? This is private property."

The men spun around and looked at him. They exchanged some words he couldn't hear and turned back to their task, working faster.

"Hey, cut that out. Who are you?"

One man, the taller of the two, heaved what must have been the last sack into the bin, gave Leo a two finger salute, and the two jumped into the truck and drove off.

"Son of a…"

Leo walked over to the waste bin and peered in. All he saw was rubble. Well, not quite. Some of the material seemed to be crudely molded out of some sort of plastic into cones. He picked up a stick and poked through what they had left. No garbage. That was good. People seemed to think a large dumpster like this one—a skip, his foreman had called it—was a public utility. If you weren't careful it could soon be filled with garbage and that meant scavengers. In the States the worry would be rats. Here, an army of monkeys and insects large enough to carry off a small child would descend on the heap and it would take more time and cost more money to clean up than a modest war.

He pulled one of the cones out of the pile and turned it over in his hand. He glanced back into the rest of the rubbish and inspected some of the broken cones. There didn't seem to be anything to worry about. Some metal shavings, some powdery stuff. He dropped the cone beside the bin, then pushed it with his toe to one side to make a stop for the gate that stood open next to the road. The foreman had complained the gate kept swinging shut at all the wrong times. So, this would hold it. Problem solved.

He closed his eyes and pulled up an image of the SUV, a white Toyota, fairly new. He had a semi-photographic memory; if he saw an object, a page of newsprint, or something similar, he could often retain a visual of most of the details for an hour or two. It was a trick that had baffled, amused, and occasionally annoyed people with whom he did business. A good memory and an eye for details were worth two MBAs—the degrees, or the people who possessed them, take your pick. The license number. He wanted the license number, just in case. He pulled a small note book from his shirt pocket and jotted down what he could remember. You never knew.

# Chapter Five

The soldier who'd shot the gorilla had to fire twice more into the beast before it finally ceased its thrashing about and lay still. It required the help of three of his comrades to drag it out into the clearing where men and boys were busy widening the entrance to the "try dig" where the new vein of coltan had been exposed. In an hour or two it would be large enough for them wielding their shovels and pry bars to start chipping out the mineral that was so valued in the both the orient and the west. This would be a marked improvement over their last site which required they pan the minerals from a stream bed. Panning was slow and tedious work with a much lower yield per man hour and consequently more abuse from their captors.

Coltan, the object of this illegal intrusion into the forest of eastern Congo, is the mineralized form of niobium, formerly columbium, and tantalalum in various combinations and mixtures. Along with the country's other mineral wealth, it is mined and marketed to slake the burgeoning world-wide thirst for electronic devices and gadgets and, as an unintended consequence, helps fuel the seemingly endless conflict wars in the Congo. Wars having casualties rivaling those of the Holocaust, wars toward which western manufacturers and eastern entrepreneurs conveniently turn a blind eye, wars lost to the public's attention by the media's obsession with Al Qaeda, Somali pirates, and the chronic troubles in the Mideast. The world's fascination with electronic devices, cell phones, GPS systems, DVD players, the list seems to grow daily, necessitates the ever growing exploitation of these minerals to make the small, efficient capacitors the devices require. Thus, boys and men, under the watchful eye of one Warlord or another, labor in the back country and forests to wrest coltan from the earth so this lust for instant gratification in the civilized world can be met.

The men, *les soldats*, their camo uniforms now rumpled and sweat stained from the effort of hauling the dead gorilla from the bush, began the process of butchering it. They were particularly pleased they had bagged a male. Its genitalia would bring a big price in Korea and China. Some of the witch doctors in the local countryside and the *moloi* to the south in Botswana would pay a handsome price for even small bits. The rest of the carcass would be sold locally as "bush meat." There would be some francs made this day.

They had not thought they would bring down a gorilla so soon, and therefore, had not brought the necessary preservatives, not even salt, to package their prize. All these supplies bounced along in the beds of trucks headed toward them but still hours away. One of the men broke out a bottle of South African brandy and poured it over the various parts they'd wrapped in towels until proper containers and solutions arrived. They all agreed that the brandy could only enhance the efficacy of these bits and pieces if and when they finally found their way into oriental apothecaries.

The men who'd been set to do the digging at the mine's entrance kept their eyes averted from this activity. They were not offended by the brutality or the obvious breach of international conventions regarding mountain gorillas. Dian Fossey and *The Gorillas in the Mist* had not been a major part of their education. Brutality had become an expected ingredient of their lives since birth. Also, they knew that no game warden or NGO activist would dare confront these men back in the wilds of the Congo. *Les soldats* were armed and veterans of fighting around the country. They would have no compunction in killing any intruder foolish enough to object to their enterprise, including them. And anyway, isn't it better to not know some things?

*Les soldats*, their butchering done, spread out into the forest, their weapons off safety. Where there was one gorilla, there would be more. Gorillas were social animals and therefore easy hunting. Two stayed back to guard the women, to keep them from running off or possibly killing themselves. The men and boys at the mine would not leave. They wouldn't dare, and where would they go?

Kgabo Modise's rise in the Botswana's police force, from the Mochudi local constabulary, to CID, then to DIS, was not, strictly speaking, meteoric. He had, in fact, out-stripped his cadre of cadets entering the police training program and had achieved his current position rapidly, but it was as much the result of hard work and luck as karma. As a young man and student at Molefi secondary school, he had shown great promise. So much so that his teachers predicted a bright future for him in the law or civil service, following the footsteps of the many other bright lights from their school—high fliers who had gone on to become High Court judges, Permanent Secretaries, and parastatal CEOs.

But then came his senior year. For reasons he never divulged, his enthusiasm for study, his school, and even his prospects dulled and unsurprisingly, the year ended with an unexceptional O-level performance. He brushed aside the urging by his principal, Mr. Basiamang to repeat the exams.

"You will not be the first to gain entry to the university and the law after a second go at the exams," he'd said, sure the young man would jump at the chance.

But Kgabo steadfastly refused and instead enrolled in the Police Academy. His family was devastated. What had happened to this rising star? Mma Motsheganong said it was woman trouble. Mma Motsheganong had a very pretty granddaughter, Kopano, who married the local bottle store owner's son, himself something of a bright light. Kgabo Modise, she said had pined after Kopano and when she jilted him for comparative wealth and ease, the heart went out of him. Modise never confirmed or denied this account but his mother was reported to have laughed very loudly when she heard of it.

The Mochudi Police Department did not qualify as a prestige posting and worse, he daily faced his neighbors and fellow students, now graduates, and their questions. But he held his tongue and worked hard at his chosen profession. He bought self improvement books and tapes and studied. He did not pursue what little night life Muchudi offered and was never seen with a woman again.

The big break for him came after his fifth year on the force. He had been chosen to attend an international conference for police—in America. His colleagues commiserated with him.

"We," they'd announced proudly, "have been selected to attend a similar gathering, but in France and as part of an Interpol briefing. Poor Modise," they'd added. "He will be sent to work with the gunslingers and cowboys in Dallas, Texas, of the USA."

Modise did not share their feelings. He knew, for example, that whatever else might be said about Americans, and there was plenty that could be said, they as a nation still remained at the top of the heap when it came to productivity per capita. He and his generation were not averse to hard work, but the transition from a British Protectorate to national independence had been rapid and lacking in some respects, at least as to how one optimally managed systems and people. He would go to the conference as much to learn the secret of this productivity as to bone up on police procedurals. He did, however, learn a great deal about the latter.

His companions had guessed wrong about his destination. Dallas was having such a meeting, but Modise was slated to go elsewhere. When his plane landed in Washington, he was met by several men who accompanied him to Quantico, Virginia, where he entered a total immersion curriculum in intelligence and counter-terrorism. He listened and he learned. He asked one agent from Phoenix if his fellow student attendees were typical of American police. He'd seen enough Hollywood police to have some doubts. The man from the American west had laughed and said no, these were the "top cops"—the best of the best.

Modise set his professional goal at that moment. He would become Botswana's "top cop." He read everything he could lay his hands on about police and intelligence work. He sent away for CDs and DVDs. He listened to and watched them over and over. He kept to himself, took on extra duties and by dint of hard work and determination, he evolved into Botswana's "top cop" and a rising star in Botswana's intelligence Directorate, the DIS.

# Chapter Six

Modise, when not immediately engaged in casework, had set himself the task of absorbing as much information as possible from all the sources available to him. He was so engrossed in studying America's no-fly list, a book with more names, it seemed, than the entire population of Botswana, that he almost missed the knock at his door.

"You are wanted in the conference room." The new recruit who had been assigned as an intern in the office looked out of place in her too-new uniform and shiny belt. Most of the occupants on this floor had a "worn-in" look about them.

"Oh yes? Do you know why?" It didn't matter if the young woman knew or not. Modise would go anyway, but he was curious whether she had acquired some listening skills.

"No, sir."

She hadn't.

He walked down the corridor that led from the president's office with some trepidation. He knew there were some heavy hitters in the room, and there had been rumors. The conference room in use this day was located in a building separate from the presidential offices. The occasional but nonimportant leaks to the press had convinced the director general to move the meetings around from time to time. The room was rectangular and still smelled of tobacco from the old days, before the current president had quit and decreed all official meetings should henceforth be smoke free. Once in the room he found himself in the presence of the Minister for Security and Intelligence, the Vice President, the Commander of the Botswana Defense Force, the BDF, and the Director General of the DIS, Botswana's equivalent to the fabled MI-5 of British Intelligence or America's FBI. Clearly this would not be a routine briefing. Modise tried without much success not to feel intimidated.

"Modise, sit please," the DG said and waved him toward a chair at the table. Modise's first thought had been to take one against the wall near the door. He couldn't see himself on such a familiar footing with these important people. "No, no, Modise, here, at the table. You have been the subject of considerable discussion."

He didn't know if that was a good thing or not.

He spent the next half hour sitting quietly as the meeting reviewed the potential problems that might spill over into the country from the World Cup matches in neighboring South Africa, scheduled for the second and third weeks in June.

"There will be opportunities for much mischief, to say the least," the minister said. Modise nodded at this acknowledgement of the obvious.

"His Excellency, the President's chief concern," the director said, "is the rather porous nature of our borders in the light of the tastes of some of the visitors who will be attending. H. E., of course, has always been concerned with the incursions of poachers and perhaps hunters, which we can assume will increase as well. It is an obsession with him. Now we add this new element."

The men around the table nodded. The president's passion for conservation was well documented and an occasional sore point with the Ministers who would prefer to focus on the economic and international matters which they believed to be far more pressing.

"The people who will find their way to Botswana, for the greater part, will be the wealthy, team sponsors, owners, and political figures of varying importance. They are more than welcome, naturally, but I am concerned about what they may wish to do with their wealth and time while in our country."

"We are speaking of smuggling, contraband and…other illegalities?" Modise asked.

"Smuggling? Certainly. That and all the sorts of things the wealthy indulge in…" The director's voice trailed off.

"Big game horns and…" Modise said.

"Yes? Continue." The DG had him in his crosshairs, it seemed.

"Yes, and other things. Rhino horns, as you know, are processed into powders or potions and sold as aphrodisiacs to the Chinese. For the Arabs, they and other species are used to carve handles for their ornamental daggers, Jambiyas, Khanjars, and so on. Then there is the ongoing market for pelts from the big cats, not to mention various body parts used in their traditional medicine. Since the animals that supply these products are all on the endangered species list or are otherwise protected, the traffic in these items has become very lucrative and, I should say, a global concern. There will be many buyers and a short supply. It could get ugly. They will be trying to slip them in from the North, I think."

Modise stopped. He had lectured these men as if they were schoolboys. They, better than he, knew the problems in this area. What was he thinking? He slumped in his chair and tried not to make eye contact with any of them.

The DG nodded and glanced around the table at the others. "You see?" he said. Modise wondered at the remark. See? See what?

"Yes, well then, we add to that the black market in ivory, artifacts, and conflict diamonds," the director added. "I am not so much worried about diamonds, though some in Parliament have raised the issue, and it is a particular obsession in the West. They have become an issue for Hollywood celebrities who have bought into the notion that the trade in—they call them blood diamonds—is the major problem when it come to financing wars on the continent. We know there are problems in that area, but in fact they play a small part of the equation. The problem for us is the sudden convergence of money, opportunity, and location. Africa is the preferred, and soon will be the only, source for many scarce and prohibited items."

"Director, you believe these exchanges will happen here? Why not in South Africa where the matches will be held?" the vice president asked. Modise had been watching him out of the corner of his eye. He knew the VP knew the answer and wondered at the question. Politics, he decided, was too deep for him. He'd stay happy as a policeman.

"There will be that sort of congress there, too, of course. But we are closer to the source of these items and the South African border presents one more obstacle they would have to surmount. We believe the big money will fly into the lodges on the Chobe and to the Okavango Delta. Both are on the border and less accessible to the press and curiosity seekers. Think of it, we border Zambia, Zimbabwe, and Namibia—four corners right on the Chobe. Then, just close by we have the Congo, Mozambique…" There was a collective murmur at the mention of Namibia. "My goodness, at the Chobe one need only accompany the elephants from the Caprivi Strip across the river in a *makoro* and there you are."

The men sat in silence digesting the director's words. The head of the BDF had taken several pages of notes. The minister, without realizing it, kept reaching for his cigarettes and then dropping his hand. The building's designation as a strict no smoking zone had not been lost on him. Modise assumed the good gentleman had an addiction to nicotine, one with which he could empathize. It had taken more willpower than he thought he possessed to stop smoking himself.

"There is one other thing." The DG sighed and looked strangely saddened. "Minister, are you acquainted with 'Orgonize Africa' or 'Operation Paradise'?"

"What? You mean that nonsense with the rubbish dumped into Lake Cahora Bassa in Mozambique?"

"Yes. Some fanatics attempted to introduce 'orgonite' as they call it, into the lower Zambezi by dumping it into the lake formed by the river's dam."

"I can see that those people might be an annoyance, but hardly a cause for concern except, as I have noted, for the annoyance factor."

"You may be right. However, our intelligence people tell us that the overriding organization for this nonsense is planning to, as they put it, 'make a statement' during the World Cup matches. The waters they've targeted are the Chobe, Victoria Falls, the Zambezi among others. They will focus their attention here as Zimbabwe is too unstable to support such an effort."

"So they dump their *motsholela* in the river. Only the fish, the hippos, and the crocodiles will care, and they not much I am thinking."

"Except they will be abusing our borders illegally along with all the more conventional illegals. At the very least it will compound our difficulties. Who shall we track? How to distinguish these fanatics from smugglers? While we waste time on them, the real criminals may slip by us. And they will be breaking the law in any event, and so whether we think they are ridiculous or not, we must respond. It will thin our ranks, you could say."

"I would say," an Army colonel sitting against the wall said, "that we will have more important things to occupy our time than harass these people. You know, there are many who believe that orgonite does what its proponents claim."

"So I hear. At any rate, they do not pose any immediate threat to our current program. They are, or will be an annoyance, a distraction at worst. Still…" The director gestured toward the commander of the BDF. "We need help. You know the borders and the animals as well as anyone in the country. We wish the BDF to be seconded to us for the duration of the cup beginning a week before and two weeks after the matches."

The head of the BDF spoke for the first time. "There will be no seconding of the men and women assigned to me. But you may expect our full cooperation, of course."

The director smiled. Modise assumed it was all he wanted in the first place.

"Then I can safely report to His Excellency, the President, that interagency cooperation in these matters is assured?" the vice president said.

"You can tell H. E. that we are all on the same page."

The men rose and gathered their notes and belongings ready to depart. The director signaled to Modise.

"Kgabo, stay a minute. I wish to have a word with you."

Kgabo. He called me by my first name. That must be very good—or very bad.

# Chapter Seven

Sanderson sat at her desk contemplating its shiny, unblemished surface. She still had difficulty thinking of it as hers. She had spent many years on the other side receiving her orders from her predecessor, Mr. Pako, and she hadn't quite gotten used to the fact that now it was she sitting behind it and giving orders to others. Mr. Pako had kept this desk free of all clutter. She couldn't remember seeing anything heavier than a single piece of paper on it. Now that it was hers it had the beginnings of a small paper mountain at one end. Charles Tlalelo stuck his head around the door frame.

"Here's trouble," she said. *Tlalelo* is Setswana for trouble and Charles had to endure at least one joke about his name daily.

"It is you who seems to be having the trouble, Sanderson...I mean, Superintendent. Your brow is furrowed like a plowed field. You are worried, I can see."

"Not worried, *no mathata*, Charles, and for you I am just Sanderson still, not Superintendent. I have a small difficulty I cannot seem to solve."

"Perhaps I can be of some help?"

"Yes. You can find us each a nice cup of tea and sit here with me and tell me the things I should hear."

Charles returned with the tea and sat opposite her. "I will tell what I can, but you must say what is it you wish to know?"

"Yes, of course, many things, one thing in particular. But first, you must tell me how the other game rangers are accepting the fact I have received this promotion to Superintendent?"

"Ah. Well, you know that some of the older men thought the job should have been theirs. They were here longer and they have opinions about women in high places."

"Who says this?"

"Andrew Takeda for one, but you are knowing how he is about things."

"That is so silly. This government is fully committed to equality of opportunity. Only these old men from before Independence don't seem to get the news. And you are right, Andrew is a strange one."

"They think they were passed over because someone in Gabz decided to address the gender issue out here in the north. I do not think you can persuade them otherwise."

"You are right about that, too, I guess. Who can say? Perhaps they are correct in thinking that."

"They will get over it, Sanderson. They like you personally, I think, and when they understand they have more to gain working for you than against you, they will come around, you will see."

"I hope you are right. As you say, we shall see. Right now I cannot concern myself with that. I have a bigger knot to untie. You heard about the shooting in the park?"

"Yes. The constable who was there with you and Superintendent Mwambe is my neighbor. He told me about it. And about you, too."

"Me? What did he say about me?"

"That you had annoyed the Baboon and not for the first time, I think. He said that Mwambe wanted a suicide and you kept insisting on murder. He said you were right in doing so but Mwambe was not happy that you were the one to point out the flaw in his assessment. It seemed to my friend that Mwambe did not want the inconvenience of an investigation. He is a good policeman, I think, and he wondered about that, you see."

"Well, that is not our concern. The police will find out what happened or they won't and Mwambe will be the hero or the goat. We have a bigger problem that his murder introduces."

Charles left and returned with more tea. This new pot emitted the sweet scent of oranges.

"And what," he said as he slid the cup across the desk, "is this great problem?"

Sanderson described the track through the trees, the breach in the fence, and the evidence pointing to its frequent use.

"We must fix it then. That does not seem much of a difficulty to me."

"No, that is not what we must do, Charles. If we close this gap the people who come into the park illegally will just find another place and cut a new one. It might take us weeks to find it, or never. We must leave this one and discover what they are doing and who they are."

"I see." Charles closed his eyes and sipped his tea. He frowned, deep in thought. Sanderson drummed her fingers lightly on the desk. Charles, she knew, was nobody's fool.

"Do you wish to stake out this place?" he said after a minute.

"No, I don't think so. For one, it will use up personnel we cannot spare, and two, if we do it will be obvious to anyone who knows anything that we are on to them. Did I tell you that dead man's car had a GPS device in it and also night vision equipment? They will not be so easily fooled."

"I didn't know." Charles sipped some more and thought some more. "Ah," he said and his eyes lit up. "Do you know if that equipment from the cinema people is still here?"

"Cinema people? What are you speaking of? I do not know about any equipment."

"Last year. Oh yes, you were on leave for Michael." Charles' sorrow at bringing up Sanderson's son, who even now lingered at home in the final stages of AIDs-related pneumonia, crossed his face. He cleared his throat in embarrassment.

"It is all right, Charles. You were saying?"

"Yes, you were out on leave then when Superintendent Pako came across a crew of filmmakers in the park. Actually, I am wrong. I think they were television people. No, cinema, for sure. Anyway, they had neglected to obtain proper permits to enter the park and to film the animals. Pako suspected they were not entirely forthcoming about their filming either. Perhaps they had other things on their mind and the camera business was a cover-up. Some of the ladies who accompanied them seemed almost too pretty to be film crew or game experts, you see? Pako can be very suspicious of people sometimes."

"Not often enough, for my thinking."

"Yes? He confiscated their equipment and said they could have it back when they returned with the correct permits from the ministry. I don't think they ever came back."

"That is very interesting, but it will help me how, exactly?"

"Don't you see? If those cameras are still here, we can take pictures of the men when they enter. We don't need to be out in the open at all."

"They will come in the darkness."

"That is so. But, you see the TV people were also taking their pictures in the night. Something to do with hyena hunting they said. They were certainly filming at night. Therefore, they will have the night vision equipment, I think."

"If we have this material, I would have seen it on an inventory, surely. But if we do, do you know how to operate it?"

Charles' face fell. "No, not really. A little maybe. I have a device at home which makes videos. I don't know, but there must be someone in the area that does."

"Well, let us see if we can find this equipment. I am guessing it ran on batteries and that they are flat by this time. But, we will see."

They left the office and went to the room in the game ranger's building reserved for storage. It took them twenty minutes, but they found the equipment in a crate tucked in at the back of the room. There was a great deal of material in it. The cameras Sanderson recognized. Tripods and microphones as well. But there were other items she could not identify. Many such items and, as she suspected, all of the batteries were flat.

# Chapter Eight

"Modise, You have had some experience with the police and the game rangers at the Chobe, I believe." It wasn't a question. "I would like you to set up a temporary station in Kasane. Then make the rounds of the hotels and so on, and brief them on our plans. We will require their cooperation in this. You realize the potential for trouble up there, I assume."

"Yes, sir, I do." Modise had to chose his words carefully. "You are correct. I have some familiarity with both the game rangers and the police. I am sure about the rangers, not so confident about the abilities of the local police."

"You mean Superintendent Mwambe. Yes, I know. You must understand this thing. Mwambe and people like him were in place before your time when the country struggled. We had raiders from across our borders, rebels using us for sanctuary, for the transport of materiel over our roads, and civil wars on all sides, and well, you see the picture. The Mwambes of the world helped us through those difficult times. They served. Now times have changed and they find it hard to adjust. Do not be hard on the man. He will come through for you in the end. He just needs a little gentle handling."

"Yes, sir." Modise saw the director's point but he had difficulty summoning up sympathy for Mwambe. But he had to deal with him, so he would.

"There is another thing, well, several things you must be alerted to, Modise."

"Sir?"

"First this, the Americans are telling us their secretary of state will be booking into the Mowana Lodge. She will be accompanied by her husband. They were here some time back, you may remember, in a different capacity. The Americans have their own excellent security, of course. We need only to coordinate with them. But now, we hear that several Mideastern leaders will be at the other lodges along the Chobe at the same time. This cannot be a coincidence on their part. No one is saying anything. They claim they are in Africa for the matches. They assume the new lodge and casino that the American and the Russian are involved in building will be open."

"Yes, sir?"

The director fumbled with his shirt pocket, the place he used to keep his cigarettes, again. He sighed and chewed on a pencil.

"This is the more important bit. The North Koreans and some high profile celebrities will be booking in the Okavango at the same time. Everything is very hush-hush and nobody will say anything but, and this you must keep to yourself, Modise, some international negotiations will be taking place under the guise of the World Cup. You know the Koreans released an American missionary as a gesture, we think, indicating that they can be approached. As Botswana is a 'Trusted Nation' in African negotiations, we will have a presence in the Okavango, do you follow?"

"In the Okavango? The Koreans and the Americans? Yes, sir, I see." Modise thought he did at any rate. The Americans would be setting up meetings using Botswana diplomats as intermediaries with the North Koreans.

"Of course events change and move swiftly so these possibilities may not come to be, and all this can disappear into the bush by next week or sooner. But in any case, we must be prepared. You understand this?"

"Yes."

"Good. Now, the next concern. How much do you know about this Orgonize Africa or Operation Paradise?"

"Only what I read in the papers and police reports."

"Not much then. Take these," the director handed him a file, "and read them on your way north. You will find them interesting and also, I think, annoying."

"I see." Kgabo would read the reports and study them as he did everything that crossed his desk. He turned to leave.

"There is one last thing, Modise. And this is something I think we will have to deal with for some time. Do you know who Oleg Lenka is?"

"Only rumors, sir. Lenka is a said to be major Russian crime boss. Is it true he is a former KGB operator in Africa and Latin America?"

"The intel from Interpol says yes. He emerged as senior Bratva figure in the nineties Kremlin with global underworld connections. I have all this in another folder for you as well. Read it when you have a chance, but first, I want you to concentrate on this Operation Paradise nonsense. At the moment it poses a threat by interfering with border security. Crime bosses are, or will be, important soon enough, but borders first."

"And that's it?"

"Not quite. You have run across Rra Botlhokwa at one time or another. Am I correct?"

"Yes sir, not personally, but I have read his file. He is a big shot with a shady reputation. The word on the street is that he could have been big in government but chose to trade in marginal pursuits instead."

"Marginal pursuits...nicely put. This is a heads-up and not to be repeated. He is connected to some very important people here in the capitol, a fact that makes bringing him down entail some serious risks for whoever attempts it. On the other hand, he has occasionally been useful to us when we have to run a dark operation, you understand?"

"Yes, of course."

"No *of course*. It is an embarrassment to us who have to see to the nation's security. But it is an unhappy fact. He is currently under indictment by the attorney general, but making the charges and bringing him to the bar is being held in abeyance for the moment. A count of how many and whose toes will be trod on is currently underway. As I said, a potential embarrassment, but it seems likely the AG will bring him to trial soon, that is if he doesn't skip the country first."

"Sir."

"Very well, that's a lot for you to chew on. Just get up there and take one thing at a time. And good luck."

Modise returned to his desk and opened the first folder, a green-jacketed one, and read the report the director had handed him. It was taken from the government's communications director.

> *With reference to a front-page Sunday Standard story, please find below insightful Mozambique Information Agency (AIM) Report. If the report is correct, the four men arrested in Mozambique, including one Tino Phutego, were on a mission to place orgonite into the Zambezi River via the dam's lake. This is part of a wider mission, dubbed Operation Paradise, by a group called Orgonize Africa to place orgonite throughout the region acting on their belief that by doing so they are restoring Africa's natural beauty, healing the earth, inducing rainfall, curing AIDs, etc.*
>
> *Orgonize Africa is part of a global network—one might term it a new age cult—that is carrying on in the footsteps of Wilhelm Reich (1897-1957), a prominent, but in the end mentally suspect, Austrian psychoanalyst who in the thirties believed that the path to a Communist Utopia lay in the release of "Orgone Energy" originally through sexual free expression. Reich thereafter came to describe orgone as a universal bio-energetic force lying behind and causing much, if not all, observable phenomena. This resulted in his creation of orgonite as a substance supposedly containing the energy force.*
>
> *Reich's New Age followers have since come to claim that orgone or orgonite was the creative substratum in all of nature.*

Modise shook his head. Who in the world believes this foolishness? But, someone most certainly did and so it was necessary
he do so, too—not believe the silliness, but that others did so and
would try to bring the stuff into the country. The people who
would facilitate the movement of this orgonite across the border
would be opening the same gates for smugglers and terrorists
as well. As long as there was *pula* to be made, there would be
people who would take the risks. These fanatics, however, would
more likely be less disingenuous and if apprehended, might be
persuaded to lead Modise and the authorities to the real threats.

He turned the last page of the stack he'd been given.

>  *Orgonite is a mixture of fiber-glass resin, metal shavings
> (iron, steel, copper or any other metal), and quartz crystals.
> This stuff is mixed into cone shaped moulds. In water the
> orgonite cones soon dissolve—but there is nothing corrosive
> about any of the components.*

The truck that had made the run to Mozambique, he read,
had been equipped with state of the art communications equipment, including satellite phones and a global positioning system.
They had very sophisticated equipment, it seemed, the sort
one needs to move across borders and national parks safely and
undetected. Perhaps it is not all it seems. Were they fanatics, or
very clever people with some other agenda hiding behind this
clowning? How easy it would be to plant a bomb in the stuff.

Modise put the file aside.

# Chapter Nine

Sanderson waved at the miscellany of cameras, cables, and cartons scattered across the floor of her office. "So, Charles, what do we do with all this now?"

"I think these things here," Charles held up a small plug-in transformer with a cord attached, "are used to charge up the batteries. I think we should start there. You didn't see any instructional manuals, did you?"

"Nothing is ever that easy, Charles. So, we charge up these batteries and then? I do not have even a small notion as to what we must do with these things. Do we turn them on and point them at the fence. Surely the batteries will die before midnight."

Charles scratched his head. "You present me with a great puzzle, Sanderson. There must be somebody around this place who knows about these things."

"Yes, that would be very nice. I am sure you are right, but I do not know of such a person." The two game rangers sat and stared at the equipment. "Wait, I do know someone who could help us, perhaps. Yes, and he will want to know of the break in the fence."

"Who?"

"He is a policeman in Gaborone. I know him from before. You remember the business with the American and the lion? I think he will know what to do with these things. If he doesn't, well then, he will know someone who does." She went to the phone, found the business card she kept in her desk drawer, and called Kgabo Modise.

◇◇◇

Rra Botlhokwa had many men in his employ. He used them as different situations developed. He made a point of keeping a certain distance between himself and them. He was not one to dirty his hands. He had learned the word "deniability" from the American newspapers. Politicians needed it, it seemed. He liked the concept. He wished also to have deniability. That was the reason the government in its many permutations had never been able to touch him, and though they would never admit it, occasionally had use of his services, but with deniability, of course. He intended to keep it that way. But this last problem caused him some annoyance.

He had guaranteed passage into the country and thence into the park, undetected passage, and there had been the shooting. The group who paid for the transit, those men came up from South Africa they claimed, but he doubted it. Congo more likely, and they were not happy. They thought he had played them off against another group. They accused him of deceit. They said he had betrayed them. They did not like that. And then there were the locals who set the whole business up. They wanted an explanation and restitution of the funds they'd paid him. That, of course, was out of the question. How would this be taken if he were to do such a thing? A sign of weakness and then…nothing good could come from that. No, there would be no restitution. He must find out how the men doing the shooting knew the time and location of the other man's arrival in the park. Someone in his employment was telling things he should not have been. He would soon regret that.

His closest assistant, a man called Noga, the snake, knocked and then entered.

Botlhokwa shifted in his chair. "You have news for me?"

"Not about the shooting, but about some things of interest to us in other ways."

"Why do I not hear about the shooting? It is not good for us, this killing. The people who depend on us for our services, who pay us, will find others to do their work. And then there is a need to have a talk with the game ranger. What does he know of this?"

"I will talk to the ranger soon. He is frightened and lying low. He will surface soon enough, him or one of his fellows. As for our people, I have talked to the most likely, the ones who would know. I must now determine who they might have spoken to. There is a weakness in the system but we will find it. But the news that you will want to hear is better."

Botlhokwa motioned him to a chair. Noga nodded and sat. He accepted the Cuban cigar offered and the two men lit up. Soon the room was filled with the strong aroma of tobacco. If a visitor were a cigar smoker, he would have been ecstatic. A non-smoker, a reformed smoker, would have staggered from the room gasping for air.

"Several important visitors will soon be with us," Noga said between puffs. "The American Secretary of State and her entourage, including the husband, will arrive during the matches."

"And?"

"There will be emissaries from some Near Eastern nations as well. They will talk politics, settle issues of sovereignty over lands they do not own, and make deals with other people's resources. It is politics as usual. And there are the rumors about the Okavango."

"And that concerns me, how? I have no interest in the Machiavellian movements of the rich and powerful. If I had, I would be president by now."

"You could be still, if you were willing to create the illusion of incorruptibility. However, the arrival of these people is important to us for several reasons. The Emirs will be in the market for some of the things and activities we can supply. The Americans may wish to confer in private with certain parties across the border in Zimbabwe. They cannot go openly. They may use their CIA people to approach us to help them, I think."

"There is no money in those transaction."

"There is good will, indebtedness, you can say, that may be useful to us in the future. It is not a bad thing to be on the CIA's list of preferred providers."

Botlhokwa flicked the ash from his cigar and stared out the window. He would be in Cape Town now except for this business at the borders. He needed to keep a tight rein on his people. He would be happy when these football matches were over and he could enjoy his wine estate again. And then, there had been the call from Gaborone earlier. He would have to spend some scarce political currency to muzzle the attorney general. Politicians!

"The Koreans, I am told, will find their way to the Okavango. The North Koreans, that is. The South will locate in one of the local lodges. Who knows what sort of business that is about. Besides wanting to meet with the Americans or perhaps the Russians who will also be here, informally of course, they will be anxious to procure hides, horns, and ivory, perhaps other things. They have peculiar tastes, I hear. Perhaps we should stock up on Snake Wine."

"And compliant women?" Noga shrugged. Some things, he reasoned, were self evident.

"You realize," Botlhokwa said between puffs, "the BDF will be out in force. They will not permit poaching of any of these things and will be patrolling the borders. They can be very difficult."

"You mean unapproachable for the sort of inducements you might offer. Of course they are. We can manage them. What we need is a supply of merchandise from Congo, Uganda, Rwanda, and possibly Kenya. Who knows what the West African people might do for us? They are all in need of negotiable currencies. And there is coltan, easy to move, hard to detect, good return on investment, you could say. It is a big continent and the borders are wide. We will be the middle men, as the American movies say. We collect fees, expedite commerce, and remain safely in the dark."

Botlhokwa nodded his approval. He did not deal in drugs, arms, or any of the illicit human traffic that coursed in and out of his country, his continent. He merely facilitated its passage from seller to buyer remaining, as Noga put it, safely in the dark. This careful positioning had kept him in place for years. It would be so in the future. Let others reap the big profits and take the risks, he'd settle for a fat fee.

◇◇◇

*Patriarche* heard the men approaching. They did not move quietly like the poachers he knew in his youth. These men crashed through the bush like elephants. That was good. He could keep his family safe and away. He picked up a stick and snapped off the remaining branches from it. A stick was a handy thing to have, He could pry roots out of the earth and if a branch with fruit or succulent leaves hung too high for him to reach, he could use it to pull the branch within his grasp. He did not think of this thing in his hand as a weapon. Such a concept had no resonance for this gentle giant.

The men moved closer. He grunted—not loudly—and the gorillas slipped deeper into the forest.

# Chapter Ten

Kgabo Modise had an overnight bag packed, a flight booked to Kasane, and was in his car on the way to the airport when he received Sanderson's call. His face creased into a frown as he listened to what she had to say. At one point, he pulled to the side of the road to jot details in the notebook he always carried with him. All the police he'd met in Quantico had notebooks like this one. He made a habit to write things down whether they seemed important or not.

"I am coming to Kasane today, Sanderson. I will visit you after I have talked with the lodge owners and local police. If the people who owned cameras were shooting at night, they will have the equipment you will need, I think. We will see."

He rang off and continued to the terminal for his Air Botswana flight north. He wondered about a film crew that never returned to retrieve their equipment. Were they stupidly wealthy, or had they leased it and skipped, or…or what? Perhaps they had come back but had been sent away again by someone else. Perhaps they were not what they seemed. Another puzzle for him to think about. He would need the particulars. He thought to call Sanderson back and discover their names. His flight was called and he left the building. Plenty of time to do these things when he arrived at Kasane later that morning.

◇◇◇

Noga left Botlhokwa's office and stepped out into the afternoon sun. He dropped the butt of his cigar and ground it beneath his heel. His mouth tasted terrible. He did not like cigars, Cuban or otherwise. He smoked them with his boss because it was a necessary ritual when dealing with him. Not everyone who sat across the desk from Botlhokwa was offered a cigar. If you were, it meant something. You had status. Botlhokwa had funny notions about some things. Noga spat and placed a breath mint on his tongue. What to do? In his world one took advantage of opportunities that often came by like a herd of antelope. If you were a lion, you took care of the antelope. You did not wait for another day, a bigger herd, a fatter prey, or, in this case, permission from the boss. You ran them down, or in his case, struck like the snake, like the *noga*.

But it required discretion. One must never bite the hand that feeds you. A side deal for some drugs, a theft of some things that just happened your way was okay. But to cross the boss was not acceptable. Well, to cross him and be caught was not. Botlhokwa wanted him to discover the man who played at both ends. No problem there. If he wanted to end up in a ditch somewhere, he could turn himself in and finish the job. Not going to happen.

He did not want to be a Botlhokwa man forever. He knew the ropes, knew the people; had dealt with them for over a year now. He'd spent months studying his man, his habits, his strengths, and especially his weaknesses. Now, he had to think about his future. The man with the tattoos, the Russian, had approached him. He made the deal. He seized the moment. He would manage Botlhokwa later. With the Finals of the Cup matches beginning soon, there would be many new opportunities…who knew? How was he to know that the carrier had rubbish in the boot? How could he guess the men would shoot him? Were they stupid? Idiots.

But first there were loose ends to tie up. He needed to find a likely candidate for Botlhokwa. He'd find a fall guy. That should not be too difficult. There were many big, slow, men in his employ. He just needed to choose one and set him up. Perhaps Cunningham would fit the bill. That would surely shake up the boss. Then he would see to the Russian and other opportunities that might become available.

Sanderson returned to her house for lunch. Ordinarily, she would have packed something in the battered tin box with the picture of the Royal Family on it. Her grandmother had stood with thousands of others in the late forties to observe this great *Kgosi*, King George the Sixth, his queen, and two young daughters. She spoke as if she had somehow known them personally.

"You know," she would say looking closely at her three year old granddaughter, "That Group Captain Peter Townsend, he was a fine catch for sure. I see him moving around in the background with the royal people. He is like a leopard that can't get to the antelope because of the lion. That Princess Margaret, she should have made her parents see that." She shook her head. "So sad."

Sanderson's grandmother was a romantic but wholly ignorant of the ins and outs of English royal politics. But she had her souvenir of that momentous visit, a square tin box that came with hard candy in it originally. She later gave it to Sanderson to use as a lunch pail on her first day of school. Sanderson had used it through her school days to carry her noon meal and later, as an adult, a place to put her meager luncheon. But today, running late and in a hurry, she had left home without it. Besides, she wished to check on her son, Michael, who lingered on, his pneumonia held at bay by antibiotics. She wrestled again with the dark notion that surfaced from the depths of her subconscious and plagued her; the idea, that perhaps these antibiotics were not such a good thing after all; that wouldn't it be better if Michael's long struggle with the effects of HIV/AIDs were to end now, quietly, peaceably? She flushed with guilt at the thought and pushed the notion back down in the recesses of her brain where it had come from. She would like to have it erased but it seemed that once an idea planted itself in your mind, it received a permanent residence permit and would stay forever.

She parked next to her red pickup, her *bakkie*, and smiled. Restoring the old Toyota HiLux had been Michael's last project. If he died, it would be his memorial.

Not *if.*

She wiped her eyes and stepped down from the Land Rover she now drove as the new superintendent of her game ranger station and turned to enter her house.

"You…woman."

She spun to see who called to her. It was neither a voice nor a face she recognized.

"Who is it?"

"You do not know me and you will forget you have seen me, you see, but I bring a message of importance to you."

"A message? What sort of message, and who are you that you bring me messages?"

The man stepped forward and stood very close to her. Too close for comfort, much too close for propriety.

"You are wanting to trace the vehicle that might be related to the death at the game park. Is that not so? It is advisable that you no longer do this. There might be consequences."

"I do not accept messages from strangers unless they identify themselves, and I do not accept threats from anybody, and I do not know what you are talking about."

Her words startled her even as she spoke them. She wondered what was happening to her. She did not consider herself a particularly brave person and yet she had just stood up to this stranger who, she now realized, was a foot taller than she, much heavier, and considerably larger than anyone she'd known except, perhaps, Inspector Mwambe. But Mwambe's size came from too much eating, not strength building and exercise. This man who threatened her looked like one of those athletes she'd seen on the telly who fought in cages and had tattoos on their bodies.

The man seemed taken aback. He did not expect this bravery from a game ranger, from a woman. He seemed about to strike her, hesitated, and stepped back.

"Remember what I tell you," he said. He turned and spat on the ground at the entry to her little court in front of her house. Sanderson clenched her teeth. The insult to her home was almost more irritating that this man's threats to her.

"What is your name, man?" She shouted after him. He waved without turning around, a dismissive gesture, and strode away. Sanderson stamped her foot.

"And what will you do if I do not listen to your threats?"

The man turned and glared. "Do not be stupid, woman. You have a daughter. Do not forget that. She is young and pretty and…" he left the sentence dangling. He didn't need to finish it.

He was right, Mpitle was young, and pretty, and vulnerable. She spent the better part of her days alone or with Michael because Sanderson had to work long hours. Michael could barely leave his bed. He certainly could do little or nothing to protect her. She depended on her village to keep her safe. But against this man? Could the villagers do anything? Sanderson stood in stunned silence and watched as the man climbed into his truck and drove away.

# Chapter Eleven

Yuri Greshenko expected a call from the freight company he'd hired to haul the room modules from South Africa to Kasane. So, the phone's brrip-brrip did not startle him. But the voice on the other end when he picked up did. He listened. A scowl settled on his face. He spoke softly in Russian, checking frequently to see if Leo or any of the close employees were within earshot, even though he was sure none of them spoke the language. His former life, however, had made him cautious.

"*Nyet*," he repeated periodically, shaking his head. He listened some more, then sighed "*Da*, okay," and hung up. He was not happy. How to explain to Leo he had to go away for a few days, perhaps longer, in the middle of this rush to finish the lodge? He'd assured Leo that his ties to his past were lost, broken, or at least sufficiently attenuated as to be nonfunctional, and all he had on his plate was his new life in Botswana. Now this.

The past has a way of seeking you out and finding you, and then sometimes punishing you for having had the audacity to ignore it. Yuri's past had searched him out and now required a favor of him, a simple task. There would be no rest until the thing was done. He did not like it. The job he could do, *no mathata*, as his foreman would say, no worries, but once done it could put him and possibly many others in an awkward position in any new situation that arose. Someone would have leverage and could use it against him. He did not wish to return to his old life, any of those old lives he'd lived before. He would need to find a way to make the thing work without a payback. He needed a diversion, a red herring.

The phone twittered again. This time it was the transport company. Good. Something he could deal with. He handled the truckers and hung up. Leo Painter stepped into the room.

"Leo," Yuri began. Leo held up his hand. He was staring out the window toward the gate.

"It's that cop," Leo said. "You know, the one from the time my daughter-in-law, if that's what she was, and her husband got into that mess."

"I remember him. He came up from Gaborone."

"That's the guy. Gabbo Mo…something."

"I think his name is Kgabo Modise."

"Right. How'd you remember that? What the hell does he want?"

Yuri shrugged. Cops were hard to figure. Best to let them do their thing. Leo chewed on the end of an unlit cigar and studied the policeman who, in turn, was kicking at something near the skip.

"What's he doing? Why is he here? Our permits are all in place, aren't they?"

"Yes, we are covered and then some. I think it must have something to do with the World Cup. The rumors are all over the place that the American Secretary of State will be staying at the Mowana Lodge and we have bookings, which I hope we can honor, for some Mideast guests as well. Maybe some geopolitical intrigue is on someone's agenda."

"What do you mean, *hope?* Of course we'll be ready. Maybe not at one hundred percent, but we'll be ready. The gaming tables and roulette wheels will arrive next week. If we offer our guests cards, dice, and make book on the matches, and keep the bar open late, we'll be okay. Might have to do a crash course in dealing, though. I hired three dealers and a croupier from Laughlin, Nevada. Temps, but they should be here long enough to teach the locals the way American casinos operate."

"He's heading this way."

The two men watched as the man from Gaborone walked toward them, notebook in hand and writing.

"Good afternoon, Mr. Painter, Mr. Greshenko. It is nice to see you here. It has been some little time."

"Hello, Inspector. Yes it has. I understand you took care of my late stepson's widow."

"We did what we had to do, sir. The case against her was mostly circumstantial and with the husband finding himself dead, there was not much else we could do, certainly not hold her. She is a very interesting woman, that Brenda Griswold."

"Interesting doesn't cover the half of it. What can we do for you? Not looking into any more murders? I'm not aware of any."

"Yes and no. I am here to apprise you of the security we will impose on the area very soon. And, in fact, there has been a murder in the park. A smuggler, we think."

"A smuggler? Of what?"

"That is hard to say. His vehicle had been emptied of whatever it carried. But I am here on other matters today."

"You mean because of the secretary of state visiting the Mowana Lodge?"

"That and the fact that we believe, with all the money and power that will congregate here in the north, there will be opportunists who will seek to market their products and cause embarrassment."

"Meaning?"

"As you know, certain animals are protected both by international agreements and by Botswana law. Rhinoceros horns, for example. Also ivory, gorilla parts, pelts, and so on. And there are always those who wish to cut the corners on the purchase of raw diamonds. We wish to give you what you Americans call the 'heads up.' We will be monitoring these activities and our borders very carefully and anyone caught trafficking in them will be severely punished. As will their employers. You see my meaning."

"Ah, so if one of my employees happens to be suborned by these traffickers, it will fall to me as well?"

"It could. The circumstances would dictate the degree of the response, if any. You are understanding this?"

"Yes. Anything else?"

"Oh yes. Drugs. We take a dim view of opiates, hallucinogens, prescriptions, or otherwise, as well. And there are other things in the wind, we hear."

"Inspector, you needn't be so hard on us. I, we, have no interest in jeopardizing this enterprise for any reason. We will keep a close watch on the staff and report anything out of the ordinary to you. Will that do?"

"Very good. Now, there is this other thing."

"More?"

"Two things, I think. First there is the news, more than a rumor, I am afraid, of Russian mobsters having their eyes on this part of the world. What you are building here will have been noticed by some of the more unsavory elements in society. This is a heads-up but one that might be of particular importance to you." Modise glanced in Greshenko's direction as he spoke.

"And secondly, can you tell me the origin of the cone-shaped object that you are using to prop open your gate?"

"Sure. A couple of goons drove up a few days ago and dumped it, and a bunch of other stuff like it, in my skip. I pulled that one out for a gate stop. Why do you ask?"

"Are you aware of a program called 'Operation Paradise'?"

"Is it a television show?"

"No, sorry, not the telly." Modise scratched his head. "It has to do with Wilhelm Reich. In the nineteen thirties, I am told, he believed that the path to Utopia lay in the release of 'orgone energy' and he came to see 'orgone' as a universal bio-energetic force that lay behind…um, various events and so forth. It is hard to explain. At any rate he created something he called orgonite, a substance supposedly containing an energy force. There are now many of the people you call New Agers following that claim, you see?"

Leo looked at Modise and then at Greshenko. He didn't see.

"Reich's successors think that orgone in this form as orgonite is the creative substratum in all of nature."

"Skip to the chase, Inspector. Hippie fads don't interest me."

"Just this—the American based 'National Center for Complementary and Alternative Medicine' regards orgone as a type of energy. According to mainstream science, it has no practical application in medicine or wider science—in other words this is all total quackery."

"That is very interesting, Inspector…I think, but what has that got to do with the trash in my skip?"

"This trash, as you so correctly label it, is orgonite. I would be interested in hearing about the men who brought it here."

"Really? Two beefy guys in hiking boots, bush jackets, and beards. Didn't look like hippies to me, though."

"Boers, probably. Anything else?"

"They were driving a fairly late model Toyota Land Cruiser and," Leo smiled and pulled out his note book, "I have their license number."

It was Modise's turn to smile.

# Chapter Twelve

"We'd be taking a huge risk, you understand." The speaker was tall and rangy, his accent from somewhere in the old Empire but difficult to place…Australia, South Africa, New Zealand, cockney, all of the above?

"It can't miss, chum," his companion said, his accent seemingly from the same world, Brit, but not quite. "They know those nutters will be bringing in the *kak* by the lorry full. Look, for the next several months or so the bloody place will be crawling with smugglers, all sorts of dodgy types, not to mention spies, potential assassins, suicide bombers, and more drunks than on Irish Sweepstakes day. With all the things the coppers have to look out for, they'll not waste much time on this stuff. Worst case, they toss it in a rubbish heap and run our guys back across the border."

"You realize that if you're wrong and they tumble to what we've got in these cones we're dead? Either we're doing time in the local pokey, or more likely, our business partners, assuming we can find someone loopy enough to back this dodge, will feed us to the crocs."

"No worries. Look, we're mixing in our stuff with these quartz bits, metal filings, powder, and fiber glass. They'll think it's orgonite for a cert. Hell's bells, it *is* orgonite. Even if they crack it open, unless they're looking, they'll need a sharp eye to separate the coltan from the rest of the junk."

"There's the third possibility you haven't thought about. People say the *Bratva* is moving in. They will claim this as their territory and then what happens to us?"

"All rumors and so what? We're small chips to those blokes—flies at the picnic. Not worth bothering with."

"I don't know. We'd be putting a half million Euros worth of minerals in that mess. That's got to mean something to somebody if they tumble to us."

"Park off, Harvey, you worry too much."

"Okay, let's say we get under the Russian mob's radar or maybe they aren't coming or don't care, like you said. How can we be sure we can deliver it? I mean we dump it in the…what? The park, the river? Then, what if the stuff disappears?"

"Easy-peasy, Jack. All we need to do is keep track of where we drop it, and it won't be the river."

"How? It's a hell of a big jungle out there."

"Not a jungle, it's called the bush. See, we drop it here and there and then log in coordinates on a GPS tracking device. Our clients will buy a list of the locations, see? Maybe we don't put all the locations on the same list. It'll depend on who we round up to sell to. They get out their GPS things, tap in the coordinates, and go pick up the goods, and if they're satisfied they return the thing and maybe buy another list. Maybe they buy the whole lot including the device. All sorts of possibilities here."

"And if they're caught?"

"If they are caught…well, we still have the locations on the master and can look for another client. Got it? And don't forget, they can pick them up at their leisure. The officials have no reason to stop them, they're all local. And if there are too many coppers in the field, they just wait for another day. I tell you, it's brill."

"And what's to keep someone else from coming along and picking them up or moving them?"

"Lions, crocodiles, hyenas, leopards, you name it. Who's going to risk wandering around the Chobe National Game Park? The only people in there, besides our mob, will be tourists with cameras on game drives and what are they told never to do? Never leave your vehicle."

"But they might."

"They might. To take a picture maybe. But it's against the law to even pick up a feather or a bone, maybe even a pretty rock, so who's going to go for this ugly shite? No way."

"I hope you're right."

"Bloody cupcake is what this is, Jack."

Modise listened to Sanderson's explanation of what had happened at the murder scene. She was careful to not be critical of Superintendent Mwambe's apparent intention to keep it a suicide if he could. Modise said he would look into that end, and she shouldn't worry herself over it. The business of the fence opening bothered him though.

"The only reason anyone would create such an opening is to avoid being recorded in the park. It's not as if the park was difficult to enter, or for that matter terribly expensive. Anyone who had any business in the area could arrange for passes, and all sorts of other quite legitimate means of gaining access. No, it is clear that the fence has been breached specifically to enable the wrong sort of persons into the park. The question is who?"

"I am thinking you will need to determine why." Sanderson said, and poured him a cup of tea. "Would you prefer coffee?"

"Tea is fine, thank you, Sanderson. I think we are knowing why. People who wish to exchange contraband, smugglers, all sorts of things, they wish not to see the light of day."

"But why in the park. Wouldn't it be easier to meet in an alley, a warehouse, somewhere easily gotten to?"

"It would, but that would risk someone witnessing the exchange, possibly. Also, in the park there is a secondary level of security, you could say."

"I don't understand."

"If you are situated in the game park you will be surrounded by the animals."

"Perhaps. It is a big park and there is much open space with no animals in it. They move about, you know."

"They do, I am sure. You would certainly know that, but do the men from the cities know it and even if they do, how will they know if this is an area where it is safe? As you say, the animals move about."

Sanderson wasn't so sure but she let it go. Modise was right about one thing; unless you worked with them every day, you would not know where and how often the predators might appear in any particular place. And if they caught your scent…

"So, what shall we do?"

"Show me these cameras you have discovered in your storage room."

Sanderson called Charles Tlalelo into the office and the two dragged the equipment they'd found earlier into the room.

"Inspector Modise, this is Charles Tlalelo. Charles, this is Inspector Kgabo Modise. He is from Gabz and is a very important policeman."

Charles extended his right hand, his left touching its elbow. "*Dumela,* Rra."

"*Dumela,* Charles, how are you keeping?"

"*Ke teng.*"

"Tell me about this apparatus."

"Well," Charles began, looking very serious. Sanderson smiled as he spoke and Modise caught the smile, nodded in her direction, but kept his expression serious. The young man was nervous and trying not to seem so. "There was a crew of filmmakers here some months ago. They were in the park filming the animals. At least that is what they said they were doing. Making a documentary for the cinema, but…"

"But?"

"I am not so sure that is what they were about. The crew, they were you could say, unlikely."

"Unlikely? How do you mean that?"

"They were several young women, very pretty young women to be exact, and they did not look to me like naturalists."

"I see. So they were filming something in the park. Why are the cameras here?"

"They left them and never returned when Mr. Pako…he was—"

"Sanderson's predecessor. I know who he was."

"Yes, well, he discovered they did not have the proper permits to be in the park disturbing the animals. He sent them packing. They never came back."

"Yes. Okay. That is a mystery in itself. This is very fine equipment. Have you looked at any of it, tried it out?"

"No. We did charge up the batteries. They were flat."

"I think I will have a look. The cassettes are still in the cameras?"

"Yes. Video tapes, expensive ones I think."

Modise snapped a battery in one of the cameras and rewound the tape. Then he flipped open the screen and played the film. Images of lions and hyenas, of several kinds of gazelles appeared. There was a blank and then there were people. Two people to be precise. Modise watched, mouth agape, as the man and the woman embraced, disrobed and…"

"Sanderson, I must confiscate these tapes. All of them. There is a reason these filmmakers did not return. I will find you new blank tapes, but these will be evidence if we ever find these men again."

Sanderson looked puzzled. Modise said he did not wish to share the contents of the tapes with her. He was sorry. It was police business. He proceeded to collect all of the cassettes and place them in a plastic bag which he sealed and initialed.

"We will speak of this another time. I will return in an hour. It is enough to say that you were correct and you were incorrect, Charles. The women are very definitely 'naturalists' but not in the sense you meant it," he said, and left with a wave of his hand.

Sanderson and Charles Tlalelo exchanged puzzled looks. Sanderson had not told him of her encounter with the threatening man. It would have to wait it seemed.

# Chapter Thirteen

Superintendent Mwambe watched Kgabo Modise as he walked up the path to the station. He did not like Modise. He represented everything that had changed from the old days. He was young. He was smart. He was successful. Mwambe had tracked this young man since the previous winter when he had insinuated himself into the business that properly belonged to Mwambe, to the Kasane Station. And now, here he is back again. What did he want this time? He picked up the Orgone Zapper from his desk and shoved it into a desk drawer. Modise did not need to know about that.

"Inspector Modise, you have honored my station with your presence, yet again. May I ask the occasion? Surely there is nothing so important in the wilds of the north that requires the attention of the rising star from the DIS."

Modise let the not-so-subtle sarcasm slide. He did not want a match with this man. He needed his cooperation, as much as he wished it were not so.

"Superintendent Mwambe, so good to see you again. I am here on behalf of the director and the H. E., the president, as it happens. There will be a heightened presence of police and security needed for the games in South Africa this June, you see."

"Heightened? I do not understand that word, Modise. The station here is able to meet any requirements and has always done so. After all the games are being played hundreds of kilometers away in South Africa. How can that affect us up here?"

"As you know from your years of experience, we have a long border and it is easily penetrated. The people coming to these games will spill over into this country. They will have money to spend and appetites that can create trouble." Mwambe started to say something but Modise held up his hand. "Furthermore, the Mowana Lodge will be receiving the personage of the American Secretary of State, and the other lodges will house many officials from the Middle East and elsewhere. There will be the usual security problems which will add to your duties here, and of course, there is always the threat of an assassination to consider."

Mwambe's jaw went slack. It was too much. He started to say so.

"Superintendent Mwambe, you will need some help here, I am sure. I am authorized to assign some auxiliary officers from other jurisdictions to you when the time comes and the BDF will increase their surveillance of the border. We will also be working closely with the local game ranger stations and—"

"I am thinking that will be a large mistake," Mwambe muttered. "That Sanderson woman was promoted over several men who were much better qualified for the position. She is not suited to the task. Her people may not be so anxious to follow her lead, you see. I think you should have her sent down to look to other duties."

"I understand your thoughts on this, but that will not be acceptable. And since you bring up her name, I understand she turned a murder over to you. What can you tell me about that?"

"She says murder, but she is a game ranger, not a skilled policeman. It is not murder until a complete investigation is completed."

"If it is not a murder, Superintendent, what then? Surely you are not thinking suicide." Modise knew that Mwambe was, in fact, leaning in that direction. "It is an absurd notion, of course. Why would someone drive all the way down from the Congo, enter the park by a surreptitious entry in the middle of the night, and then shoot himself. No, it is most likely he went to meet someone and that someone betrayed him, don't you agree?" At the mention of a possible meeting, Modise noted that Mwambe became visibly uncomfortable.

"A full investigation will tell us what we need to know about this business."

"Yes, of course. May I see the vehicle? Oh yes, and the medical report, if you will."

Mwambe's expression became thunderous. Modise knew he was treading in where he needn't, but he also knew that Mwambe might very well let this business slip out of his hands. His instinct told him it might be important well beyond another murder and that it might, like a crocodile who lurks just below the river's surface, rise up to bite them later.

"Modise, it is not necessary for you to investigate. I am in the process of doing so, and this station is fully competent in the procedures to be followed."

"I am sure you will do a fine job, Superintendent. I have every confidence in you, but I have a secondary purpose in mind. I need to inspect the vehicle and read the report. Please allow me this small thing."

Mwambe sorted through the stack of reports on his desk and all but threw one folder at Modise. "The vehicle is in the impound portion of the parking area. You may see it there," he turned and stalked away. Modise sighed and sat down to read the report. After a few minutes he stepped out into the foyer and flagged down a junior officer and requested he make copies of the contents in the folder. He then let himself out the rear door of the police station and walked to the old Land Rover. He circled it twice before opening the driver's side door. Evidence of the gunshot wound still stained the upholstery and had attracted many flies. He crouched and scrutinized the door opposite. The door frame sported a neat hole. He called over one of the officers Mwambe had evidently sent to observe him.

"Do you see that hole in the door frame?"

The young man seemed confused at being addressed but recovered. "Yes, sir, I do."

"What is your best guess as to the source of the hole?"

"I cannot say, sir."

"Think, man. What does it look like?"

"A hole."

Modise shoulders sagged and he turned his head toward the officer. "Try again, only this time try to remember you are a policeman. What's your name?"

"Derek Kgasa, sir. Might it be a bullet hole? It is round and it has penetrated much steel, I am thinking. So, a bullet hole?"

"Brilliant, Derek. Now I want you to produce some evidence bags and see if you can dig that bullet out of the door frame. Do not worry if you have to take the door apart. It is more important we find the bullet than preserve the truck, you see?"

Modise left Derek Kgasa to the task he'd assigned him and stepped to the rear of the Land Rover. "The report said there was nothing in the cargo area of this vehicle. Is that correct?"

Derek looked up from his efforts to disassemble the door and nodded. "Yes, that is so. I was here when it was towed in. The only things in the back were some rubbish, bits of plaster or something like that."

"Didn't that strike you as odd, Derek? If this man was murdered in the park doesn't it strike you that he must have had something that someone else wanted and they took it before they left?"

"I had not thought of that, no. That is very interesting. So, it wasn't a suicide?"

Modise didn't answer but shook his head and opened the rear of the SUV. "What's this?"

"Sir?"

"Is this the rubbish you described? Hand me another evidence bag. How are you doing with that bullet?"

Derek handed Modise a clear plastic bag and gave one last tug at the window ledge. The door liner fell away and the bullet dropped onto the floorboards.

"Bag that." Modise carefully turned his attention back to the rear of the SUV. He swept the bits and pieces of resin into a bag, sealed it and turned back to the station. "I must resume my conversation with your boss. Please bring him to me in his office."

# Chapter Fourteen

"What was that all about?" Sanderson asked an equally puzzled Charles Tlalelo. "He went out of here like his britches were on fire."

A spark of comprehension flickered in Charles eyes. He grinned. "Perhaps they were."

"What are you going on about, Charles? What do you know of this?" Sanderson felt left out. She did not like it. Men, she thought, had ways of communicating that sometimes sailed over her head and it annoyed her. In truth, she realized that her sex was often accused, rightly, of the same mystery, but that did not make it any easier for her.

"The ladies in the cinema recording, Sanderson. I said they did not seem to be 'naturalists.' I meant they did not strike me as people who were qualified to study animals in the wild. Then Modise said—"

"I heard what he said, Charles, but I am thinking not as you did."

"He said I was right and I was wrong. You see? The women were naturalists in the other sense of the meaning."

"You have lost me."

"The French I was required to learn in school would put it, *au natural*. They were recorded in the state of nature and..."

Sanderson blushed and understood. "They were making filthy pictures, you think?"

"Most certainly. I think it is now safe for you to book this equipment permanently into our inventory. Those cinema people will not be returning to claim their cameras and tapes unless they wish to spend some important time in prison."

Sanderson shook her head and wondered at the male sex in general. What sort of people made such films and why did men seem to crave them? Did they not have someone to visit, someone of their own at home to love?

"What is it about that which so fascinates men?" she asked, not really expecting a reply.

"It is difficult to say, Sanderson. But since the world gifted us with the internet, it is there for anyone who wishes it."

"Really?"

"Oh yes. Just type in any word, the more specific, I should say the more graphic, the better. And there you will have pictures, videos, names and addresses, and opportunities to spend money, download, meet someone who says she shares your interests… whatever you wish."

"Amazing. This is true?" Charles nodded. Sanderson inspected his expression for traces of guilt. She saw some and assumed he spoke from experience.

"Imagine, Charles, the trouble the poor man who forgot to retrieve the cassettes and cameras found himself in when they cleared out of here. His boss could not have been happy with him, for sure."

Charles nodded but his eyes told her his thoughts seemed far away. Sanderson let out an exasperated snort. "You are as bad as the rest of them, Charles."

"What? What am I? Sanderson, what do you mean?"

Sanderson waved him away. Men!

"There is a policeman up from Gabz, Mr. Botlhokwa. He has been to all the lodges and to the police station. I do not think it is a good thing."

"He can know nothing of any of the business with the man in the park. Someone shot him and that person cannot be connected to us, as we did not have anything to do with that. We only guaranteed entry to the park to the man who is now, unfortunately for him, dead. We have provided that service before and everyone knows it. What is the criminal outcome from that?"

"If they find that shooter and if they roll him over he will lead them to someone local and that someone will be one of our people."

"Ours? Are you so sure? Then you must step up your inquiries, Noga, and find this rogue lion who is hunting in my territory. Find him and put him down."

"I am working on it. If I can find the men who bought the information from him, I may have better luck. I am wondering if they have contacted you."

"No. But sooner or later, Noga, they will surface, you can depend on it. I do not believe they got what they were expecting from the man, and they will soon be complaining about it to us. Then we will backtrack to our man, you see?"

"Or the police will have them first and then, whether it was our doing or not, they will be in here breaking up the furniture,"

"That will never happen. There are too many people who have invested in our, as you put it, furniture. Also, these same people will need our services in a few weeks when certain arrangements need to be made to transport certain people across the border, or away to private places without anyone the wiser. No, we have nothing to fear from the officials this day."

"Across the border? What do you mean?" Noga quickly picked up on the not so subtle reference to important people. Rumors of the impending visit from the Americans and the Middle Eastern delegates had been discussed by nearly everyone in the area for days. This might be the time to reconnect with the Russian, but he would have to be very careful. What he needed was a quick solution to this problem of the rogue in the bush. Botlhokwa would be put to sleep, so to speak, if he could deliver this man, any man. It wouldn't make any difference in the end who Noga ended in throwing to the dogs—anyone. Botlhokwa would be pleased that the breach had been filled, and would be less likely to notice any new activity on Noga's part.

"All in good time, Noga. Just be ready to serve the purposes of world peace—for a price, of course." Botlhokwa chuckled at his own joke and waved his man away. "Peace for a price. That's a good one."

◇◇◇

"What I mean, Charles, is that I do not understand how you think about these things. I am studying your face and all I see is a far away stare. You have conjured up in your mind how these ladies may have appeared naked, have you not?"

"Certainly not." Charles face took on an expression of shock. Sanderson was not impressed.

"No? Describe them to me, the women as you remember them. Were they white or colored?"

"They were white. They were Swedish, I think, or from that part of the world where women have that yellow hair and big... blue eyes."

"Swedish? You are sure of that?"

"No, I...they were definitely white women, *ntle* even, but the men were not."

"Not? Not beautiful or not white? How did they look then?"

"Asian or something along those lines. Not typical white men."

"I see. So, how are you imagining those women now, Charles?"

"Sanderson, that is not fair. I am a game ranger like you. I only am concerned for the problems those cinema people may have created with the animals."

"And I am thinking that you look like one of those men who travel to Swaziland each year or to Nongoma and King Zwelithimi's Emyoken, pretending to be Zulu so that you can witness the Reed Dance and all the young girls dancing with their breasts exposed."

"Why would you think such a thing, Sanderson, I would never do that. They expose their...chests at that dance?"

"Fifteen thousand of them, perhaps many more, it is reported. Dancing as near to naked as you could care. Do not tell me you do not know of this. Shame on you, Charles."

# Chapter Fifteen

Modise waited for Superintendent Mwambe to finish his sulk and return to the office. He knew the big policeman wished he would go away, knew he resented what he assumed to be interference from the capital, but he could not concern himself with Mwambe's petulance now. Something about this murder in the park did not add up and the sooner he or Mwambe's people unraveled it, the better. The vehicle had been carrying orgonite rubbish and who would steal that? There were people, he knew, who had no patience with this business. He numbered himself among them, but surely no one would kill a carrier of the materials to stop it. Arrest, harass, humiliate them, yes, but murder? It didn't make sense. Surely Mwambe would see that. And, he had the license plate number of the men who were seen dumping the same stuff in the American's skip. Lab tests would show if they were from the same source, but he felt he had enough for him to move forward. Suicide? What was he thinking?

He ran his hands across the desk's smooth surface and opened a drawer or two. He saw the Zapper and recognized it for what it was. Mwambe was a believer in the benefits of orgonite. That might either explain or complicate things. He quickly closed the drawer and lifted a piece of paper from the pile on the right hand side of the desk.

Mwambe loomed in the doorway and took his seat behind his desk. "My aide informs me you wish to see me again. What is it this time?"

Modise ignored the superintendent's rudeness and outlined what he had been thinking. Mwambe's expression slowly transformed from irritated to curious. Modise explained that the bullet fragment found in the Land Rover's door frame might or might not be suitable for ballistics but as the caliber made it clear it most certainly did not come from a pistol. Further, the orgonite in the rear of the vehicle might or might not be from the same source as that from the skip. So, not a suicide and evidently linked to something else. If they knew what, they might have a lead to follow.

"But, it doesn't matter at this point, Superintendent. What we must do is find these men who disposed of the orgonite and question them. They do not need to know what we can or cannot prove, you see?"

"And how," Mwambe grumbled, "are we to find these men who were seen at the American casino? Surely you do not think they are cruising about on the streets of Kasane."

"Ah, that is where we are lucky. I have a license plate number. It is South African and perhaps stolen or from a rental vehicle, but it is a start. You can have your people trace it, put out a bulletin for patrols to look for it. You know the drill."

"I do. Let me have that number and we will see."

"Good. Now, there is one other thing. Sanderson has found a breach in the park fence close to Kasane. It appears this is the spot where the murdered man came into the park."

"You wish me to send a detachment to seal the fence? That would be Sanderson's duty, I think."

"No, I don't want it sealed. I think we should pretend to know nothing of it. I believe it would be better to have her put it under surveillance and see who else comes through."

"A break in the fence makes no sense. You are from the south. You do not know these parts as I do, Modise. What reason some person has come up with for cutting the fence I cannot imagine, but it is a silly idea. The park is crisscrossed with tracks where guides drive their safari trucks. The airport is within the parks boundaries, for heaven's sake. This is a wide open range. Anyone can, if they wish, and with the proper vehicle and a map, drive into the park and onto these tracks and go where they wish, do what they wish. As long as they do not tempt the animals, of course."

"That is true?"

"Nearly enough. A gap in the fence near Kasane is for convenience, I am thinking. It is for people from outside the area, foreigners and so on, who do not know better. They would need to be directed and someone like…well, someone who trades in illegalities, you could say, would use that entrance for his clients who would most likely be ignorant of the nature of the park. Our local malefactors will know their ways in and out, and certainly need no help of that sort."

"You were about to say a name. You said 'someone like' and then stopped. Who were you about to point a finger at?"

"Rra Botlhokwa came to mind. But we have not been able to prove anything against him as yet. And he has friends in high places, I am led to believe. We are not going to accuse him of anything without a very strong case."

"Fair enough. What other local illegal activities were you hinting at?"

"We have occasional poachers. They come in from the Caprivi and Zimbabwe, of course. The safari guides will tip them off if they see sick animals, cats mostly, and they slip in and help the poor beast out of his misery. They will leave the carcass for the *manong* and *dipheri*, the scavengers." Mwambe shook his head at thought of vultures and hyenas worrying a carcass. Modise shuddered at the image of scavengers dining on it. "Poaching has picked up since the president left the Army in others' hands. When he ran the army it was poachers beware, for certain," Mwambe said.

"With the probable influx of rich tourists in June, will they be more active?"

"I believe that is a thing that goes without saying, Modise. It is supply and demand. Rich tourists always have peculiar tastes in what they will pay money for. There are men who still wish to bag the big five."

"Big five?"

"Yes. To shoot one of each, a leopard, a lion, a rhinoceros, an elephant, and a cape buffalo. These are the most difficult animals to hunt on foot. It used to be a rite of passage you could say, among the rich and idle. I thought you would know that."

"My mistake. I did know, my mind was elsewhere on arrests and so on. Go on."

"The hunting, however, will be done elsewhere. Zimbabwe or perhaps Angola, but not here. Too dangerous if caught. It is not an activity where a bribe will buy a blind eye and a deaf ear. Still, they must get to the hunting grounds and back again with protected material so…well, there will be opportunities. And then there are the odd things others want. Well, the Asians and Arabs, for example, they will go for the odd bits and pieces. Strange people."

"That is true. Well, I leave it to you to monitor the locals who facilitate these activities and also a keep a sharp eye on our devious friend, Rra Botlhokwa. Also, we will monitor the gap, and perhaps post some motion-sensitive cameras in the park to find these people and any new ones who, I have no doubt in my mind, will arrive in your town any day now."

Mwambe nodded his assent. He held up the paper with the license number and raised his eyebrows in a question.

"Yes, certainly, let's get that looked into, Superintendent. I have a feeling that if we can bring these men in, we will save ourselves a pile of trouble in the future."

Mwambe stood to leave, but not before letting his gaze roam across his desk behind which Modise had ensconced himself. It was an invitation for the interloper from Gaborone to leave and return the station to its rightful leader. Modise shrugged and stood.

"One last thing, Superintendent Mwambe. I am hoping you can put aside your dislike for Sanderson the game ranger sufficiently to work with her on these intrusions into the park. You understand I am here on the direct orders of the DG and H. E., the President. It will not do to have any disruption of this operation. Certainly not for personal reasons." Modise took his leave without waiting for a reply. Mwambe had the message. It would be up to him how he responded, and if the response would allow him to retain his office or find himself in early retirement.

# Chapter Sixteen

Rra Botlhokwa was not in the habit of accepting criticism from any one and certainly not from people whom he judged to be inferior to him in either station or intellect. He gritted his teeth as he listened to this very loud man who called himself Sczepanski, who had all but barged into his office. When he paused to catch his breath, Botlhokwa raised both hands in front of him and hissed.

"Quiet please," he said, and gave his guest a malevolent stare as fierce as a person whose visage could only be described as moon-like could muster. "You must let me speak before you say, or perhaps, do something that could do you a great disservice." He lit one of his Cubans. After he had a satisfyingly heavy cloud of smoke between the two of them, he placed both hands palms down on the rosewood desktop.

"Now, as to the man who sold you this information, first, we do not sell information. If we contract to guarantee entry into the park—this is hypothetical of course—that is what we would do. No more, no less. If it became generally known we sold out our clients, well, how long do you think we would stay in business?"

"My men say they spoke with your man." Botlhokwa started to interrupt but the man shushed him. "No, no it was definitely your man. At least, he said he was your man. He had done some things for us in the past for which he was paid certain sums, I should say. He was yours, I assure you. He told us there would be a delivery made in the park. He said it was a Congolese outfit delivering goods through Zambia. The Congo is a supplier of many things that cannot be easily obtained. We took him at his word and paid him. There was nothing of value in that truck, no horns, no contraband, nothing, just some plaster rubbish. I am here to retrieve my money and suggest to you that my employer is less than pleased with this situation."

Botlhokwa studied the man for a full minute. He seemed to be telling the truth. More importantly, he did not seem in awe of him. Most men who ventured into his presence were, or pretended to be. Who was this man and who was the employer he alluded to? He would need to find out.

"Do you have a name for me? I will gladly give back your money, but as I do not have it, I must extricate it from this person who you say works for me. You understand? If this man took money from you in my name, he did so without my knowing and did not remit the money to me. If he, in fact, is one of my people I will do more than just extract the money from him, I promise you."

The man opposite shifted in his chair.

"We do not have the name. I will have to go through my books and find it. He was your man *Rra*, I am sure of it."

*We?* Who would *we* be? "Fine, bring me the name and I will see to it. But without the name I can do nothing and I don't think you will either."

The man heard the edge to Botlhokwa's voice and narrowed his eyes.

I do not like this man, Botlhokwa thought. He hoped the Noga would turn up a name soon. If he didn't, well he was doing all he could do, wasn't he? There'd been rumors circulating in Cape Town. Rumors about a criminal syndicate wanting to come north into his territory. Well, we shall see about that. He might work with these men, but it would be on his terms. Otherwise…It had been years since he'd called out the dangerous men he kept on retainer across the border in Zimbabwe, but he would do so if he had to.

*Patriarche* heard the crashing in the bush as the hunters closed in on his family. He grunted for them to move farther up the hill and away from the threat. Never able to move with stealth, their departure was obvious and noisy. They knuckle-walked as quickly as they could through the brush, the females pausing from time to time to keep track of their young. One infant fell behind and its distress call caused *Patriarche* to stop. The female wheeled and charged down the hill. A volley of shots rang out and the sounds of the hunter's triumph rang out across the hillside. *Patriarche* reasoned the young one still lived. He knew its mother did not. He stared in the direction of the sounds. The group huddled close to him. They waited for his direction. They would be safe enough for a while, but they should move on. They were running out of space. *Patriarche* sniffed the air. Mixed in with the odor of gunpowder, he picked up another, equally dangerous scent. They had invaded a leopard's territory. He huffed. They would stay here the night. Tomorrow? Who knew?

◇◇◇

"Charles supposes the cinema crew who left us this fine equipment were filming restricted footage." Sanderson could not bring herself to say pornography to Modise. She didn't know why. Perhaps it was because she had a daughter and she knew that these sorts of men, the men who made those awful DVDs, preyed on girls Mpitle's age. She also knew that there were times in the lives of some families when a daughter in that business, if only for a very short time, meant the difference between starving and eating. And of course, however certain the girl or her family were that it was *only this once,* it never ended there—not until the girl had been exploited by all sorts of very bad men, not until she came home feverish and sick with HIV/Aids.

She clenched her fists at these thoughts and felt anger in her heart for the people who did these terrible things, and then at men in general whose sick need to view women in this way created the market that kept the producers in business. It was always the same: the rich and self indulgent with their appetites created the market that exploited the poor, and required the police to spend scarce resources to stop it. Drugs, pornography, it was all the same. Their money was blood money paying for pain and death. The drug cartels, the pornographers, all relied on so-called good people to continue their awfulness. She smacked the desk with her fist.

Modise jumped and reading the expression on her face took a step back. Whatever she was about in her mind, he seemed to say, he did not want to be too close when she expressed it.

Sanderson caught her breath, shot an angry look at Charles who, like Modise, stepped back, puzzled.

"I am very angry at the thought of the park being a place where this awfulness is taking place."

"Well, Sanderson, you can rest assured they will not be back. At least not to film. But that will not stop others from trying somewhere else. It is a shame, but all we, the police, can do is be vigilant."

"I am not sure it is enough. If people do not buy this filth, there is no reason to make it, yes? You must stop it at the consumer end, I am thinking. Perhaps Charles can give you some leads in this matter."

Charles looked genuinely shocked. "Sanderson, what are you saying? I am not a person who frequents the places where this business goes on. I merely pointed out to you what anyone, no everyone, knows. That pornography is ingrained into the culture. It has been for years, I think. I saw a very fine program on the telly about some place in Italy where they had a big volcano problem many years ago, thousands, I think, and the walls on these houses that they uncovered after all this time had pictures of…those sorts of pictures. It has not always been so bad a thing it seems."

"That those people did these things is no excuse."

"Do you think I am likely…Sanderson, simply to know these things is not the same as condoning, utilizing them or… or anything. What are you thinking?"

Modise paused and then sat at Sanderson's desk, just as he had at Mwambe's. And for the same reason—to assert his authority and bring the conversation back to where he needed it to be.

"Enough, Sanderson. I agree with you completely," he said, "But this gets us nowhere. I need your thoughts…yours too, Charles, on how we can monitor the park when the press arrives in a month or two. Mwambe tells me the gap in the fence is for outsiders, people who do not know how really easy it is to enter the park. He says the poachers would not need it. Is that so?"

Sanderson took a breath. Her anger subsided sufficiently to address this problem. "I am sorry, Charles. I had no right to accuse you. So, as to Mwambe. He is correct in that. The gap is convenient to Kasane, and so has the advantage of providing quick access to the park. Otherwise you must do some driving about on bad and probably unfamiliar paths. If you do not know these tracks, they can be dangerous."

"Who would know of these?"

"The guides from the lodges all know them. And then there are the local people. You know there are still some people living in the enclaves near the water. They come and go. Mwambe may think they are poachers but they live off the land—at least some of them do, and they have hunted it forever. They fish but will not take an animal. I cannot be so sure about their friends and relatives from across the river, and then there are the illegals from Zimbabwe. They flee the chaos in their country and the foolishness of Crazy Bob. If there is a problem with them, it is the poverty they experience that will make them easy prey for exploiters."

"Well, we must work with what we have, I guess." Modise would have liked something more concrete, but it was early still.

# Chapter Seventeen

"It's dead simple. We find customers, we find suppliers, we put them together and take a nice finder's fee."

"I'm not convinced about the simple bit, but if we're caught, we're perished and that'll be the dead bit."

"Don't be such a puss, Harvey. I've explained it to you a dozen times. Now, your job is to scare us up some buyers. That should be easy enough for you. You've been mucking about in the minerals business for donkey's years. I'll see to the suppliers. There's always some power hungry warlord or Mugabe wannabe out there who can supply the goods to get the cash he needs to pay for his personal war."

"Jack, you could sell ice to Eskimos, I know. I just think we might be headed into something that could bring some very nasty types into our yard. Never disturb a hornet's nest, I say."

"Hornets? Oh, come on, mate."

"I'm serious, Jack. Like you said, I've been mucking about in this business for a long time, and I will tell you there are people who can smell a wonky deal at thirty paces. Coppers, officials, governmental types, and even some do-gooder U.N. people worried about the wars up north. They are all over the lot looking for just this sort of dodge. It's uncanny, but I've seen it up close. Some of those people've been in the intercession business for years."

"Now, surely those blokes you can deal with if you have to."

"Maybe. Worst case, they shut us down. It's the others, the stone cold chaps with eyes like ice, lads who'd kill you as quick as look at you if they thought you had something of value in your kit."

"Harvey we're covered here. Whether they can smell them or have super powers and can see through walls, dodge bullets, and drink river water, the scam here is they won't tumble to us because they'll think we're a pair of nutters flogging orgonite all over the place. If they object at all, it will be because we get in their way while they're out in the park doing truly dark deeds."

"You'd better hope so, Jack. Okay, I will go through my contacts and work up a list of possible customers. Some are easy, low risk, some are the other way about."

"We'll start with the low risk. Who would that be?"

"There are a few companies that can't compete in the global market, and many who would be middle men in the market. They've got financing problems, or have been elbowed out of the way by the big guns in Asia, mostly. The government will not be happy if we start moving this stuff into the wrong places. There is a market in place for coltan. I just need a name or two and we're in."

"The government. This is the strangest country I've ever had to work a grift. These people are determinedly honest. They seem incapable of straying. They say they will not allow corruption to seep into their affairs."

"That is true now. Give them time and a healthy dose of Western civilization and then see how straight they stay. I'll give them ten years, tops. Progress under capitalism always has a price, and that price is the corruption that always follows greed."

"You are a terrible cynic, Harvey. But, I hope you're right. I like working here. Who are the high risk customers?"

"The usual—the greedy, the slightly bent, the dealers who are low on the supply chain. There are always people ready to broker anything that's hard to come by. You realize, of course, that we will need to have the stuff analyzed. That is a specialty skill. We will have to find someone who can do that for us and keep his mouth shut."

"No worries. I have some people in mind that can handle that."

"Can you get the coltan? And if so, how much?"

"My man in the north says they just opened a new pit and it looks big. Sky's the limit, he says."

"I still think it's risky."

"Life is risky and listen, he says there might be gorillas in the area where the pit is located. Nice secondary market. He'll sell the bush meat and we'll distribute the interesting bits."

"Jack, I'm drawing the line here. If we get caught moving coltan we have a minor felony on our sheet. If this government catches us with endangered species products they will lock us up and throw away the key. No gorillas. Period."

Leo Painter allowed as how he could manage for a few days without him. Greshenko guessed Leo didn't buy his excuses entirely, though. He knew something was up, but hadn't said anything—yet.

"But while you are in South Africa, drop in on the shippers in Cape Town and double check their capacity to get those modules up here on time. Oh, and see if you can scrounge…finagle…" Greshenko had a puzzled expression on his face, "Okay, how do you say in Russian, something like to steal honestly?"

Greshenko shrugged and shook his head.

"Okay, you do…whatever you would do if you needed something and didn't have time to bargain or pay right away."

"Ah, some little playing of the shell game?"

"Whatever you say. I want a block of tickets for the finals of the World Cup matches. It's early yet and there has to be someone who can make that happen, maybe our shipper. Like, if you were to hint we might be putting our business out for bid, they might find a way to come up with some tickets. Anyway, see what you can do."

"These tickets are for who? Or should I say what?"

"Premiums, Yuri. Part of the package. Customers who stay with us after or before, watch the games free and in comfort. Marketing."

Greshenko didn't say so, but he was sure his contacts, the men he had been bullied into meeting, would have no trouble finding as many tickets as Leo wanted. Whether he would pay their price was something else entirely.

"I will talk to some people. You know that most of the tickets to the boxes and lounges are consigned already or sold. I may have access to a small block of first rate tickets and more of the general admission variety."

"Do the best you can. It's just an idea, not a requirement. If we can't lay our hands on a sufficient number, we can always scalp them."

But, tickets notwithstanding, he could not stop now. He must do what they asked and hoped they kept their word. He didn't believe it but, as they had pointed out to him in painful detail, he had no options. Do as bid or end his days in a very cold place from which there would be no hope of escape. Greshenko nodded and pulled the handle of his bag up. "Very well, then, I will see you in a few days." He rolled the bag out to his waiting taxi.

"Airport," he said, and climbed in.

◇◇◇

Sanderson saw Tlalelo and Modise to the door and shut it behind him. Could this internet thing be true? Surely the government would not permit it. She positioned herself behind her desk and stared at her computer screen. What to do. Did she need to know about this thing? Would her knowing be of help? She didn't know. How could she?

She pulled up her internet browser. Computers were not something she completely understood. She thought of her daughter, Mpitle. She would know how to find this out but… that was the point, wasn't it. She did not want that to happen. Mpitle, so young and in so much danger with the HIV/AIDs all about. She shook her head and thought a moment. What do I type in this Google box? Did she know any of those words? She did, but knowing was not something she wished to admit.

Her computer screen, pale blue and nonjudgmental, seemed to wait for her to decide. Did she want to proceed or not? Finally she typed in two words and hit enter. A screen filled with sites appeared. She clicked on the first offering and stared, her mouth agape as images of women flooded the screen. They were naked, of course, but the things they were doing! It was true. She clicked back to the search results and read that there were over three thousand sites with this rubbish on them.

She quickly exited, erased her search history, and contemplated the now pristine screen. Why was this permitted? Who looked at those pictures? Why? And where were those girls' mothers who allowed this to happen to their children?

# Chapter Eighteen

Sometime in his early life, *Patriarche* had learned to use a stick. That happened before he became the leader of this increasingly threatened family group. A branch had apparently fallen from a tree and stuck vertically in the turf. Instead of knocking it over as he might have in the past, he grasped it with both hands and pulled it straight toward him. It unearthed a succulent root. A second scratch with the stick yielded the same results. He discovered the small end of a stick could push through the tangle and turn up an edible root more efficiently than grubbing in the dirt with his massive paws. At that moment *Patriarche* became what anthropologists would describe as a "tool user." Somewhat later he discovered that a longer stick could be used to pull down tree limbs otherwise just out of his reach and make their leaves more accessible. He tried to teach the ways of the stick to the other gorillas. Some caught on; most remained unimpressed. He kept trying, however.

Throwing the stick at limbs to bring down a shower of leaves, fruit, and occasionally nuts and seeds had only occurred to him in the last several months. He had become proficient at the art. Once, when he'd thrown the stick into a tree top, he'd brought down a bird's nest. The eggs broke when they hit the ground and he'd tasted the yellow mess. It was food, no doubt. He did not try to knock down anymore nests but he remembered how it had been done. If he and the others had to change their territory or move to a less lush area, they might have to learn to eat these things that fell from the trees. A bigger stick would bring more things to him.

Now as the sun rose in the east, stick in hand, he surveyed his family grazing quietly in the bush. He sensed more than knew, that down the hillside the infant gorilla was still alive and calling for its mother who would never answer. How much longer it would remain alive he could not know. He smacked the earth with his stick and it broke. He grunted and went searching for another, a stronger one. He would find a bigger stick and he would learn to throw it better. Then he would show the others how to do it again.

◇◇◇

Leo Painter's reply when asked how he'd produced counter moves to various efforts by rivals intent on upsetting his plans would always be, "I may be slow, but I'm not stupid." Advancing age and the residual effects of multiple coronary accidents had not in any way diminished his intuitive grasp of situations that posed a threat to him or his business, although he readily admitted he'd slowed down considerably. And while he no longer held the day-to-day management responsibilities of Earth Global, the company he'd built from a small oil wildcatting firm to one of the world's largest energy and mining consortiums, he still had a business to attend to. His casino and hotel on the Chobe occupied his full attention and he sensed that for some reason Yuri Greshenko had gone off the rails. He did not doubt Greshenko's loyalty. He had no reason to. It wasn't a matter of blind loyalty or friendship. He just knew enough about his partner to realize it was not in anyone's interest, his or Greshenko's, to mess it up. So, this rapid and nonessential departure to the south could only mean that something very much off the books lurked out there somewhere.

Leo sorely missed his contacts in the States. Were he back home in Chicago, he'd need only to pick up the phone, make two or three calls, and he'd have a pretty good line on what pit Greshenko had fallen into. But this was neither Chicago nor the United States and the people who could deliver the information he wanted did not operate here. He positioned himself behind the battered desk that would serve as his office until the administrative wing of his hotel was completed and drummed his fingers. In the past this would be a two-cigar think. But cigars were off his list of permissible things along with double martinis before lunch and a few other small vices he'd once enjoyed but now only relished as memories.

The telephone system had a call logger built into the system. Leo had insisted on that from the outset. He had had to order it special from the States and at considerable expense. But it had been one of those things he'd come to rely on in his past life, one of his "I-may-be-slow- but-I'm-not-stupid" props and he accessed it now. Who had Yuri been talking to besides the usual business and personal calls he made. It would be a start.

Because she'd been so distracted by the topic of the filmmakers and the subject of internet sex, Sanderson had neglected to tell Modise of her encounter with the stranger who'd threatened in such a disturbing fashion. So much had happened so quickly and Modise…well, he distracted her too, she had to admit. He moved like one of the big cats, not a lion. Lions were not the graceful ones, only the largest. Although she'd been told the tigers of India were bigger, she found that hard to believe. In Setswana his name *Kgabo* meant monkey, but she did not think of him that way. Ape, maybe, but not a monkey for sure. No, she imagined him more as a leopard, one of those black ones that she'd read about that mostly live in Asia.

"This is such foolishness," she muttered and put Kgabo Modise out of her mind.

She had arranged to take her daughter to the shops and that meant returning to her home, parking the government Land Rover, and starting off in her red Bakkie. She was very firm on that point. Personal business meant using her personal means of transportation. She knew perfectly well that many, indeed most people employed by the government, took as a perquisite of that employment the use of their government issued vehicle. She did not. To and from work only. So, it was in her red Toyota HiLux that she drove into Kasane, not the Land Rover. It was a perfect disguise, you could say, if she wanted to go unnoticed. Old and battered Toyota pickup trucks were as common as ticks on a rhinoceros in this part of the country.

She was about to make the turn to the road that led to her daughter's school when the man, this threatening person of hers, stepped into the street and started toward her. She slid low in her seat and hoped he did not see her. But she saw him. Panicked, she put the truck into gear and thought to pull away, but he turned abruptly and seemed to follow another smaller man who seemed familiar, but his back was turned and she couldn't be sure. Sanderson eased her truck into motion. She would trail this lummox who had threatened her. Perhaps he would lead her to his home or work place and she would identify him. Knowing these things would surely help Modise.

◇◇◇

Superintendent Mwambe reread the cable from Kinshasa. He should contact Modise with this information. It would help with his investigation. It annoyed Mwambe that Modise had intuitively hit on the central fact of the killing—that the dead man was part of the Orgonise Africa movement and had come to the park ostensibly to distribute orgonite there or in the Chobe River. There had to be more, of course, but...he dropped the cable onto a pile of papers, straightened its edges, and decided he would wait and call Modise after lunch. He needed time to consider all the possibilities this knowledge presented as well as to affirm his jurisdiction over the investigation. Gaborone needed to understand that up in the north the police were perfectly capable of handling any and all situations with out the interference of young ambitious operators like Modise.

And there he needed time to consider how to deal with Andrew Tanaka. Such a fool.

# Chapter Nineteen

The group of people Mwambe's cable referenced sat around a table in Kinshasa and considered their options. The plan to introduce orgonite into the Chobe seemed brilliant at the time. Thus far, only small amounts had been placed in northern Botswana. With the excitement of the games arriving soon, now seemed a perfect time to correct that. If they could put enough of this revitalizing substance into this river it would easily find its way along the river's course on into the Zambezi River, and to Mozambique. Where they had previously failed at Cahora Bassa would be taken care of this time. The fact that it would also drift through Victoria Falls would be another great benefit. One only had to witness the mist billowing out of the fall's gorge to see how it could not fail to put energy into the land.

There had been some lengthy discussion about the energy migrating along the rivers. The people in London steadfastly insisted that the orgonite had to be placed in specific areas; that it did not migrate from the cones which held it. If that were the case, they insisted, one need only to introduce it at the headwaters of the continents great rivers and the task would be complete. But the younger, indigenous members of the movement had seen the blocks of material slowly disintegrate over time and reckoned it only reasonable that once this process had started the effects of the orgonite, the released energy, would drift inexorably downstream, refreshing and healing the countryside as it did so. That they should spot the material periodically along the course of the rivers and spread across a great expanse of land represented something of a compromise.

They all knew from experience that a river in full flood did not behave like one during a time of relative drought. Indeed, a flood tide could bring water from the Okavango onto the Chobe and refresh the swamps between them. It didn't happen often, but it did occur. Water in swamps would not fulfill the promise of distribution they anticipated. Thus, the plan to introduce orgonite in concentrations in certain areas rather than simply drop it into the Kwando in Angola and let it flow southeastward through the Chobe to the Zambezi and on to the sea in Mozambique.

They neither thought nor cared that William Reich's ideas about the orgone energy were peculiarly focused on its sexual and mental benefits and had little or nothing to do with revitalizing land, much less an entire continent. And what he would make of all this was never mentioned, much less discussed. Movements, great or small, once separated from their founders often acquired a life remarkably different than that which was initially envisioned, and Operation Paradise was no exception. If you believed, as these young people did, that you held in your hands the means to rid the continent of HIV/AIDs without having to acknowledge the societal, behavioral, that is to say the human element in its spread, why question premises? And one must add to this account the healing it offered from drought, poverty, and the residue of centuries of oppressive colonial rule. In the face of all this, they could not let this small setback stop them now.

The group mourned the loss of their comrade, determined to send his widow some money if they came across any to spare, and began their search for another vehicle and driver. Their mission was of too great importance to pause now, either for reflection or mourning.

◇◇◇

Leo Painter studied the printout of Greshenko's most recent phone calls. The international ones he could explain for the most part. The ones to Gaborone also except…Greshenko told him he had had no contact with the country of his birth for years. His temporary resident permit, however, had been issued to Yuri's Russian passport. Leo never asked how this could be. He assumed that Yuri's former connections to the nether world of international crime managed it for him. He also knew that Yuri had filed for citizenship in Botswana and that effort had landed in a sea of red tape. Yet there could be no mistaking this number. What would a Russian restaurant in Gaborone want with him? More likely, what would the denizens of such a place want with him?

Leo wondered if his revelation would create an unnecessary snarl in his carefully planned retirement. He no longer wished for, much less relished, the sort of plotting and scheming that had characterized his earlier life as a CEO, and all the corporate wheeling and dealing it entailed. "The simple life," he'd said six months ago, "from now on peace and serenity, thank you."

So, what had Greshenko gotten himself involved in now? He had no idea what it might involve, but he knew he would not like it when he found out. Once again, he longed for the resources, the investigators and yes, the muscle, he could muster back in the States. He could call them, he supposed. They might have some suggestions, some alternatives. It would be worth a try.

He'd confront Greshenko the instant he returned. International intrigue, if this is what it is, did not figure in Leo's future. And anything that threatened his hotel and casino threatened him personally.

He did not need this.

◇◇◇

The street appeared nearly empty. It would be another hour before luncheon and people would spill out of offices and buildings. That he would be noticed was not in question. A white man carrying a large overnight bag loitering in the mall's food court would be obvious to even the most inattentive passerby. And he felt sure the men who awaited him in the restaurant had him in sight as well. But caution had become a habit in his past life and he allowed it to click in now as well. He walked with deliberate slowness toward the entrance marked *Pectopah* and *Reseturente* on the opposite side of the corridor. He needed to know if others, not his contacts, were interested in him as well. If he did spot them he'd keep walking and wait for another call. Aside from the fact he was white and carrying a satchel, there did not appear to be anyone even remotely interested in him.

As he suspected, however, he *had* been monitored from the restaurant. The young man who acted as *maitre de* gave his ID a cursory glance and waved him into a booth in the back. A moment later a tall man, whom in the old days Greshenko would more than likely have labeled a Cossack, gestured for him to follow. He was ushered through the kitchen area into a small sitting room and told someone would be with him shortly. Requiring a person, who had one could say certain deficits, and who was, therefore, in his summoner's power, to wait was an old psychological trick. It was not lost on Greshenko. The visa, which permitted his continued residence in the country, and therefore his very future, could very well depend on the outcome of this meeting. Leo, with all his political connections in the United States, did not have much sway in this venue. So he waited in silence, eyes fixed on the wall opposite, and wondering where they had planted the listening devices.

In something less than a half hour a grizzled man entered followed by a billow of thick smoke which reeked of the sort of tobacco that only Russians and Turks could abide. Yuri had all but forgotten that aroma. It brought back memories, very few of them pleasant. The old man sat and studied him. He, in turn, studied the old man. He could read his history by the tattoos on his arms, at least those he could see. This man had been around. Greshenko had never reached the point of wearing his résumé, as it were, as skin art. The practice which started in the gulags as far back as Tsarist Russia had pretty much ended by the time Greshenko found himself in the service of these men.

"You're part of Lenka's organization?" he asked.

The big man coughed, one of those "been smoking cheap tobacco products for over thirty years" coughs that sounded as if his lungs would soon fly out of his mouth and slide across the table. He caught his breath, wiped his chin, and grinned, Greshenko caught sight of the stainless steel in his mouth. He *had* been around a long time.

"Perhaps, my son, and perhaps not. That is knowledge you do not need to possess at this moment."

So, the rumors he'd heard before he left Chicago were true. The *Bratva* had established a base in South Africa and, with Bout out of the picture, this had to be Lenka. It had only been a matter of time before they moved north. He contemplated the man across from him who still tried to clear his throat from the after effects of the coughing spell. We are two of a kind, he thought. Separated by decades and history but after that, where was the difference? Time and tide, he thought. Weren't they both too old to play this game? Very possibly, yet here they were. This man from the Russian *Bratva* who represented as well the *Bratva's* reluctant bridegroom—the smoldering embers of the old KGB—and him. Only Greshenko believed he'd left this life behind, but it seemed he'd anticipated his freedom to soon. Now he wondered if he would ever be free.

These were implacable men, he knew. Men who would kill you as soon as look at you, who would kill your wife and children, your uncles, aunts, and anyone near to you just to make their point, to assure compliance. One did not cross them. One did not resign from service without some higher-up's blessing. The organization's tentacles reached into every continent, every nation, and every disagreeable, dirty, and dishonest enterprise from arms running, prostitution, drugs, smuggling, to those more esoteric preoccupations known to men with certain peculiar predilections.

The business he was to be recruited into would soon be laid out for him. And as with the smoke, his response to its requirements, he guessed, would be neither pleasant nor possible to refuse. And the after effects would cling to him for a long, long time.

# Chapter Twenty

Sanderson followed the man for a hundred meters. She noticed that he did not make an attempt to contact the man he seemed to be following. When the first stopped, so did her quarry. What is this all about? Another hundred meters further along and the small man stopped once again, looked furtively over his shoulder, nodded toward the follower, and veered into the parking area next to the police station. She knew this man. He worked for her. Andrew Takeda. The follower, this harasser of women, turned in as well. The Police station? What happens here?

Sanderson pulled to the side of the road and parked her *bakkie* so that she had a view of both men. They sidled to a corner of the car park and up to one another, and started a conversation. So, it seemed that this following was part of something else. Why did these men wish not to be seen together on the street, but in a car park next to the police station? Something here did not make much sense. Andrew. Why would he be talking to this man? Did he send this man to threaten her because of her promotion? Well, she did not scare so easily. She would have a long discussion with Andrew, and decide if he needed to remain employed in her unit. What were they talking about? She wished she could hear what these men were saying. She searched her pockets and found her cell phone.

Her daughter had shown her how to use the camera function. At the time she thought having a phone that took pictures a rubbish idea. Now she was not so sure. She held it up and took a series of photos of the two men. They were a distance away, but perhaps they could be enlarged. Modise would know. She turned the key in the ignition and started the engine. Nothing more to be done here. As she engaged the clutch, she caught sight of Superintendant Mwambe out of the corner of her eye. He stepped out of the door and into the car park. As he did so, the two men disengaged and drifted apart. The large man exited the area the way he had come and headed directly toward her. Mwambe apparently noticed only Andrew and joined him.

She fought her fear of the approaching man just long enough to take one more shot of Mwambe and Andrew. Then she pulled away and drove off in a hurry. She hoped she hadn't been seen. On reflection, she didn't care if she had.

She would call Modise.

◇◇◇

"Mr. Painter." The foreman on the construction site looked fearful. "It wasn't my fault. Sammi borrowed my telephone to call his wife and then put it on the ledge for me to gather up later. I told him not to, that the last time someone did that the phone disappeared, but he didn't listen."

"You are telling me that your phone was stolen? I supplied those phones so that I could stay in touch with you. They were not for personal use, and certainly not to be handed around like chips at the lunch table."

"I am sorry. Sammi said it was an emergency. His wife is pregnant and he had a feeling."

"A what? He had a feeling? He is gifted with second sight?"

"Pardon?"

"Are you telling me he thought his wife might be in trouble and he knew it?"

"Sammi knows things, Mr. Painter. The *moloi* says he has the connection to the spirits."

"If he's so connected to the spirits, then what did he need your phone for? Wouldn't he have already known what had or had not happened?"

The foreman only shrugged. The question did not make sense to him. There were people who talked to the spirits, and there were those who did not. One does not question these things. Americans, he thought were a peculiar people and sadly lacking in this simple wisdom. "Sorry," he said and held out his hands in an attitude of supplication.

"Okay then, do you have any idea who might have taken the phone? They cost money, you know. Much *pula*."

"Oh yes, I know."

"Then why not go and demand that he return it. Why talk to me?"

"That will not be possible, sir."

"Not possible? Why not?"

"No. You see, it was the monkey that took it. When Sammi put it on the ledge, he forgot about that gray monkey that hangs around here. It is a mistake we made when we started."

"Whoa, you lost me. You say the monkey, that big one that pops up all the time looking for lunch handouts, took the phone? Why is that a mistake? I mean I guess it must be, but...you've lost me again"

"No, no, I must make my meaning clear. The monkey stole the phone. Where he took it is anybody's guess. We could dial the number up and perhaps we will find he has dropped it nearby, but I do not think so. I saw him head into the park. No, the mistake, Mr. Painter, was for the men to ignore the signs saying not to, and then they feed that bad monkey in the first place. That is why he is always here and why he has taken up stealing as a pastime you could say. He took Joseph's measuring tape yesterday and other things have gone missing."

"What other things?"

"Well the lunches, as you mentioned, cold drinks, and well, under the tree where he likes to sit we find small tools that he takes, plays with, and then drops when he is done with them. He is a very curious monkey, that one."

"Curious George, no doubt. Can you chase him off?"

"Perhaps, but I don't think so. Monkeys do not run off if only you yell at them, you see. No, he will not be chased off. There is a way, but it is frowned on and is probably illegal. The game rangers will be very angry at us."

"How, 'frowned on?'"

"It is illegal."

"So you said, but...?"

"Beer, Mr. Painter. He is fond of beer. It comes from living near the game lodges. People leave their cans half empty lying about and the monkey, he has developed a taste for it. We can feed him much beer. He will become drunk and we carry him off to another place far away, perhaps into the park with the other animals. He won't come back so soon."

"But it's illegal."

"Yes."

"Do it. But call the number first in the off chance he dropped the phone nearby. I don't want any trouble with that woman game ranger. Been there, done that and..."

Excuse me?

""Never mind. Do what you have to do and if it isn't available, I'll see about getting you another.

"Yes, sir."

Leo watched the man walk to his comrades speaking rapid Setswana. The men grinned and searched their lunch boxes for cans of beer. Leo decided he did not want to see this. Deniability, that was the word.

◇◇◇

The man Greshenko met with had a job to do, and seemed to say he intended to do it. No one had to like what they would do. A job is a job. This man was no different than the hundreds of manipulators Greshenko had encountered along the way—in the army, the governments of more than one country, crime bosses, politicians, and international industrialists. He had become cynical in the process. This occasional marriage of Russian intelligence services and the dark side of society, the

*Bratva,* was not new or unique, but it still made him uneasy. He was not naïve enough to believe this new love for Botswana meant it was completely corruption free or that it would always provide that safe haven for him, but he also knew that any country that had established a permanent commission to root out and expose dishonesty at every level had a better chance of staying clean than the ones that had institutionalized their dysfunctional behavior, and masked them with commissions and boards assigned to investigate breaches of ethics.

But how do you withstand the *Bratva?* You don't.

So, it was with sadness that he climbed into the taxi that had been summoned for him. He dropped his overnight bag, now heavier by the addition of nearly a half million dollars in *pula* notes, on the seat next to him. The remainder of the equipment required to complete this enterprise would be sent to his hotel the following day along with detailed instructions. He sat back and gave the driver the address of his hotel. It would not be the last time these men approached him, that much had been made clear. He wondered if he should make a run for it. What were the chances?

This will destroy Leo.

# Chapter Twenty-one

Leo Painter said nothing when Greshenko returned except to note that the trip seemed to have taken less time than he thought it would. Greshenko only nodded and stepped to his desk. The afternoon passed as the two men worked separately on that portion of the build for which they had taken responsibility. Greshenko, though, seemed distracted. Leo waited. He knew his friend well enough not to press.

Toward dinner time, Leo received an international call from the CEO of Earth Global, Travis Parizzi, who wanted to know how the project was going, and to give him the name and number of the contact he'd asked for. Parizzi didn't ask Leo why he needed that particular name and address. If Leo wanted him to know more he would undoubtedly have told him. He probably sensed that the query had something to do with an undertaking about which he did not wish to know. He had dealt with Leo in similar matters in the past.

Leo thanked him and hung up. He swiveled around in his chair and studied Greshenko.

"It is nearly time for dinner, Yuri. Mrs. Painter is over at the Marina Lodge playing bridge and will have her dinner there with her new-found friends. Let's you and me slip up to the Old House and get a steak."

Greshenko hesitated. He shifted some papers about on his desk and looked uneasy.

"We'll have a drink or two and you can tell me what's bothering you and," Leo paused briefly for effect, "what the Russians wanted from you."

Greshenko's expression revealed nothing but Leo knew he'd touched a nerve. He smiled and raised an eyebrow. "Yeah, I know about the calls to and from the restaurant, and if you push me hard enough, I can probably find out who they are and what they're likely to be about anyway. So tell me, what's going on Yuri?"

"It's complicated."

"Life is complicated. At least the bit that has meaning is. Animals have uncomplicated lives. A cow worries about nothing much at all—better forage, full udder, that's pretty much it. 'Happy as a clam,' the saying goes. But people are remarkably different…so what's the big deal?"

Greshenko looked around the room and frowned. Then he signaled for Leo to follow him outside. The two men walked toward the road in silence. Leo looked at his watch.

"The docs say I am supposed exercise every day. Bunch of horse hockey if you ask me. You know what Mark Twain said about exercise?"

Greshenko shook his head.

"He said, 'I don't have anything against exercise, I just don't see the virtue in being tired.' I agree. So, we'll walk to the Old House for our steak. That will be my stab at healthy living, and it will give you time to arrange the disinformation you are contemplating telling me into a format that you think I will buy. Then I will tell you it's all bullshit and then you will tell me the truth."

The two men walked east on the road the half kilometer to the Old House, a restaurant of dubious ambience and presence, but which served the best steak in the country. Or at least Leo thought so. There were people in Gaborone who disagreed and many in Chicago who still thought the Windy City had invented the steak house, but Leo put that down to urban snobbishness, chauvinism, ignorance, or all of the above. He'd toyed with the idea of purchasing the restaurant, moving it, lock, stock, and barrel, to his property and attaching it somehow to the hotel. He had not completely dismissed the idea. He worried, however, if the high-end look of the hotel/casino could accommodate this rustic, tin roofed, oversized shack. He couldn't make up his mind so he'd not made the offer.

The restaurant was crowded with locals and a few tourists who, to Leo's amusement, were staring dubiously at the walls, decor, and the other customers. He supposed they were contemplating the possible risks to their health if they actually ate the food. If they had a look at the kitchen they'd no doubt run screaming into the night.

They found a table against the wall away from the door. They did not need a menu. The Old House had an eclectic array of offerings from pizza to Chinese, but the only thing worth eating, Leo claimed, was the T-bone steak. They each ordered and called for Saint Louis beers while they waited.

"Are you going to give up what you're trying to sit on or do I have to use my sources?"

"Ah Leo, it's complicated."

"So you said. And I said life is complicated. Knitting an argyle sweater is complicated, or so I've been told. I've never attempted to knit so I could be wrong, but it certainly looks like it would be. Have you ever dismantled a sewing machine? Complicated as hell. Shall I go on?"

Greshenko held up his hands in surrender. "No, stop. Next you will be telling me how to turn potatoes into vodka."

"I had no idea vodka was made from potatoes. How *do* they do it?"

"It's simple. First you...never mind. Okay, some of my former countrymen and colleagues have me in a tight spot."

"A tight spot? What sort of tight spot?"

"You know of my past, yes?"

Leo nodded. He did. He'd made a point to learn as much as he could about Greshenko before he'd been recruited to take the trip to Botswana in the first place. A man who knew his way around the shadier side of the law, the Russian Mafia to be precise, would be useful, Leo believed, when dealing with bureaucrats and businessmen. Two discoveries had altered that estimate almost immediately. First, Botswana was the least corrupt country in Africa and one of the least in the world, and second, Greshenko wanted out of the life a failed Russian military had forced him into in the first instance. Botswana offered an escape for Leo, but more so for Greshenko.

"I know about the Russian Mafia, of course—"

"Mafia, *mafiya*, is the Russian word. Mafia is Italian. But we say *Vory v zakone*." Greshenko scribbled on a piece of paper. "Like this," воры в Законе. "It means *disciplined thieves*, but not quite. The groups have been around since the Tsars, believe it or not. Communism, neo-capitalism, the Tsars...nothing stops people who trade in the dark. Now we just say *Bratva*, the brotherhood. And then you know, also, I still travel on a Russian passport. I have false ones stashed here and there, of course, but they are of no use to me now."

"Disciplined thieves, very apt. Change *Bratva* to Congress and it could apply to some politicians I know, too, a lot of them actually. Yes, so, as they say in Hollywood, let's cut to the chase. What's up?"

"You are a very cynical man for one so blessed with the fruits of your capitalist system, Leo."

"Cynical? Yes, I suppose I am. It comes from the sure knowledge that if I wanted to, I could under the guise of campaign contributions, buy myself a congressman, or several, and certainly their votes. So, moving right along..."

"Okay, out of the blue, I receive a call from one of the underlings who says he is calling on behalf of the government. The term is used loosely here, you understand. The government will not confirm any of this. It is a contractual arrangement."

"They are out-sourcing?"

"Ah, yes, that would describe it, surely. So, they know me, of course, and they know my past connections and, this is the important part, they know of certain actions and reactions in my past that are still on the books, you could say."

"Sorry, you lost me. Yuri, circumlocution is not your style. What exactly are you getting at?"

Greshenko glanced around the room and lowered his voice. "Okay. In the past I was indiscreet legally. I have some outstanding warrants circulating. They can extradite me back to Russia anytime they want to for those things. They said they would make that happen if I did not help them with this small thing. Or, and this is no idle threat, they will kill me and anyone associated with me."

"Oh come on. Gangsters are mostly hot air. Why would they do that?"

"Leo, please believe me. You only know your mafia and most of that knowledge is from Hollywood or HBO. This is not *The Sopranos*. Those men are gentlemen crooks compared to this crowd. Your mafia will rub out a man and then send his widow flowers. But the *Bratva*? They will send her a bomb."

"Jesus. Really? Okay, you said a small thing? What sort of small thing would you have to do to make these guys leave you alone?"

Their steaks and sides arrived. Neither picked up a fork. Greshenko waited until the waitress had gone away and continued.

"You understand, Leo, they have me by the…how do you say? Shorts. If I refuse, they will call the local police, and I will be on a military aircraft and on my way to Moscow in a heartbeat… maybe worse. Even if the local government stalls—say you pull some of your strings and get the U.S. involved—it will end my chances for citizenship, and eventually I will have no means of staying here. Where would I go then?"

"I see and I don't see. You are in a jam. I get that part. The… what did you call them? The *Bratva* are threatening you. I get that part, too. What do they want from you, and what guarantees do you have that if you comply they will forget all about you?"

"That is the hard part. What they want me to do is dangerous. It could compromise many other people, and perhaps end in your having to leave Botswana as well. That is, if I am caught. And the answer to the second part is that I have no assurances at all they will not come after me again if they need something else. It is not a good prospect. I am short on options. And then there is the casino to consider."

"You better tell me everything. Then we'll see if we can un-complicate it. As you say, I do have sources. And I also have options they, and you too, may not know about."

# Chapter Twenty-two

"The Russian on the Permanent Residency Permit spent the best part of two hours in a restaurant with some very shady characters yesterday afternoon. What do you suppose that meant?"

Modise listened with half an ear. His latest telephone call from Sanderson distracted him and he hardly heard his boss. Kgabo Modise had no idea, but if the characters were who he suspected they were, he could guess. Lenka.

"Sorry," he said. "I have a call here from Kasane. It is about that shooting in the park, I think. What were you saying?"

"Our people reported that the Russian, Greshenko, spent some time in the company of people thought to be associated with the ex-Russian intelligence assets. You know how that works. They would have been his co-workers in the past. At least some of them would have been. It's hard to draw the line between their mafia types, the former KGB operatives, and the new order. It has become like smoke and mirrors with them. One can't always tell where one begins and the other ends. Lenka, it seems has his eyes on opportunities in our country. So far it is mostly working the information mill for his contacts in the embassy. Let's hope it stays that way for now."

"Probably not worth the effort to keep them apart, but is his meeting with them so unusual? He is a Russian national living here on a Residency Permit. He has a history with them. Wouldn't they be interested in his comings and goings?"

"Yes, that is so but the way he entered the building it seemed odd to our people in the field, so they reported it."

"Odd?"

The director sifted through the reports on his desk and withdrew one. He jerked his head forward which caused his reading glasses to drop from his forehead to the end of his nose.

"He left his taxi at the mall parking lot and walked the distance to the restaurant which is, as you know a bit of a hike. Why not have the taxi drop him off at the front entrance? He carried a large overnight case with him." Modise shook his head. "We have to ask, why does a man bring his suitcase to the food court? They also report that they couldn't be sure, but the case he carried seemed heavier on the way out than on the way in."

"With respect, Director, that is a stretch, don't you think? How can someone fifty or more meters away possibly know if a case is heavier? And even if it were, what significance does that carry?"

"None at all on the face of it. They also report he received a visitor that night in his hotel room. The person in question is one of the men on our watch list. He is a seller of illegal and questionable merchandise. He carried a roll-along in and left without it."

"No idea what the luggage contained?"

"Oh yes. Ideas we have, evidence of wrong doing, none, you see."

"Yes, so you wish me to explore this coincidence with Mr. Greshenko when I return to Kasane?"

"Yes. With the American Secretary of State arriving soon, it is imperative we confirm what that case contained."

Modise's phone rang again. "Excuse me, Director, it is the police superintendent from Kasane on the line." His boss signaled for him to take the call. "Yes, Mwambe, you have news?"

"Indeed, Modise. We have traced this license number you gave to us. The number plates were reported stolen in Jo'berg two months ago. This morning they were turned in to the station by a road vendor who found them behind his shed."

"Very good. I don't suppose anyone has reported number plates missing in Kasane."

"Not yet, but I am guessing they soon shall unless, of course, they went to Botlhokwa for replacements."

"How would that make a difference?"

"It is said he has useful numbers for sale. All untraceable. We believe he takes or buys them from abandoned vehicles, and collects stolen plates from neighboring countries. Very hard to track, you see."

"Very good. Stay on it. We will find those men eventually. And thank you."

Modise couldn't be sure, but he thought he heard a muffled 'Ha' on the other end. Well, so be it. Mwambe had issues. Modise didn't have time to deal with them. Not today.

"There is another thing. We have identified the victim. He is Congolese and harmless, we believe."

"Harmless? What does that mean?"

"What brought him to the park was not dangerous to anyone but himself, I would say."

Modise let that go. He'd get back to Mwambe and that nonsensical analysis later that day when he returned to Kasane.

◇◇◇

Leo waited for Greshenko to collect his thoughts. There was no need to rush and clarity would be preferable to haste in any case.

"Perhaps this is not the best place to speak."

Leo glanced around the crowded restaurant and shook his head. "Actually, Yuri, I think this may be the ideal spot. I'm guessing here but what I'm hearing, or more accurately, what I am not hearing, is that you are in some deep shit and might be under surveillance. Am I close?"

Greshenko nodded.

"Then to be seen eating dinner with your partner in a local, crowded restaurant would seem the most innocent venue for us. If we were to traipse off into the bush or deliberately set up a meet where we could not be observed, it would be a tip-off you were up to something. So, smile and talk to me."

Greshenko nodded once and forced a smile to his lips. "Very well. I'll skip the history lesson. You know most of it already. As I said, I must do this thing and if I refuse, I will be found, best case, missing. Worst case, dead, you see?" He signaled for the waitress to bring another round of drinks and asked for a dessert menu.

"I met with the unofficial arm of Russian Intelligence you could say. Never mind who they are. They run for my old country the sorts of things your government refers to as 'black ops.' Freelance contractors would best describe it. Only not obviously connected to the government, you understand?"

Leo did, or thought he did. What the CIA and other intelligence gathering arms of his government did or did not do he'd mostly learned from fiction and the internet and in as much as both of those sources were dominated more by imagination than fact, he couldn't say with certainty if what he knew had any connection with reality. He did understand, however, why the government might purchase toilet seats for seventeen hundred dollars. The money to run those programs had to come from somewhere. What he knew of the Russian equivalents was even vaguer. It didn't matter.

"Okay. I meet with these men at a Russian restaurant in the big mall. It is not very busy. No surprise there. I don't think there is a big demand for Russian cuisine. Chinese, maybe, but not Russian."

Leo circled his hand. "Get to the point, Yuri. I don't need to know about either the restaurant or their problems."

"No, of course not. Okay, they lay it out to me. Do this or else." Greshenko paused and drained his bottle. The waitress reappeared with new drinks and the menu. "I have in my room a suitcase full of highly sophisticated listening devices and another filled with money. I am to place these devices in our rooms where the Arab nationals are staying. Then, I am to bug...is that how you say it? I am to bug the Mowana Lodge where the American Secretary of State will be staying."

"Jesus, Yuri, how do they expect you to do that? You heard what that cop said. If anybody tries anything like that, the whole lodge and everybody in it gets hammered."

"Yes, well that is what the money is for. They assume that if the offer to allow me in the rooms is high enough, their fear of discovery will be overcome."

Leo pushed his plate aside and contemplated the corrugated tin ceiling for a moment. He withdrew his evening cigar, the one he'd been saving for later, and lit up. Greshenko folded his napkin and swallowed half the contents of his beer in a single tilt.

"You know, of course, you're being set up. One way or the other, no matter what you do from here on out, you're screwed."

Greshenko stared at the red and white checked, oilskin table cloth. "Of course."

"Look, if you're successful, they will be back for more. If you fail, they'll leave you twisting in the wind. If you mess it up—a little of both—or worse. You're in a no-win here, Yuri."

Greshenko sighed and waved his hand. "But what are my choices? I am speaking to you as my friend. If you had not arranged for me to accompany you here in the first place my life would be...would not be so good. My only course is to flee. I must dump this stuff, use one of my old passports, and disappear."

"That's one option, surely, but not the only one and maybe not the best one. They found you here, they will find you wherever you go."

"You have an alternative for me?"

"I might and I might not. We're done here and I need to make a few calls."

# Chapter Twenty-three

Jack and Harvey may not have been the sharpest tools in the shed, but anyone looking at their body of work would have to admit they usually deployed original techniques to separate people from their money.

"Jack, wait 'til you hear this. I got it."

"What? More buyers, sellers, capital? What have you managed to dig up for us?"

"The way in. A safe, sure, and, I might also say, guaranteed entry into the park. All we need to do is show up."

"What's it going to cost us?"

"That's the good part. Nada, nil, nothing. The guy's going to usher us in and thank us to boot.'"

"How?"

"You'll never believe this. I'm in that little coffee shop getting us our mornings, and I happen to look at the wall and there're all sorts of posters and notices. There's one for a meeting. 'Operation Paradise' it says. My bell rings. Something I've heard about I think. I'm thinking about the orgone energy caper we've heard of, so I reckon I'll check in on those birds. I slipped around there last night to have a peek. Talk about your fanatics."

"Here, hand me the sugar bowl and get on with it, Harv. I ain't got all day."

"Steady on. I'm in the back listening, you know, just trying to get the lay of the land, you could say, and this chap in a uniform sidles up to me. He's suspicious, see, because I'm not a regular, and I guess they get a lot of newspaper people and troublemakers crashing their meetings. So he asks what my business is."

"What'd you tell him?" Jack stuck a match and lit a small kero stove and placed a kettle on it.

"I tell him the unvarnished truth short a few details, of course. Like I said, I'd been listening to these screwballs for a half hour or so and picked up the lingo, so I said. 'We're bringing hope and healing to the Chobe.' Like that."

"Hope and healing? What are you going on at, Harv?"

"Just that. He says, 'Orgonite?' And I says, 'Yes, a great deal." He says 'Who sent you? We never had a white man in here before.'"

"How'd you handle that one?"

"Oh, I was brilliant. I'd been reading their handouts. All about the worldwide network of saviors, you could say. Some pretty important folks have their names attached to this business. Anyway, one name catches my eye. So I tell him his nibs, TPW, himself is behind our effort."

"The Prince of Wales. You're bonkers. How'd you come up with that one?"

"You are not paying me mind, Jack. I told you I had their handouts and there in the literature is a reference to Charlie himself, big as life. I figure it can't get any better than that, so then this chap says he'll help us."

"And how is that going to go down?" Jack filled a pot with hot water and dropped in a tea ball to steep.

"I mentioned he wore a uniform, right? Okay, so he's a game ranger and has access to a set up, an entrance through the fence he knows about. Seems there is a fair amount of traffic through there. He said he'd meet us inside but I said no, not necessary. That we have our orders as to where we were to seed—that's how they describe what they do, seeding the continent with orgone energy— and we could manage. So, after that he gives me directions where this hole is and how to open and close it. Then said to be careful."

"Careful of what? He's the guy in charge. What can go wrong?"

"Actually, he's not in charge and is pretty snarky about that, I learned over a beer later, but that's not the point. He said a week ago one of their people tried to bring in the stuff and someone shot him and took off with the goods."

"Wait a minute, some fellow went into the park with this chap's okay and some other bloke shot him and took the rubbish? That don't make sense, Harvey."

"That's what I said, and he says…he's a little paranoid besides being angry about a missed promotion…that there are forces at work to stop the mission. The old colonial powers, he says, want to regain their lost territory or some nonsense, and they can only do it by keeping Africa weak. That's why he was suspicious of me, see? They think if they get strong with this jiggery pokey…well, the whole enterprise don't make sense but who cares? I expect he thought I was one of those old colonials come to spy. But he knew about Prince Charlie sure enough. I told you, they're all missing a few cards from their deck."

"But he's going to let us in and maybe take a bullet. Bloody nice of him, that."

"Actually he said it should be safe now, or safer, because the police were on it. I got the impression that the local coppers had an interest in the project somehow."

"Interest in the orgone thing? That's a neat trick. Okay, I accept it for now. Keep checking. My news is I've heard from our self-proclaimed general in the north and he has the goods for us. He also has a buyer or two. He thinks of us as the middle men. You know, delivery boys. We'll disabuse him of that later. We are not in the business of working on commission."

"He won't come after us?"

"How can he? We'll sell the stuff and we're off to where the sun and surf call our names and—"

"Bob's your uncle."

"Exactly"

"It still don't feel right."

"Sanderson, we have identified these pictures for you. You know, of course, that the one man is your associate, Andrew Takeda.

The other fellow is called Noga, no first name. He is reputed to be high up in Botlhokwa's organization. We received some information, a rumor actually, that he has stepped over the line a time or two to work some private deals on his own. That may or may not have earned him in Botlhokwa's distrust. There is also a report he is overseeing some new actors in the area, but we cannot confirm that either."

"Why was he meeting with Andrew?"

"We are not sure. Can you suggest anything? Takeda works for you, after all."

"Nothing. Well, perhaps, but I cannot credit it. I was promoted over him. He had seniority and was Mr. Pako's choice to take over, but someone in Gabz overruled it and I was chosen. Andrew did not take it so nicely."

"And this suggests that he engaged this Noga person to threaten you?"

"It is all I can think of. What else could it be?"

"A possibility surely, but there is another. Since we acquired computers and the go-ahead from the President's office, we have put into place the means to check financial transactions. It appears your Mr. Takeda has received sums of money over the years. He deposits them in an account that he does not acknowledge as his when it is tax time. We believe he is being paid by someone for services he would rather weren't generally known."

"Services? What sort of...he was selling information about the park or the animals?"

"More, we are guessing. Access probably. If you wish to move something through the park, wouldn't it be better if the authorities could make that happen?"

"He let people in? But what is the point? Anyone can enter the park if they wish. There is a fee but it is not so great that a bribe is necessary."

"I am thinking of your cinema people, the ones who left their equipment behind. How did they manage that without someone's help?"

"They were shooting filthy pictures, weren't they?" Modise nodded. "He could have done that. And that would clear Mr. Pako because he caught them and sent them packing."

"So it would seem. And there are other possibilities. Perhaps they are irregular but innocent, perhaps not. Will you search your records for the last several years and see if you can discover a pattern of instances…things out of the ordinary that might line up with these deposits?"

"Do I need a list of the transactions?"

"No, not right now. I prefer you do it blind. I trust you, Sanderson, but I don't want you to be tempted to connect one thing to another to make a case. If this man is dirty, we will find him out soon enough."

"I will speak to Andrew. He must be put on probation pending a hearing."

"No, do not do that. Not yet. He is a little fish and may lead us to bigger ones. We can reel him in anytime, but with border activity heating up I would rather have someone in place we know about than have to find a new one which they would recruit. The temptation for riches is too great."

# Chapter Twenty-four

The cargo plane, a refurbished DC 3 and relic of thousands of hours in the service of one suspect owner or another, lifted off the ground and banked sharply left to avoid the Rwandan hills that loomed several kilometers ahead. Below a few natives shook their fists at the plane as it soared overhead scattering their cattle. The pilot, a veteran of the backwoods forays in one continent or another, lit a cigarette from the butt of the one he'd just finished and stubbed the first out on the cockpit bulkhead. His companion eyed the mess on the floor, the accumulated stubs, paper cups, and tissues, and wrinkled his nose. The pilot merely shrugged.

Once clear of the area, the passenger powered up his Iridium phone and punched in a series of numbers.

Pause.

"Dmitri, here is Sergei. I must speak to the boss." He waited until a second voice came on the line. "We have a problem with the little general it seems. He has reneged on his commitment to sell to you, and has consigned the goods to another group. He says they will pay more and in Euros."

Sergei listened for a moment. "I don't know who the other party is. Not one of ours, I am thinking. What?"

The plane reached its lowest cruising altitude and the pilot turned an inquiring eye to Sergei, who waved him off temporarily.

"No, he had a platoon of his troops at his back or I would have. They pretty much surrounded us. Some of those militiamen couldn't have been more than kids. Not a good age to issue a seventies-era Kalashnikov. They don't seem to know what the safety is for either."

Sergei listened some more while wagging his hand at the pilot who, it seemed, wanted a destination.

"Yes I reminded him of our deal to take the coltan, but as I said, he just laughed at me and hinted he was not committed to us if he could get a bigger price. I said the price does not change and he gave me one of those looks, you know, and said 'Too bad for you. Tell M. Lenka it was not a matter of *honneur parmi les voleurs.*' I didn't ask him what that meant. They speak French or something up here."

The pilot, his impatience growing, wagged the plane's wings and glared at Sergei.

"So, he will travel back to the forest and his new mine tomorrow. What? Yes, very well. I will take care if it at this end." He turned to the pilot and shouted. "Sudan. We are to pick up Tarq and drop him off at the little airfield where we sold the guns, you remember? Our little general is about to be replaced."

The plane banked and set a course north and slightly east. The pilot lit another cigarette, coughed, and settled back in his seat.

*Patriarche* waited. There were no new movements from the men in the valley. He relaxed. The troubling thoughts passed. He retrieved his stick, the biggest he'd ever used, and swatted at a tree branch. A shower of leaves fell to the ground. He pawed through them. Several seemed sweeter to his taste, they were the lighter shaded ones. He looked up and saw that at the topmost branches, there seemed to be many more of these better tasting leaves, but they were out of reach. He threw the stick at the nearest of the unreachable branches, He missed and his stick sailed in a low arc away from him and hit one of the other gorillas in the head who, in turn, barked in pain. It looked at *Patriarche's* stick, picked it up and threw it back at him nearly hitting him in the chest. He scowled and roared an admonition at this impudence, but did nothing else. They were not enemies.

*Patriarche* tried another toss, this time with more success. The other ape, watching, tore a branch from a nearby tree and stripped it of its smaller branches and leaves. He glanced in *Patriarche's* direction and threw his stick in the air as well. He was better at throwing, it seemed. *Patriarche* grunted his approval. By the end of the day most of the males and a few females had now mastered the stick, some better than others. It must have been the better tasting leaves.

The negotiations in Somalia only required a few minutes. Tarq—no one knew his real name, only that he was an American and he'd been trained by one of their military services as a sniper—climbed aboard the aircraft with his sidekick and spotter, a woman whose Arabic name sounded like Condoleezza, but whom Tarq simply called Rice. They carried back packs with provisions for several days, a spotter's scope, and the Mosin-Nagant sniper rifle he'd been issued by the organization. The pilot reached for his package of Marlboros. American cigarettes were a perquisite that came with his employment with Lenka. Before he could light one, however, Tarq slapped it from his hand. It rolled across the cockpit floor and dropped into a crack next to Sergei. No word was said. The two men glared at each other. The pilot returned the pack to his shirt pocket with a grunt.

Sergei watched this exchange with amusement. Pilots were always so arrogant. He was pleased to see this one put in his place. No one dared to annoy Tarq. Men like him drifted at the edge of the darkness like the big cats, only they were infinitely more dangerous.

"Tarq," he said as the plane taxied into what little wind there was, "What is your real name?"

Sergei didn't expect an answer. He only wanted the man to know he'd seen and approved of the cigarette business.

"Booth," Tarq said. It would be the only words from him for the entire trip. Sergei could not tell if he told the truth or simply added another layer of anonymity to his already murky persona. As soon as the plane was airborne, Tarq sprawled on the floor among his equipment and slept. Rice, it seemed, knew neither Russian nor English and had nothing to say in any case. She stretched out in the rear of the plane on a pile of duffle bags that smelled suspiciously of marijuana. The four traveled toward Rwanda in silence.

They landed in a spot close enough to the mining operation in the Congo for the sniper and his spotter to hike in and back out without trouble, but far enough from the general and his troops to not arouse their suspicions or signal their presence. They might be curious, of course. News of the plane would reach them soon enough. But they also knew that the men they dealt with were known to have interests across the breadth of central Africa. Tarq and Rice quickly disembarked. They agreed to a pickup the same five days hence. The two figures, back packs in place and the rifle sheathed, melted into the forest. Sergei circled his hand over his head signaling the pilot it was time to go. The plane's engine picked up RPMs, taxied, and then flew east.

The pilot lit up.

Sergei called Cape Town with an update. He settled back in the left seat. An hour, hour and a half at most, Sergei thought, then home and a bottle of chilled vodka, some caviar, and Serafina…or perhaps her sister.

He'd have to think about that.

# Chapter Twenty-five

Andrew Takeda found himself on the carpet. Not Sanderson's as he'd supposed he might someday. After all, everyone knew his disappointment about being passed over for promotion and his less than graceful acquiescence. But today he stood in front of Superintendent Mwambe. Mwambe was his friend and coworker in efforts to seed the Chobe. Yet here he was and Mwambe did not look happy.

"So, Takeda," he said.

Not a good start. Normally Mwambe would have called him by his Christian name, but not today, not Andrew, just Takeda.

"We have a serious problem, it seems. Let me correct that, you have a serious problem. A problem which may hurt the effort of all of us, you see?"

Andrew thought he did, but hoped he was wrong.

"There is this murder in the park, which I assume you must have witnessed, and now the police outside of this jurisdiction are making inquires. It did not take much to discover the contents of the SUV. They have linked the murder to orgonite. It will be only a matter of time before they will find you and then me. I am not wanting to place myself in the middle of such an investigation because of your foolishness."

"I don't know how this connects with me, Superintendent." Andrew thought it best to use Mwambe's title and play dumb.

"When we met in the car park, I noticed that man Noga lingering at its edge. I have the strong impression that the two of you had been in conversation."

Andrew focused his attention on the floor. Then he stammered, "I was under the impression he was one of us."

"Us! That's idiotic. Why would you think one of Botlhokwa's henchmen would be interested in saving Africa? He is only interested in grabbing and running. He would sell the entire continent to the highest bidder and throw in his grandmother as the deal closer. What did you say to him?"

"Nothing, nothing at all. He met me in the street, said something about knowing the park and so on. I assumed—"

"You assumed? Assumed what? There is a very dead Congolese in our morgue and a whole shipment of orgonite in the American's skip, which we dare not retrieve. So what could you possibly have assumed that would have produced such a catastrophe?"

"As I said, that he was one of us. So when he asked what was happening, I said some very precious material would be passing into the park the next night. Meaning, of course the orgonite."

"You knew him from before, I think."

"I don't know what you mean, I don't know him—"

"Do you take me for a fool? Botlhokwa has been moving in and out of that park for years and someone has enabled that. That someone, it seems, is you, Takeda. I overlooked it because I could see no harm in what transpired and I did not want my friend Pako to find himself in hot water. This Sanderson I do not care about. But here is the dilemma we find ourselves in."

"Dilemma?"

"Be still. Yes, dilemma. The DIS has a man here. The DIS is worried about the border and the silliness going on in South Africa with the football matches. This incident will not go away. I cannot cover for you. They will find you, Andrew, and they will find Noga as well. You have very few choices. You might lay low and hope all this will go away, but—"

"All this? What do you mean?"

"Andrew, do not be stupid with me. You are beginning to sound like my nephew, Derek. The man was murdered in the park. You supplied information to a shady character about his presence. I must assume that Noga thought your idea of *precious* agreed with his and that it meant precious in the monetary sense. So he went to steal it, or he sold that information to someone else who did the stealing. I am betting on that story, by the way. Noga is Botlhokwa's man, and he does not get his hands dirty if he can avoid it. It is his way. But either way, you are an accessory to murder, Andrew. Get that straight in your brain."

"I didn't—"

"It doesn't matter what you think you did or did not do. As I was saying, you can lay low and hope it goes away. But my guess is it won't. Or you can come clean. Turn yourself in to me for arrest and examination. That will mean you will also give up Noga and he will not be pleased. There may be side consequences to that. I would say collateral damage. You should send your family away for a while. Your third choice, you can expect the people from Gabz to pick you up and then all three will come down on your head."

"Mwambe, we have been friends for many years. Your cousin is married to my aunt, surely—"

"Three choices, Takeda. Family cannot save you this day. I will give you one hour to make up your mind. But in case you missed it, your career with the government is over."

"One hour only?"

"One hour."

Mwambe glanced out the window and watched as Kgabo Modise parked his rental in front of the police station. He slammed the car door shut, opened and checked the contents of a folder in his hand, and marched through the front door. Mwambe had an uneasy feeling about that folder.

It seemed Andrew Takeda would not have an hour after all.

General le Grande, commander of the militia currently occupying the site of the coltan dig, seemed very proud of himself. He had rebuffed the Russian thug who thought he could push him around. These European gangsters, *les bandes criminelles,* they believed, like their colonialist predecessors, they could lord it over simple African folk. Now this group knew better. And if these other white men from the south who wished to buy the coltan thought they could fool him, they would soon learn their lesson as well.

Le Grande carried a swagger stick fashioned from an infant gorilla femur. A bit of the donor's fur had been woven into a strand and attached to its distal end which, when *le généralissime* flicked his wrist just so, would snap. If it happened to catch someone's wrist in the process, it could raise an angry welt. His followers had learned to stay out of range.

He stepped from his restored GAZ-67b four-by-four which had been newly painted an olive green, and had a fifty caliber machine gun mounted in the rear. It had seen better days a long time ago, but he was very proud of this truck, his *voiture blindée,* with his personal gold and blue flag attached to the right front bumper. He strode toward the growing pile of coltan and inspected it with a practiced eye. There would be many Euros here. Perhaps, he thought, if he could mix enough look-alike shale in with it he could double his profits. He did not know where he could find such *fausse minéraux* but he would ask around.

He strolled over to the other side of the camp acknowledging his soldiers salutes with a touch of his beret with the swagger stick and a quick snap. He wished to inspect the gorilla parts. The meat to be sold as bush meat had already been carted away. The rest of the body parts lay in untidy piles sorted by type and presumed market. He was pleased and told his troops so. They grinned perfect-toothed smiles and shuffled their feet.

"*Où sont les gorilles maintenant?*" he asked.

The men pointed toward the forest and up the hillside. Up there, the gorillas are there.

Le Grande pivoted, snapped his stick, and announced there would be a hunt which he would lead as soon as he returned from meeting with his staff at headquarters. In a day or two they would harvest this animal crop.

"*Ce que Dieu a semé, nous récolterons,*" he said and smiled. What God has sown, we shall reap.

The men cheered. Killing defenseless gorillas would be a welcome change from the killing of defenseless people. *Les soldats* did not harbor much in the way of guilt or remorse over either prospect. Months of pillage, rape, autocannibalism—the latest addition to the accretion of mindless brutality and violence that characterized their chosen avocation—had inured them to any such benevolent thoughts. They had exercised these despicable behaviors on rival tribesmen, passersby, innocent villagers who might have stood between them and their opponents, and others who were sometimes former neighbors and occasionally kinsmen.

Gorillas, they believed, did not count. Although during the rare moments that might be thought of as reflective, they recognized the beasts bore an uncomfortable resemblance to themselves. But as they existed only as soulless animals, they need not be reckoned among life's necessary elements. They wouldn't admit to it, perhaps were not aware of it, but the primary difference between them and the gorillas was that the latter did not kill for either pleasure of profit. They were gentle vegetarians who must be pushed to extremes before they would show even a trace of aggression.

Ten kilometers to the north, and moving through the bush at a killing pace, Tarq and Rice closed in on the camp. Like the soldiers, they had no compunctions against killing people either, but did when it came to lesser primates.

Hunters of all sorts coursed through the forests.

# Chapter Twenty-six

Leo stepped out of his office and strolled to the bench he'd had his carpenters construct for him under a baobab tree. Like the Mowana Lodge to the east, Leo wanted a large baobab to serve as a signature for his hotel. Unlike that at the Mowana, which sat in the back portion of the hotel, Leo's baobab would grace the entrance. He had the business cards and camera-ready graphics already at the studio. He'd been told the tree with its huge girth was hollow. He wondered if it would be possible to cut a doorway into it. A Dutch door and the tree could serve as the night security post. He would have a gate. It would be down after…ten, midnight? He'd ask around. The people in this country were so peculiar about disturbing wildlife. He didn't know if trees counted.

He should be content. But not now. Not with this Greshenko business. He lowered himself onto the bench with a grunt. Something he did more often lately. Age acquires some inevitable negatives, diet and nutritional good behavior notwithstanding. He needed some alone time to think how best to break it to Yuri that he'd contacted Kgabo Modise, the cop from Gaborone. His contact at the CIA had made it clear that from the viewpoint of the people in DC, if Leo were to call in the problem officially they would have no option but to detain Greshenko, seek to have his residence permit revoked, and possibly remand him into the custody of the Russians. They suggested the locals might have a gentler solution. So, he'd made the call to Modise who said he'd be by as soon as he finished some business at police headquarters. An hour or two.

He'd had the builders place the bench so that it faced the casino and he could sit and monitor progress made day to day. As he settled on the wooden slats, he wished he'd thought to bring a cushion. Age! He let his gaze wander over the project. It would be ready for Greshenko's promised surge of guests. That should have cheered him. It didn't. Leo exhaled, wished he'd taken better care of himself in the past so that he could still have his afternoon cocktail and cigar. That wasn't asking too much. A movement to his right caused him to swing his gaze around to a pile of concrete blocks a few meters away. He squinted against the sun and realized that the monkey, he assumed the same one that had stolen the cell phone, had taken a position on the blocks and had something in its hand. Or did monkeys not have hands but paws? W. W. Jacobs wrote a story, *The Monkey's Paw*. So, paw it is. He looked again. Clearly the beast had gotten a hold of something that did not belong on the concrete blocks. He stooped down and gathered a handful of debris and threw it at the monkey.

"Hey, get out of here. Shoo."

The monkey dropped whatever it had been holding, bounded across the yard, and with a leap that was nothing short of spectacular, sailed into the trees. It turned and screamed at Leo who assumed he was being castigated with the simian equivalent of obscenities. It then made a gesture which confirmed his assumption.

Leo walked to the pile and retrieved the object. "Sammi," he yelled, "What the hell is this thing and why did somebody leave it lying around?"

"Sorry, Mr. Painter, it is my fault. That is my youngest boy's gaming device. I took it from him this morning as punishment. It was in my back pocket and I thought maybe it will be damaged there so I took it out. I am thinking I will put it in a jacket pocket and then the foreman called to me into a conversation and I forgot."

"You nearly lost it to that monkey. That's the same monkey that filched the cell phone, isn't it?"

"Oh, yes. You can tell by the white tuft over his eye, you see. I think he must have had a run in with a big cat when he was small and escaped with a cut over his eye."

"I thought you all were going to get rid of him. Get him drunk and dump him in the park or something."

"That was the plan, yes, but the park people are giving the very fishy eye to everyone who is entering the park, except the game drives. They are concerned about the murder, you know. I think now is not a good time to do that."

"Well if we can't have him drink beer, how about something that will do him in? These monkeys are like rats, for crying out loud. If this were Chicago, I'd set out poison and that would be that."

"Oh no, that cannot be. If we are caught killing the animals it is off to jail for a very long time. It is not worth a cell phone or this game toy. We will be more careful, I promise."

"Careful or not, this is the new rule—you lose something to that little thief, replacing it is on your dime."

"Dime?"

"*Thebe,* then. The costs of replacing whatever is lost will come out of your pay. Do you understand?"

"Oh yes. Certainly. That is very fair."

Leo wasn't sure it was, but he wouldn't say so. If the threat of lost money helped stop the problem, then he'd let them believe it was so. If and when it happened again, he'd decide whether to enforce the rule. He returned to his bench. The light-fingered antics of the monkey were the least of his problems. What would Modise do to Greshenko and how would that affect the casino? Well, the cop said we were to report any and all illegal activity. They will have done it. That ought to score a few points in their favor.

But the real worry would be the reaction of the goons who'd put Yuri into the game. Leo guessed that if all that Yuri had told him were true—if half of it were true—there'd be hell to pay in the morning. Well, you reap what you sow, he'd been taught and it looked like some of Yuri's bad seed had finally germinated and produced a crop. People on the shady side of the law didn't always spread the best seed around.

The Bible, if he remembered the story correctly, and that would be a stretch, taught that you had to let the crop mature and then pick out the weeds from the good grain at harvest. Tares among the corn. Too early and you couldn't tell the good from the bad. He conjured up an image of his grandmother reading from her Bible dictionary. She took her Bible seriously. She had a dictionary that allowed her to look up things like tares. Who said tares anymore? As a child Leo had listened politely to her. He loved his grandparents. But as soon as he was out of the house, all thoughts of the Hereafter were left behind. Now? Perhaps he should pick up the Good Book, you never knew. *Bearded dirndl.* What did that have to do with this? Ah, it was the name of the weed that looked like wheat until it reached full maturity—this from grandmother's dictionary. You had to wait 'til that happened and then you separated the wheat from the weeds. The latter were burned in the fire. Grandmother had looked at him with flinty eyes and urged him not to be numbered among the weeds or he'd burn in the eternal flames. The image a demon in a red union suit brandishing a pitchfork and herding him into the eternal flames had terrified him. He'd promised to never be a tare, a weed, a bearded dirndl, although the idea of growing a beard did have a certain attraction to an eight year old.

On reflection, he wasn't entirely sure, at the remove of nearly sixty years, that he'd managed to avoid the weediness he'd promised her he'd eschew. He shuddered. He no longer believed in the fiery furnace, but was less sure about retribution or the lack thereof at some point. He shook his head and longed again for one of his banished cigars. Why could he remember all this youthful imagery and not what he'd had for lunch the day before? *I must be getting old, maybe senile. What a terrible thought. Someone…who? Can't remember.* Someone once said "the trouble with Alzheimer's is: when you finally realize you have it you can't remember where you hid the gun."

He sat back down on his bench and waited for Inspector Modise. He really needed to concentrate on something brighter. But that would have to wait.

# Chapter Twenty-seven

"I'm worried. This whole business has moved from something that was simple to something very complex, Jack."

"In my experience, Harvey, anything worth doing usually moves that way. You show me a simple job, and I'll show you a low return on investment."

"Right, if you say so. Okay, I met with the guy I bumped into at that squirrely meeting, and he said he could provide some locals to help us make the orgonite. They seem pretty happy about the process, though they did wonder why we were assembling it here. In the past they said it came in from outside the country and their job was to just place it."

"What'd you tell them?"

"I made up a book about the London office had determined that the stuff worked better if it was made fresh before it was put down. All bollocks, of course but they seemed okay with that. Who knows?"

"Here's the plan then. Have them make up the cone things with a hollow inside. Then when the goods get here, we can pop it in a plastic bag, shove it in, and seal the bottom. That way our buyers can retrieve it without a lot of fuss."

"I don't think they'll buy into plastic. It will cut down on the power."

"Harvey, have you slipped round the bend? What do you mean, 'it'll cut down the power?' The whole business is bogus.

Who the bloody hell cares? Tell them there's new research. Plastic acts as an amplifier or some such guff."

"Sorry. I'm trying to think like them."

"Right. Good luck with that. Then we'll tell the lads that they can't be part of the final loading. Too dangerous. Tell them we have a new formula direct from old Whosis himself."

"Reich? He's dead. Been that way for years, you could say."

"Say we found some old notes of his what say using this new approach would up the power. I don't care, just keep them the hell away."

"I'll think of something. Okay, then we stuff the cones, seal them, and drop them off in the park. How's the buy going?"

"Super. I have the money. It's going to cost a bit more than I hoped what with the interest they're asking but we'll book a packet."

"Where'd you find it?"

"There's a group of European investors anxious to buy in. They are most likely mobbed up, but they have the cash. We get the stuff for quarter of a mil, sell for a half quick like, and we're in the chips, lad. Two hundred and fifty thousand Euros. Think of it."

"Right. I ain't counting my pennies 'til they're in my pocket. When will the stuff be here?"

"On its way. That local wheeler dealer, Botlhokwa, is handling the transfer through Zambia or Zimbabwe. It should be here any day now. Somebody named Noga is our contact."

"I'll get the chaps going on the cones."

"So, Superintendent Mwambe, you have saved me time by rounding this man up and putting him under arrest."

Mwambe thought Kgabo Modise seemed very pleased with his good fortune. He didn't know how he thought about that, though. Did he really want this upstart from Gaborone liking his efforts? Bad luck for Andrew. So much for a grace period.

"Andrew Takeda, before I charge you I wish to suggest that you can do yourself a large favor by coming clean."

Andrew's eyes widened and Mwambe could almost see the wheels turning behind them. Would his friend try to slither out of this with a pack of lies and make his case worse in the hopes of keeping his employment, or would he come clean? He knew Andrew could tell a pretty tall tale if he wanted to.

"I don't know what you are saying." Takeda glanced hopefully at Mwambe, who merely shrugged.

"You don't? That is very strange indeed. Perhaps you would like to inspect these photographs. I must apologize for the quality. They were taken with a cell phone, after all. You will be interested in them as well, Superintendent."

Modise tossed Sanderson's processed and enlarged pictures on the desk. Mwambe nudged them with a stubby finger. "Who took these pictures?" This did not look so good. Someone seeing these for the first time would think he and Andrew were somehow in some dodgy business with the big man, Noga. Did Gaborone have agents in his jurisdiction he did not know about? This was serious.

"It is not important who took them. What is important is what is going on here."

Mwambe sat back in his chair which protested with a loud squeal. There could be no saving Andrew now. "We were just discussing this very situation," he said. "That man in the picture having a chat with Takeda here is a man called Noga. I do not know his full name. I am not sure anyone does. He is one of Botlhokwa's people. I am under the impression that he may have been alerted by Ranger Takeda that someone would be entering the park at night. Isn't that right, Takeda?"

Takeda wiped his palms on his trousers and swallowed. Mwambe could see the emotions race behind the poor game ranger's eyes. Fear, doubt, cunning, and finally, resignation. For him, the game was up.

"As I told Superintendent Mwambe here, I had some contact with this man before. I believed he was one of us, you see."

"Us? Another game ranger? I don't think so. Who, or what, is *us*?"

Takeda lowered his gaze to the floor and then, a decision made, shot Mwambe a defiant look. "Us. That would be myself, Mwambe here, and a dozen other men who wish to see the countryside restored and the land healed."

"You say the superintendent is involved with this man?"

Time for Mwambe to assert himself. "Modise, you are ahead of yourself."

"Am I? This picture seems to tell a different story, wouldn't you say?"

"No, it does not. Takeda means that he and I and others are convinced that orgonite will have many beneficial effects for the country." A safe description and near enough to what he believed. "We meet and plan how we might accomplish this great thing. We arrange for the orgonite to be brought in and so on. That is all. Takeda met this man and foolishly thought he held that same beliefs. Understand, because he is a rogue does not mean he cannot be concerned for the home continent."

"I am sorry, but I am not following you. Please explain this sequence of pictures and the connection between them."

Takeda took a deep breath and let it out. He was defeated. "It is like this. I know this man and believed he wanted to help with our project, you see. I mentioned a 'precious cargo' would soon arrive. He thanked me and that was that. I cannot believe he would go and shoot somebody—"

"I believe you have left something out of your story," Mwambe interrupted. Now was the time to distance himself from Takeda. Friendship is one thing, a career in jeopardy and disgrace quite another. He was a policeman after all.

"What? What did I leave out?" Takeda's eyes pleaded. Mwambe ignored them.

"You witnessed the shooting in the park, did you not?"

When Mwambe made this accusation Takeda collapsed. His body language up to that point had been alert and cautious. No more. If he didn't know better, Mwambe would have said he shrank by about half.

Modise stared with dead eyes at Mwambe. "You knew of this arrangement?"

No time for equivocation now. "I knew he would be in the park to meet the man sent from Kinshasa and receive the orgonite, yes. We all did. I simply waited for him to come forward and tell me what he saw that night. That is why we insisted on the suicide story. I wished for some time, you see? When Takeda didn't do his duty, I called him in, and here he is. And, also, here you are. If I have erred in this matter it is in overlooking the illicit entry into the park. It is something you will discover, Modise, which is not always considered an illegality in these parts. After all, the Chobe is our homeland and orders from the government not withstanding, we maintain we hold certain rights to it."

Modise studied Mwambe for a moment. "And were you aware that this man has made a small extra income over the years by allowing others into the park?"

Mwambe shook his head. "I did not know for certain, but I am not surprised. Until that new superintendent for the game rangers took over, it was a common practice, something many did. This is the north, Modise. Except for the lodges and tourist places, the economy is thin here. We do what we must to survive."

"You, too?"

"Not me, no."

"Then I would like you to please explain the pictures to me again."

# Chapter Twenty-eight

Noga had his orders. Botlhokwa wished him to bring a shipment from Congo into Zambia at Kasumbalesa and see it through to Kasane. The material would be delivered to an address he would only receive after he'd crossed the border. Botlhokwa made it clear Noga did not need to know what the truck carried. His job consisted only of assuring its safe passage, no more. Noga was annoyed by this apparent snub by his boss. He had stared angrily at Botlhokwa for nearly a full minute before the latter spoke.

"So, you are angry at me, Noga? You think as one of my most trusted employees you should know what it is you bring into the country?"

Noga nodded.

"Yes, I suppose you would. But there is this small difficulty. I charged you, you recall, with finding out who introduced this man into the park only to give him over to be murdered. 'Oh,' you said, 'I will find this man immediately.' But you failed me in this. I am thinking this double dealer must be very clever to elude discovery by my man, Noga. It is surely a great puzzle. This is the very interesting part…you will appreciate this…that game ranger, Takeda, is taken to the police headquarters. Why is that, I ask myself. Then I remembered this is the man about which you have spoken to me in the past. 'He,' you told me, 'secretes many people into the park for a small bribe.' A pittance to what we might realize on the deal of that sort we agreed. And I sent you out to discover what this man is up to."

Noga opened his mouth to speak, but Botlhokwa scowled and waved him to silence

"And here is a most peculiar thing. You do not return to tell me. So, now I am thinking, well he has some other matters on his mind, he will tell me eventually. It is, after all, no threat to our business. So I wait some more."

Noga had no response for this. None was expected. Botlhokwa drummed his fingers on the polished surface of an elaborately carved antique library table. A remnant of past colonial overrule.

"I can add, Noga. I know that two plus two equals four. You decided to do some business on your own, something you have done before. I have overlooked this activity in the past. If it doesn't hurt me too much, I can overlook a small loss of revenue that would ordinarily come to me. But this little enterprise went badly, I think. Did the cargo turn out not to be what your people expected and they want their money back? So it would seem."

Botlhokwa leaned back in his chair and sipped mint tea from a delicate Royal Doulton cup. He waved his hand absently in Noga's direction and shook his head.

"So that disagreeable man, Sczepanski, tells me. But you are not to be found, or rather the culprit who did the double deal is not to be found. It is very confusing. But you knew that, of course. And so, this odious man approaches me. This man with a strange name is a small fish, it seems, in a very large pond. A pond, I might add, filled with many such fish and a few dangerous and hungry crocodiles."

Botlhokwa rose from behind the table and walked to the window where he paused staring out into the afternoon sun. Noga could not see what held his attention. Perhaps there was nothing, this was all to create an effect. He lit a cigar but did not offer one to Noga. A bad sign. He spun and faced Noga, and blew a plume of smoke in his direction. The grit on the warehouse floor scraped and ground as he pivoted.

"So, now I have a predicament, thanks to you. You did not find the double dealer, naturally, because you are the double dealer."

"Rra Botlhokwa…" Noga began. Again he was waved to silence.

"What am I to do then? I could turn you over to those men. I don't mean the Boers to whom you sold the information. I mean the men at the top." Botlhokwa shook his head and drew on the cigar. "If I did, they would gut you alive, Noga, and before you passed out from the pain they would remove your eyes from their sockets with their thumbs. They are not nice people, I have discovered."

"Rra, I—"

"Be still. But I must also see to my reputation. I do not collapse for these people so I cannot turn you over so quickly. I will have to rectify my position with these men and it will cost me. While I do that, you will remain out of sight and try to remember whose hand it is that feeds you. Here is how you will redeem yourself with me, at least for now. You must leave the country for a day or two and see to this shipment. I will negotiate with these men. You will bring in the cargo and deliver it to the consignee as I direct. What happens to it and to you after that will depend on whether they, and I, are satisfied with the outcome of some complex negotiations. It is best you do not know what you are bringing in. Temptation might trigger some rash action on your part that could only compound my problems. It is enough to know that it is very valuable, and therefore very dangerous to be in your possession. There are men who would kill to get their hands on it, you see? What you don't know cannot hurt you. In the meantime remember this, you are alive because I permit it, and only so long as I permit it."

Now, Noga sat in the passenger seat of the battered pickup. It had been marked with the logo of one of Botlhokwa's construction companies. Botlhokwa had several businesses that covered a cash flow that would otherwise raise the eyebrows of the authorities if they were to be made public. In the truck's bed were a miscellany of tools nestled in among some bags labeled *sable* and *ciment*. The truck's suspension had been sorely tested by the weight of these bags innocently marked as sand and cement. Noga made a point of not thinking about their real contents. He did consider some alternatives and then let them go.

He sat stoically in the cab with the motor idling, one of a long string of trucks and cars in line of waiting to cross the river on the ferry into Botswana. They would have to clear a customs inspection before they did so. He'd timed the crossing so that he'd arrive when the ferry would be at its busiest and its inspectors most harassed. He hoped that would earn them a quick wave through. If there were trouble, whether they managed to get the bags to the other side depended on Noga's connections with the locals. He had made a crossing of this sort before but usually in the opposite direction.

Noga did not recognize his driver. One of Botlhokwa's new men. His shirt dripped with sweat. The ambient heat and humidity would normally cause that to happen but not so heavily. They finally pulled up to the inspection point. Noga did not recognize the officer. He tensed and felt for the roll of Euros in his shirt pocket. Would this man accept a bribe?

"What is in the bags?" The uniformed agent said pointing to the cargo behind the cab. Noga signaled the driver to be silent.

"As you can see, we are bringing some supplies in for a job in Kasane."

"Oh yes? There is no cement and sand in Botswana and you must import it from the Congo?"

Noga smiled. "It is a special job. The rich American, you know the one who builds the casino, wishes concrete to be made with this special sand. He is very peculiar."

"Special, is it? Please to show me."

Noga could only hope that what the bags contained would pass for what their labels promised. He stepped from the truck and made a small slit in the topmost bag. Dark, coarse, granular material that easily could pass as inferior sand spilled out from the edge of the cut.

"You see, sand."

The driver of a large tractor with its enormous trailer behind them revved its engine.

"Can we move along here, please," he shouted, and tapped his horn.

The border agent waved Noga and his truck through. It would go more easily on the Botswana side of the river. His cousin, Danko, would be there to pass him through, minus a few of the Euros, of course. They disembarked from the ferry on the Botswana side of the Chobe. His cousin leaned on the door and accepted his present, then flagged them through.

Noga had gotten a good look at the "sand." Although his experience with it was limited, he knew coltan when he saw it. Botlhokwa had been right; it might tempt him to do something rash, indeed. He would have to think about what, if anything, that might be.

# Chapter Twenty-nine

Modise left Mwambe blustering about his reputation, his past service to the country, all of which he made clear had occurred before he, Modise, was born. Modise felt reasonably sure that the superintendent had no connection to Takeda's petty criminal career, but he wanted him to stew a bit about his decision to not pull the little game ranger in earlier. It might not have made a difference, but at the same time it smacked of favoritism, and that did nothing to advance the image of the police. At least they now knew that there were two men involved in the shooting and that Noga was probably not one of them. Painter, the American casino builder, had seen the same two men at his skip. That connected the license number plate, albeit a stolen one, and the two men to the crime.

"Mwambe, when you have finished lecturing me on your history and patriotism," he'd said before he left, "you will fill out a report with the pertinent facts in proper order for me. I have nothing but respect for you and your long service and I do not want to see it ended prematurely, so you will please indulge me in this. Before you do that, however, this man must be arrested and booked. He can call his solicitor or whomever he requires, but for the next few days I need him under lock and key and out of sight."

"I do not see the need, Modise. If he can raise the necessary bond funds, I do not see why he cannot return to his home and duties."

"I need him out of the way because I do not wish this Noga person or any others to have access to him until we can wrap this business up. An open warrant, Mwambe, please."

He left the superintendent's in a righteous funk but also with a directive to increase the surveillance for the Toyota and the two men.

His next stop would be with Sanderson to discuss her camera surveillance, and then on to Painter who'd called earlier about some crisis or another of his own. Perhaps he would remember something else about the two men.

Boers!

◇◇◇

Sanderson waited for Modise in her office. Her aide, Charles Tlalelo, brought tea and sat with her.

"So, Sanderson," Modise said as he breezed through her door. "I have given your problem some thought and I have brought you some paraphernalia. Do you have your camera equipment available?"

She pointed to the corner where Charles had assembled the apparatus. Modise strolled over and picked up one of the cameras.

"You must place these in service on a tripod with this attachment on the power switch. There is a place for it here, you see?"

Sanderson peered over his shoulder and Charles over hers. "What is this thing?"

"Ah, you will see in a moment. Now I suggest this camera be placed across the road from the gap in the fence." He opened the tripod, affixed a camera to it, and set it up on one side of the room. "You must disguise it with branches. Also, I have brought a covering for the camera. It is called a ghillie suit, a thing that soldiers wear when they are hiding. Snipers mostly."

He pulled material that Sanderson thought looked like a limp bush from a paper bag. Charles reached out and took the suit from his hand and flipped open so that it floated onto his shoulders. He grinned at the effect.

"You did that very well, Tlalelo, have you used one of these before?"

Charles grinned some more and slipped the suit off. "No sir. I saw it at the cinema, Mr. Tom Beranger and Billy Zane wore them in it and—"

"Yes, that is very interesting, but—"

"Where can one get these things, Modise? I think we might find them a very useful thing to have with the animals."

"You can draw them from government stores with the proper paperwork. Here, I will write the number down for you." He consulted the paper that had fallen from the bag when he'd withdrawn the suit and copied a number on a scrap of paper. "Now, drape it over the camera like this but be sure the lens is clear. You will note this lens has a non-glare coating on it and that is good."

Sanderson had not noticed anything of the sort about the lens, only that there was a cap on it that must be removed at some time.

"Across the road?"

"Yes, facing the gap. Then you will place this," he lifted a small box-like device from the assemblage of equipment and held it up, "motion sensor next to the fence aimed along its length. Disguise it as well. I will set it so that it will send a signal as long as there is motion and when there is no more, it will shut down." He placed the sensor on a table on the opposite side of the room.

"It sends a signal? How?"

"It is a wireless device and this thing I just showed you that you must attach to the camera is the receiver. If there is motion at the fence, the camera will become live and record everything. Your equipment is fitted for night vision and the lenses are very good. Watch."

He waved his hand in front of the motion detector. Sanderson heard the camera click and thought she also heard a hum.

"You see? Leave it to those people to have the very best equipment for their movie making. We should thank them."

He did not elaborate on *those people* but Sanderson knew what he meant. She felt herself blush and hoped he did not notice.

"When there is no further movement after a full minute it will shut down."

"That is very nice but I am afraid that camera will run all night or until the battery goes flat."

"Why is that?"

"Animals, Inspector Modise. Night time for people means bed, for the animals, movement. There is a small group of kudu that are making that area their habitat right now. They may be moving about all night."

"That is why you must aim the beam from the sensor parallel to the fence. If the kudu are on the other side, they will not trigger the device you see, but an intruder must approach the fence, break the beam, drive through it and…well you see how it must be."

Charles had listened attentively to Modise. He nodded vigorously. "I have it," he said.

"You are certain, Charles?"

"Yes. I am. Do not worry, Inspector Modise. I have been studying this equipment and I have one of these TV cameras, well one similar to it, you could say, at home. I am familiar with the general principle."

"Good, then it is settled. Unless you object, Sanderson, Charles will be seconded to oversee this project. After it is in place he can test it, and then we shall see who uses this entrance and perhaps even discover why."

Sanderson was pleased that Modise handed the task off to Charles. He had promise and needed a chance to shine. Also, these cameras were a thing she did not fully understand.

"One last thing, Sanderson…"

"Yes?"

"Your ranger Takeda is under arrest and in jail for taking bribes and allowing unauthorized persons into the park, very possibly the cinema people who left us this very fine equipment. You will be short-handed, I am afraid."

"He is arrested already?"

"Yes, Mwambe has already picked him up. Apparently they had a connection."

"The superintendent also?"

"Yes, but peripherally. Your Takeda is also implicated with the murder you discovered. It seems he guided your dead man into the park."

"He will lose his job."

"If he is convicted, yes."

"I have the report you asked for. Will you still be wanting it?"

"Yes, thank you, it is further evidence if we need it. Who knows what Takeda will say when he has had a chance to discuss his situation with his solicitor."

Sanderson did not like Takeda and the news he might be less than honest did not surprise her, but the thought of his family and the shame he brought them saddened her.

"So, Sanderson, there is one last thing."

"I thought you said that Takeda's arrest was the last thing."

"Yes, well…I am staying in Kasane for the time being, and I wondered if you might be available for dinner tonight."

This time she really did blush. "Tonight? I would like to, but my daughter, my son, I must be home to…And the cameras must be placed."

"If you permit, Superintendent," Charles said with a grin, "I will be happy to attend to them, the cameras, and your children until you return. If you will call them to expect me—"

"That is very kind of you Charles, but I can't—"

"It is settled then," Modise said. "I will meet you at the Marina Lodge at seven. They say the food is excellent." He left before she could protest.

"You need a break, Sanderson. Be happy. I will set up our surveillance equipment and join you at your house to look after Michael and Mpitle. Do not do anything naughty up there at the Lodge though."

She smacked him on the shoulder.

# Chapter Thirty

Tarq and Rice pushed their way to the mountain's crest. It had been a grueling trek from the tiny airstrip where they'd been dropped to this point. They'd hacked their way through the Congo's jungle being careful to avoid the militias that combed this area seeking women to rape, villages to plunder, and children to enslave. Tarq had no assurance that his target would be in place even if they managed to avoid that plague of human locusts. He hated the senseless killing to which the militias seemed addicted. If a person needed to die, it should be clean and quick. These militiamen, some no more than twelve years old, were as savage as hyenas, he thought, and just as ugly, taking pleasure in the pain and suffering they created. It was as if someone had unleashed a battalion of serial killers on the land. He shuddered to think what life would be like if there were a truce. Could these insensate young men ever return to normal living and relationships after participating in years of unmitigated violence and merciless brutality?

The man and woman moved slowly and carefully through the underbrush. They rarely spoke. Rice knew enough English to follow Tarq and he in turn had acquired enough Arabic so that they could, if they wished, converse. But before a job, they spoke only when necessary. They slept in separate sleeping bags, and anyone observing them from a distance would have assumed they were no more than business associates, brother and sister.

They would be wrong. When their work ended they would backtrack through the jungle, fly to the Seychelles, and take up residence in their condo on the beach. They would eat, sleep, bask in the sun, and make love until they received the next call for their services.

Rice slipped binoculars from her backpack and scanned the area below them toward the encampment. A kilometer away and perhaps the same distance below she could make out the rough placement of tents and shacks set up near the coltan mine. She motioned for Tarq to look. He lifted his sniper scope to his eye and swept the area. Men milled about, rifles slung across shoulders, apparently preparing to move out. But to where? General Le Grande exited the only decent looking tent on the site. He pivoted and flashed some sort of stick at the troopers. It would be a stretch, but if the little man would hold still long enough, Tarq thought he might be able to make the kill from where he stood. Then they could return to their rendezvous point. It would be risky. If he missed he wouldn't get another chance, at least not in this venue, and they would have made the long hike in for nothing. The general would hightail it back to his main headquarters, and a wholly different strategy would be required to take him out there. Not an option Tarq relished. He'd wait for a sure thing. They would have to move closer.

He pulled his ghillie suit from his pack and indicated that Rice should do the same. They wrapped themselves in the camouflage and began the slow process of moving downhill toward the camp. Periodically Rice checked for changes. After twenty minutes of cautious maneuvering she held up her hand.

She indicated with her hands that Tarq should look down slope, that the men were moving in their direction.

Tarq lifted his head fractionally and confirmed it.

"This way. Why?"

Was it possible they'd been seen, been betrayed? He closed the bolt of his rifle over a cartridge, patted the holstered 1918 Colt .45 on his hip.

At that moment he heard rustling in the forest nearby. Too soon for the troops and their leader. He swung his rifle around; its scope now secured to its barrel, and scanned the underbrush.

"Gorillas. They are coming here to hunt the apes. We can move faster now. They will be in the forest on their way up the mountain and not expecting to see us or anybody except those bad boys."

Rice nodded. They crouched and scrabbled down the hillside on an angle that should put them in position to intercept the hunters below the point where the gorillas grazed. Twenty meters further, they entered the westernmost end of a forest glade perhaps ten meters wide and at least fifty long. Perfect. The general and the cockroaches he called his *soldats* would have to cross this area out in the open to get to the gorillas on the hillside above.

Tarq calculated possible lines of fire and chose a spot that would allow him to draw down on anyone emerging from the tree line. He hoped the general would live up to his reputation for bravado and be the first one through. Tarq did not wish to shoot any more men than necessary. He understood, but disliked, the concept of collateral damage. A clean kill was best. One shot and then a high speed bug out.

He'd been trained for this life by the United Stated Marine Corps and had it not been for a bad run of luck involving the wife of his CO and a resultant dishonorable discharge for adultery and striking an officer, he might still be in their employ. On the whole he thought the exchange from highly regarded but underpaid grunt to wealthy assassin had worked out pretty well. Whether shooting the Corps' idea of a bad guy or some other organization's was, for him, a distinction without a difference. Bad guys were bad guys, period.

Rice switched from binoculars to her spotter scope and lined up distances and elevations while they waited for the general and his hunting party. She told each off as she sighted down the glade. Tarq muttered, "check" each time she called a mark and adjusted his sight settings on the scope. There was no wind. The only possible difficulty he envisioned would arise if the gorillas moved through the glade before the soldiers arrived. He couldn't worry about that now. He rubbed the palm of his hand down the length of his rifle, pulled gently at the scope to assure it had seated firmly, and readjusted the camo sleeve that covered the whole. He liked this rifle and scope but still missed the one he'd been issued in the Corps. The Mosin-Nagant M-40A3 had good balance, and excellent optics in the scope. As well as it performed, though, it was still a relic of the Second World War. After this payday he would have one of Lenka's people find him a Sig Sauer SG 550 fully equipped. That was a piece! He lifted his head up to take in the whole of the shooting field, turned toward Rice and smiled. A thin smile. She blinked her response. They were ready.

If the gorillas were aware of their presence, and he guessed they were, they did not seem to care one way or another. They continued to graze their way toward them through the forest floor. Only the old silverback seemed to be aware of something out of the ordinary. He raised up and scrutinized the trees down the hill. Tarq blinked and thought maybe he might have imagined that.

Thirty seconds later, he heard the movements that apparently had attracted the old gorilla's attention. These hunters were not very skillful. If the gorillas were to realize the danger they represented, they had ample opportunity to flee. But they lingered. Tarq settled into his shooting position and touched Rice's shoulder. She lowered her body beside his. Only a matter of seconds now.

The first man into the glade was not the general. Two more stepped clear. Tarq realized the gorillas had become unnaturally quiet. He risked a look up the hill where the group of apes had been. They had moved, not away from, but toward the men. Odd. Tarq turned his attention back to the glade. He heard Rice hiss. The general had stepped forward. He stood, Napoleon-like, in the center, his rifle slung loosely in the crook of his arm. Tarq settled the crosshairs on the general's core. A head shot would be surer but riskier. At the same instant, the gorillas seemed to rise as one and advance on the men. The soldiers hesitated, not expecting this move. Some raised their rifles and took aim but the general seemed to wave them off. He could not make out the man's words but an order had been given and the men hesitated. At that moment the unthinkable happened.

The silverback had been carrying a large stick. He lifted his arm and threw it with considerable force toward the general. The other apes followed suit, apparently with no intentional aim at a target. They simply let fly and then rearmed with rocks and forest debris. The silverback's stick caught the general on the temple. He dropped like a stone. Tarq could not see how badly he'd been hurt, only that he didn't move once he fell. The apes moved closer now screaming and beating their chests, rocks and sticks flying. The soldiers, with their leader down, panicked and raced back down the mountainside. The silverback shuffled to the prostrate general and picked up his rifle. He held it by the barrel, as he had the stick earlier. He used it to smash the man's head several times. It sounded to Tarq like the time he'd taken a baseball bat to a watermelon. The gorilla stared at the bloody end of the rifle, swung it around, and shattered it against a tree trunk. He dropped the pieces next to the man and he and the rest of his group retreated back up the mountain and out of sight.

Tarq waited until he felt certain the apes had cleared the area. He quickstepped down the hill to the general. The man was very decidedly dead. He snapped a picture with his cell phone, grabbed the ID from the general's pocket, and turned.

"We're out of here," he said to Rice. They shed their ghillie suits and retraced their steps out of the area.

Except for the long trek through the jungle, it might have been the easiest paycheck he'd ever earned.

# Chapter Thirty-one

Modise listened stone-faced to Leo Painter. He thought the attempt to sell intel to the Russians by a local gang of thugs verged on the fantastic. He knew about the *Bratva*, of course. Notices about it, its known activities and personnel, had been discussed at the Director's briefings when the agenda reached global threats and Interpol intel. He had the file he'd been handed by the DG as well. He'd studied pictures of the major players and thought he could recognize many of them on sight. But, up until now, its known activities south of the Zambezi had been largely confined to South Africa. The possibility that it had spread its tentacles into Botswana and the Chobe was cause for serious concern. He would need to contact the Director General at once.

"Are you sure of this, Mr. Painter?"

"It is what Greshenko told me. I have no reason not to believe him. Before I asked him to come to the Chobe with me last year I had him vetted by a very reliable private investigator who told me that Greshenko used to run with those people. If he says the Russian *mafyia* is here and selling its services to Russian Intelligence, it would be silly for me not to believe him."

"Have you contacted your embassy, the United States authorities? They will want to know, certainly."

"I made some informal calls to some people I know in the State Department and elsewhere. They did not offer much in the way of relief for Greshenko. As I hear it, he's as well off playing with the bad guys as with the good guys. I'm hoping you can do better by him."

"Yes, I see. The circumstances of his past are most unfortunate, I think. You know it does not make him the sort of person for whom a government like ours does favors."

Modise turned his gaze away and studied the men applying stucco to the walls of the hotel in front of him. He stood and began to pace. He reached into his pocket and pulled out his notebook, flipped it open, and held it up to his ear. A confused look, followed by a sheepish smile, and he placed the book on a low wall nearby and fished out his cell phone.

"Inspector, I would not leave that thing on the wall. If I were you."

Modise stopped pacing and looked at Leo. "There is a problem?"

At that instant, the gray monkey made a lightning dash toward the wall, Modise's notebook his destination.

"Hey, get away from that," Modise shouted and bent to retrieve a scrap of debris which he scaled at the monkey who, in turn, veered away and scurried up a nearby tree to await another larcenous opportunity.

"That sucker does that all the time. We've lost tools, cell phones, and God only knows what else to that little bastard. Maybe your police can arrest him."

"If we arrested every monkey who steals we would have none in the trees to amuse your guests."

"I would not miss them, Inspector."

"Ah, but the tourists would, I believe." He pocketed his notebook and turned his attention to his phone, his back to Leo who strained to catch a word or two or make out who the inspector had on the line. But as the talk was in Setswana, a language he had not yet mastered, he failed.

The conversation, if you could call it that—Modise mostly listened—lasted nearly five full minutes. Leo scuffed his toe in the dirt and waited.

"Mr. Painter, my superiors will require more time to consider how best to handle this situation. I reminded them of the threats made to your Mr. Greshenko and the likelihood his controllers will be expecting results soon."

"More than that. I hope you also told him that if Greshenko is taken out of the picture, it means someone else will be sent in his place and we will not know who that person will be. Greshenko is your proverbial 'bird in the hand.'"

"Bird? Yes, I suggested we would be wise to keep the operation in your friend's hands rather than taking a risk that a stranger might be sent in his place. Is that what you meant?"

"Yes, that sort of bird, you understand correctly."

"The DG suggests you proceed but only in part. What you do in your hotel is your business, he says. Placing cameras and microphones in the units is highly suspicious behavior, perhaps unethical even, but only becomes a problem when used in a covert or illegal manner and only then depending for what purpose, you see?"

"Not really. Are you saying we should go ahead and install them?"

"In your buildings, yes, but in yours only. If Greshenko's controllers get word of work in progress, it will hold them at bay for a while. Long enough for us to decide what to do next."

"I'm being told to bug and setup secret surveillance of guests in my hotel rooms?"

"Bugging, surveillance? Um…I think you did not hear me correctly, sir. I am sure I distinctly said the government would have no difficulty with your attempt to provide a cutting edge fire warning system in your rooms. Of course you understand the equipment must key to switch on only when your smoke detectors activate."

"My smoke detectors activate? Oh, fire warnings, right. I'm not as quick as I used to be, Inspector. Sorry about that. Yes, indeed, we are very proud of our system for helping guests safely from their rooms in case of fire. Smoke detectors do their thing and the system jumps to attention. Indeed, we call it the Fuggo system."

Modise raised his eyebrows. "Fuggo?"

"F. G. H. O.—Fire, Get the Hell Out."

"Very clever. I must remember that. Well, put your man to installing the Fuggo. We will of course, wish to have a close monitor on your system as well. Perhaps we could build in a delay of some sort. You know how that is, time to assess the actions before sending them along. We are not sure."

"And the rest of the job? What does Greshenko tell the bozos about installing things in the Mowana Lodge?"

"We will have an answer for that in a day or two."

"And what happens to Greshenko when this gets out?"

"If it gets out you mean."

"I think I mean, when. If he does this job, he will be in their pocket forever. I don't want that to happen. But if he gets caught, does time, or whatever, they'll have no more use for him."

"And they may eliminate him as he is the link to them. But if he doesn't and he stays in their service, you could say, we would have use for him."

"You'd make him a double? Modise, you might as well put a bullet in his head right now."

"You are too dramatic, I think."

"How well do you know this *Bratva*?"

"Well enough."

"I think not."

"Still, for the moment, he should proceed as we have discussed."

"I hate it when big institutions decide the sacrifice of a life is justifiable if it serves the greater good, especially when it's someone else's life."

"Stay with us, Mr. Painter, we do not wish any harm to fall on your friend."

"Words, Modise, words. Governments trade in them. But I don't suppose we have any better options, do we?"

"No."

# Chapter Thirty-two

The two men Modise had referred to as "Boers" had their SUV headed toward the park. Their orders were to ferret out the men who'd short-circuited Lenka's purchase of the Congolese coltan. A pickup truck with construction company markings on its door passed them headed in the opposite direction.

"That's him."

"Who?"

"Botlhokwa's man that took our money and sent us into the park for nothing."

"Where?"

"He just drove past us in that *bakkie*. Turn around and follow him."

"We're supposed to be looking for the men who took the big man's coltan."

"Never mind that now. I want that *kaffir*. Turn around"

The driver twisted the wheel over hard and cut across the road. As it happens, heavy traffic is a relative rarity in Kasane, and except for a police car approaching from the west, there was none now. The SUV's tires left a fresh patch of rubber on the macadam as it wheeled around to follow the truck carrying Noga. The police car braked and then picked up its pace and trailed them in turn. The constable who happened to be driving could not be sure, he'd had at best only a quick a glance, but thought the men in the car might be the two men Superintendent

Mwambe had mentioned at roll call the day before. They were wanted for questioning in the park murder. The constable leaned toward the microphone on his collar and spoke. Apparently to call in his position and what he'd guessed were the possibilities with respect to the passengers in the SUV. After some minutes, devoted to what may have been an argument, the constable shook his head and keyed off.

The man in the SUV's passenger seat strained forward. "Where is he headed?"

"You're asking me? Who knows? We'll just have to follow and when we find the right pull-off, we stop him and have a conversation."

The second man grinned and retrieved his rifle from the behind the seat and slid open its breech.

The road swung south and east. The truck headed away from Kazungula toward Nata some three hundred kilometers away. Enormous commercial rigs, diesel engines chuffing noisily, and their trailers lined the west side of the road waiting for their turn to cross the river into Zambia on the ferry.

"As soon as we clear these monsters, pull him over."

"There is a car behind us. It started following us in Kasane. I think it's the police."

"*Scheiss,* what do we do now?"

"I'll pass the truck. Let that bird see us. I'll give him a sign to pull up after the police get tired of following us."

"What if they don't?"

'We'll pull over and take care of the copper. Then we'll see to the truck."

"I am not liking this."

Constable Kgobela had a particular and personal interest in chasing the SUV with the two men. He'd suffered through Mwambe's impatience at the crime scene in the park, his stubborn insistence that the dead man had committed suicide in spite of the obvious evidence to the contrary and the game ranger's suggestions, and now this reversal with neither explanation nor clarity. Something had happened after the DIS man from Gaborone showed up for sure. Either way, Kgobela would like very much to arrest these two. If suspicion of murder were not adequate, certainly he had reason enough to pull them over for their irresponsible driving. He pulled a bit closer to the SUV as it swung south on the Nata road.

His radio crackled.

"Kgobela, is that you? Are you there?'

"Derek, we have been through this before, you must learn correct procedure. That is not how you are to contact someone on the radio."

"Yes, yes, I know, it is complicated, but I am learning, I think. Yes, well…anyway, this is urgent. Superintendent Mwambe says you are to pull back and wait for backup."

"That means he is coming to make the arrest himself?"

"I cannot say. Probably. He has some difficulties with headquarters, I think and needs to show…well, you know how he is. He has left in his car and will meet up with you soon."

"But he does not know where I am."

"Oh, yes, as to that, he is on the alternate radio frequency. You are to contact him there and give him your location. Under no circumstances, he said, are you to stop these men by yourself."

"It is too late for that. They are pulling off the road even now. They have a *bakkie*, I think one of Botlhokwa's, that they have been tailing. I am stopping now. Tell your uncle, the superintendent, I am four kilometers south on the road to Nata on the east side, if that helps."

Kgobela signed off and eased his car behind the SUV. The men had already dismounted and were approaching the pickup. One of the men pivoted and watched the police car arrive and then grinned. Kgobela thought that seemed odd under the circumstances. He braked and reached for his baton. He hoped there wouldn't be any use for it but that grin suggested there might be trouble. Too late, Kgobela saw the rifle at the grinning man's side.

◇◇◇

By the time Superintendent Mwambe had deciphered his nephew Derek's messages and tried and failed to contact Kgobela himself, nearly twenty minutes had elapsed before he pulled up behind the police car. A bit farther along, a pickup truck, the one apparently belonging to Botlhokwa, sat with its motor idling and seemingly empty. A uniformed body lay face down between the two vehicles. Nothing else stirred. Mwambe stayed in his car waiting. A large trailer truck roared north, its air wash rocked the car. Mwambe had drawn a pistol from the gun locker before he'd left. At the time he didn't know why. Instinct, he'd assumed. Now he realized what the spirits had been trying to tell him.

"Derek, call for backup immediately. I want them armed. Also, I will need a forensic team here. Do this right now."

The car jumped again as another truck rocketed by. Mwambe eased open his door, and being careful to stay behind its protecting steel, stepped out onto the verge. He slipped the pistol into his hand and peered over the window sill. Still, nothing stirred. He swung his gaze toward the bush. No one but a fool would venture too deeply into it. Most wild animals did not venture so close to the road, but you could never count on that. Elephants might decide to cross at any point. They claimed the right of way and were granted it.

Satisfied he was alone; he stepped out from behind the car door and walked to the body. Constable Kgobela lay in the dust. He'd obviously been shot. The wounds on his back indicated the bullets had passed clean through. With no walls, trees or other obstacles to capture them, there would be none for ballistics to analyze. Too bad about that. He stepped carefully around the body and approached the other vehicle. It had a passenger after all, crumpled sideways across the seat. He too, had been shot at close range by a quite powerful weapon. The chances for ballistics test improved in the shooting within a closed space.

There was nothing more Mwambe could do but wait for his people to arrive. Modise would have a field day with this. He gritted his teeth at the thought.

Two bodies.

# Chapter Thirty-three

Noga stared down at the business end of the rifle barrel. He had no illusions whether the man brandishing it would pull the trigger if so inclined. He'd just seen him kill a policeman and the driver. The two men forced him into their Toyota. Then they'd driven a kilometer south of the encounter and veered off and bounced into the bush for another two. They had stopped and shoved Noga out onto the ground. They'd climbed out and now faced him.

"So, Mr. Botlhokwa's man, you owe us some money, I think."

Noga recognized the men, of course, and it was true he'd taken money from them but couldn't be sure why they thought they deserved to have it returned. Well, he guessed he did, but he reasoned his end of the bargain was to identify a possible cargo to steal, not to guarantee its ultimate worth. These men had made it clear to Botlhokwa that that they did not consider that to be the case and Botlhokwa, in turn, had come down on Noga when he'd discovered the truth. That Takeda…if only he'd been clearer about what he considered precious. Now the ranger sat safely in jail while these men threatened to send him to join his ancestors. Noga had long abandoned the Christian notion of heaven but as he contemplated the business end of the rifle, he longed for a reasonable substitute. Clearly, no matter what he said or did in the next ten minutes, that thing might very well go off and he'd be away to some other place.

"The money. You will please give it back to us, now."

Noga sighed. "I cannot do that. Sorry." He squeezed his eyes shut and braced himself for the rifle's report and bullet's impact. Nothing happened. He risked a look at the men. They stood frowning. One scratched his chin through his scraggly beard.

""What do you mean you can't repay us our money, boy. You will. One way or another, you will. By Gott, even you must be worth something to somebody. We could sell you dead or alive back to your Botlhokwa."

Noga's mind raced. There had to be a way out of this. The English and the coltan might work.

"I have something better for you."

"Better? How better? You for sure have something we can take back to our boss?"

"I just delivered a very valuable cargo to some Englishmen. If you take me to your boss, I will tell him what it is, where it is, and how to find it."

"You will tell us now and we will decide if you live long enough to talk to anybody."

Noga knew he had them. Boers could be so thick at times. "If you kill me, you get no money, no cargo no…well, you will be where you were before you caught up with me only even less likely to find a pay-off."

"You think that is important to us?"

"I think so, yes. Listen, there are two things you should be thinking about. First, whether I am telling you the truth or not. I might really have something to sell. If I do, and if your bosses are who I think they are and they find out you killed me without checking, you'll be next on the firing line. Yes?"

The two exchanged looks. Noga knew he'd touched a sore spot.

"Maybe. What is the second reason?"

"You come from the south somewhere. South Africa probably, and you don't know any better, I guess but—"

"What do you mean, but?"

"But…you have taken us deep into the bush. This is lion country and they are always hungry. A pride of them could come crashing through these bushes any time now if they've caught our scent. If so, you will be some big cat's lunch. We need to get out of here and quick."

As if on cue, they heard rustling in the bush nearby. All three dove for the Toyota, scrambled in, and slammed the doors.

"Just hurry up, you bastard." The driver slapped the SUV into gear and they wheeled away, crashing through brush, small trees, and nearly took out their transmission as they lurched across a dry streambed. The gazelles which had created the panic in the first place, bolted in the opposite direction.

Noga had bought himself some time.

Modise left Leo Painter and headed back to police headquarters. He needed to give Mwambe a heads-up about the trouble brewing at the American's casino. He needn't tell it all just yet; just enough to prevent an investigation if someone were to report suspicious activity at the casino. In fact, he hoped they would. It would be a good sign about the security system he hoped he'd established.

He couldn't be sure how Mwambe would react to a caution couched as "in the best interest of government security." The Americans were always finding themselves in hot water when they claimed "national security" as their reason to stifle information.

As he approached the parking area, he was nearly sideswiped by a convoy of official vehicles headed out the gate. He flagged one down by flashing his police ID.

"Where are you going?"

"Is that you, Inspector Modise? Oh, well, there has been a shooting on the road south to Nata. One of our officers has been shot. Two Boers—"

Modise did not need to hear the rest. He braked, reversed, and wheeled around to follow the stream of cars and vans heading back out of the village. A shooting? Boers? This was something for sure. The last time there'd been a shooting involving a Boer had been the infamous Mariotta Bosche, who killed her lover's wife a few years ago. Big scandal. She'd been hung, much to the consternation of the international press. Could these be the same two implicated in the park shooting? That small killing in the park was growing into something more than a misfired hijacking.

Ten minutes later he pulled up behind a police car and walked toward the scene. Mwambe appeared to be in charge and busy. Modise hung back and watched. He would give the superintendent some space. As much as he disliked this overstuffed policeman, Modise conceded he knew how to do his job when he chose. Today, it seemed, he did so choose. A few meters away, Modise saw the body on the ground—the constable. Evidence techs were at that moment easing a second body from a pickup truck farther along the track.

"Ah, Modise, you have heard?"

"Superintendent Mwambe, I have. Your man is killed by Boers? Our Boers?"

"Possibly, possibly. Constable Kgobela is dead and so he cannot tell us who pulled the trigger on him, but we believe it is those two. He called in that he had taken up pursuit of two men matching the description of the men we sought. The vehicle matched that the American gave us but not the number plate, of course."

"Of course. I am sorry about your officer."

"He died doing his duty. He was Rra Kgobela's son, the man that ran the fruit market, and Mma Carl, his mother. They also lost a daughter, his sister, last year. So much sadness for them, but, if you must die young it is the better way, is it not?"

Modise nodded. It was. "What are the chances for a ballistics match?"

"Too soon to tell, but the man in the *bakkie* died in the vehicle. That means there could be a projectile in there somewhere."

"Good. When we catch up with these two men we will want it."

"You believe we will catch them then?"

"Oh yes. They have returned to the area. They are either very stupid, very sure of themselves, or truly believe we have no case against them. Oh yes, we will have them."

Mwambe smiled and nodded. Poor Takeda was forgotten for the moment.

# Chapter Thirty-four

Sanderson and Charles Tlalelo arrived at her house at the same time. She, flustered, introduced Charles to Michael even though he had visited many times previously.

"Tell Mpitle about Charles," she said.

Michael raised his hand in greeting. Charles seemed startled at the young man's appearance, It had been some months since he'd last seen him and the effects of HIV/AIDs changed him dramatically.

"*Dumela,* Michael, *le kae?*"

Michael smiled. His voice was so weak; Charles could not make out what he said. So much sorrow for Sanderson, Charles thought. If this assignation with Modise did nothing more than put some cheer in her life, it would be worth it.

Sanderson disappeared into her bedroom. He heard her crashing about and muttering about having nothing to wear. Women always said that, didn't they? Mpitle, the teenager who turned many heads in the village, banged in the door and jumped at the sight of him. She may not have remembered meeting him earlier.

"I am Charles Tlalelo," he said. "You have forgotten me, I think."

Mpitle looked at him uncertainly.

"Mpitle, is that you?" Sanderson called. "This is Charles from the station. Say hello to him. He will be staying here while I am away this night."

"Where are you going?"

"She has a date with Inspector Modise, from Gaborone" Charles said and winked.

"You are going out with a man, Momma?"

"No, a hippo. Of course, a man. Is that so strange? You think I should remain an old widow woman forever?"

"No, of course not." Mpitle did not sound convinced. "But why Rra Tlalelo is being here? Michael and I can take care of ourselves. We always do."

Sanderson stepped from the back room wrapped in a robe. She pursed her lips and nodded toward the bed where Michael lay, his forehead beaded with sweat. She shook her head.

"There had been a development in that murder in the park you have heard me speak about. A man, a very large man, has threatened to hurt you if I do not do certain things. I do not think he will, but I cannot take the chance, so Charles will spend the evening here with you two. He will not disturb you so you can concentrate on doing your homework."

Mpitle rolled her eyes. "This is so silly. I am a grown woman and—"

"Charles has the rifle with him just in case. You see it is serious, Mpitle, so do not argue with me on this. Now, I need you to help me find an appropriate dress."

"A dress? Momma, when was the last time you wore a dress? You live in that uniform of yours. I do not think I will recognize you in a dress. The neighbors will call the police alerting them to a stranger in the neighborhood."

"I do not need to be hearing your sass, lady. Now help me with this decision or I will take you father's belt to your backside." Mpitle giggled at the idea. "Don't think I won't."

"Yes, Momma, and I will be the next president of this country."

"You could be if you wanted. But that would require a much more determined effort in schooling and that begins with your homework. Now, come in here and let us see what we can make of these many garments. Lord have mercy, I don't think any of them are less that ten years old."

Charles settled in the good chair and opened his paper. He had his rifle across his knees but hoped he'd not be called on to use it. He hated firearms.

Modise glanced at his watch. He had time to check a few more things and return to his room at the Marina Lodge to freshen up before collecting Sanderson for their dinner engagement. He'd made reservations at the restaurant earlier to assure it could seat them. He waved goodbye to Mwambe and returned to the privacy of his car. He made three calls to Gaborone and then sat contemplating the setting sun and the growing threat to his country posed by international crime syndicates.

He slid the red-jacketed file he'd brought from Gaborone out of the leather case he kept with him always and added to it the notes he'd just jotted down. Things will be difficult, the DG had said. Difficult? If the Lenka organization decided to move north to the Chobe, maybe impossible unless an army were assigned to him. And then what to do with Greshenko. Clearly he had become a liability. If he were made a "double," as Painter suggested, his future life expectancy would drop to under five years, and even that was a stretch. He flipped open the file to the first page and read, wondering how much of this he should share with Painter and the other hoteliers on the river.

The South African authorities had confirmed Olegushka Zhoravitch Lenka's presence in Cape Town. So it was certain. The major Russian crime boss had opened up shop and was looking northward. Modise flipped through the pages.

*Lenka has moved between various locales, Sharjah, Antwerp, and Rio de Janeiro. Like his contemporaries, including the presently incarcerated and disgraced Victor Bout, he is a native of the old and the new Russia, the USSR as it had been, and the state that now operated in its place. Born in Novograd, educated in St. Petersburg, this former KGB operator emerged as a senior Bratva figure in the late nineties. His group now operated through multiple fronts including Nexus*

*Aviation which is currently one of the larger commercial air carriers linking Africa, Latin America, Middle East, and Asia. And it has a significant air service infrastructure at O. R. Tambo airport in Johannesburg. Lenka's network linked these services operating out of East Africa—specifically to Uganda and Rwanda, where they apparently are involved in a variety of enterprises in and out of the Democratic Republic of Congo: Specifically guns, spares, drugs, as well as legitimate and quasi-legitimate cargoes such as coltan.*

How do you curb a criminal organization that has its own air force?

*In addition to employing ex-Soviets as muscle, his organization employs locals as "boots on the ground" in its markets. In Southern Africa this meant the presence of ex-liberation era combatants both white and black.*

That would explain the Boers. Like the ex-Soviet cold warriors, there were hardcore elements from such notorious units as the *Koevoet* and De Kock's infamous *Vlakplaas* who had not been able to reconcile to the prospect of a Rainbow Nation finally at peace with itself. The scary part related to the intel that linked Lenka to the militias in Eastern Congo, groups known up and down Africa for their horrific brutality toward women, children, and rival tribes. Modise had heard stories from his opposite number in Kinshasa, stories that only lately began to appear in the Western press. And all this, it seemed, went on with the tacit acquiescence from Rwanda and Uganda. Modise shook his head. Was there no end to this European obsession with exploiting Africa? Were not several centuries of colonial pillaging enough for them?

*The Russian intelligence arm, the FSB, wanted to know what Americans and the Arabs might be up to.*

So, it appears they had not turned up the North Korean connection yet. At least he hoped not. The FSB must have solicited Lenka's organization to generate the intel they wanted which would allow them to maintain a position of deniability if it were revealed that such surveillance had been done. But, of course, Western intelligence agencies and Botswana's DIS couldn't verify any of this yet.

Until now. One final entry, an apparent late addition, deepened his frown:

> *The South Africa government has notified the UN Security Council that it recently seized a shipment of North Korean arms bound for Congo in violation of Security Council Resolution 1874 which bans all North Korean arms exports. Experts from the council's North Korea Sanctions Panel have been tasked with probing the case. Western sources reported South Africa acted after receiving a tip from a French shipper. Inspection by authorities determined that the cargo contained spare parts for T-54 and T-55 tanks.*
>
> *Last December, Thai authorities also seized thirty-five tons of arms originating from North Korea, including missiles and rocket-propelled grenades, from aboard an Ilyushin cargo plane which landed for refueling in Bangkok. The crew was detained. They claimed they only carried oil drilling equipment bound for the Ukraine. The five crewmen, a Belarusian pilot and four Kazakh, were charged with possessing illegal weapons and ammunition, smuggling, and failing to report the cache.*

Could this have been one of Lenka's planes? The report did not mention him or Nexus Aviation. Russian pilots had the reputation of being able to land practically anywhere.

> *This is the second instance in which Thailand has played a role in interdicting illicit arms trafficking. Earlier it was credited with the apprehension of Victor Bout who was attempting to supply one of the Colombian drug cartels.*

Modise closed the file and replaced it in the case next to the green one that detailed Operation Paradise. He was struck by the irony represented in the two files in his attaché case. Both detailed threatened incursions into Botswana. But while the first posed a real and probably long term menace to the country, its people, and its economy, the other would be at worst, no more than a nuisance. Yet both required a wide deployment of law enforcement personnel, thereby thinning their ranks to the detriment to their effectiveness.

Modise sighed, closed the case, and let his mind drift back to the predicament in which Painter and his friend now found themselves. It would be difficult to retrieve anything good from it, he felt. And with the World Cup coming up, Lenka would certainly be attracted to the possibilities associated with the games—gambling, bet fixing, procuring high class escorts, and supplying those special needs the wealthy and privileged seem to crave. He will have his eye on Painter's Kasane operation and must have spotted Greshenko early on. If Painter thought that Kasane could be a civilized, mob-free gambling zone…he will soon find that compared to what could be coming together on the banks of the Chobe, Bugsy Siegel's Las Vegas would seem like a church outing.

"Modise," he murmured to the empty car, "you and your colleagues will soon have your hands full, that's for certain."

He started the engine and headed back to Kasane. He had more cheerful things to occupy him back there.

# Chapter Thirty-five

Botlhokwa had had his eye on the American's casino project since they'd first met months before. But the hoped for opportunity to squeeze money from the American had evaporated when the authorities moved in after the American's stepson was killed. Still, he had some ideas in mind with respect to the project. For example, protection against unhappy locals and employee labor relations. He could provide that and more in exchange for an equity position. Certainly, this American would not like his employees out on strike. And there were always chances of fires, accidents, and, well, you never knew. The possibilities spread out before him and gave him a warm feeling.

He had not expected any visitors and was startled when that odious man Sczepanski barged into his office. He it was who'd badgered him before about Noga, when neither of them knew at the time that Noga was the one who'd bilked the two Boers out of money. What did he want now?

"I am accustomed to having people knock before they enter," Botlhokwa said. He shot the intruder a look as icy as he could manage. It immediately faded when he saw the automatic in his visitor's hand. At least now he understood why this oaf had not been stopped by Henry Cunningham, a very large man to whom he paid substantial sums to protect him from these inconveniences.

"Cunningham, are you alright?" No answer.

"Your man, Cunningham…is that his name, truly?…He is not in a position to speak at the moment. He is in the company of several of my aides but will be allowed back to his post when we have completed our conversation—or perhaps not. Now," the man settled into the chair opposite, "to business."

No options to hearing the man out occurred to Botlhokwa. He nodded and leaned back in his leather chair behind the great mahogany desk that he claimed had once belonged to Cecil Rhodes. His guest leaned forward, flipped open the cigar humidor on the desk's edge, and helped himself to a handful of the *Cohibas*. He stuffed all but one into his inside jacket pocket, bit off the end of the remaining one, and lit it. He tilted back on the fragile chair's back legs and swung his boots onto the desktop with a thump. It was all Botlhokwa could manage to not react to this rudeness. Not to mention the danger to his priceless furniture, at least not yet. They had Cunningham, but they would see that two could play at this game.

"You were tasked to find our merchandise."

"Tasked? I am not someone's errand boy. I agreed that I would, for a reasonable fee, find the coltan your employer misplaced. I have done so. I am waiting to hear from my man that it has arrived safely at its destination. That is all."

"Even as we speak, your man is currently locked up in our warehouse keeping company with a Doberman pinscher that suffers from what you might say is an erratic disposition. We never know what that animal will do next, but if your man stays very still, he may live long enough for us to dispose of him later in a less painful way."

Botlhokwa swallowed and reached for one of the remaining cigars. "What do you mean, he's locked up?"

"Locked up? What is there to know? He is sitting on a chair murmuring soothing words to a lunatic dog. He would be tied to the chair, but for this dog. But locked away is just that. You see, you were not completely candid with me the last time we met. You said that you did not know who had cheated us, but you assured us it was a rogue acting in your name only. You said you would find this man and make restitution and so on."

"Yes, and I will."

The man let his feet scrape off the desk top and crash to the floor. He stood and leaned so far across the desk that his nose was no more than ten centimeters from Botlhokwa's.

"Do you take me for a fool? Do you think I am just another one of the petty grifters you are used to dealing with?"

"Petty…I do not deal with petty anythings. My connections reach into the highest level in the government. I—"

"You are small potatoes to us. You continue to work your small dodges here because it pleases us to let you. You are thought to be useful. You should concentrate on staying that way. When that is no longer the case, you will disappear. Do you understand?"

"Just who do you think you are? Let my man outside go, and we will see who is 'tasking' whom."

"Let him go? Certainly, if you insist." He barked an order to someone on the other side of the door. Botlhokwa did not recognize the language at first. Then he heard the gunshot and realized it didn't matter.

"So, we have let your man go. To heaven or hell, I don't know him well enough to say. Now, we will continue our discussion. As long as we find you useful, you will continue to operate exactly as you have. Forty percent of your gross profits will be remitted to us and you will make your people available to us from time to time for, shall we say, special projects."

Botlhokwa's cigar had dropped to the floor at the gunshot. It had started to singe the silk Qom-Mohsenzadeh carpet he'd bought in Iran. That was before it became unwise to travel in that country. He did not try to retrieve it. He stared slack-jawed at the man sitting across from him.

"You are from…who? Which family? Bout is out of circulation, maybe dead, and that means you must be with—"

"It is not important to say who, you understand, not just now. As I said we have your man who calls himself Snake. He has had some words with us, and so we know now that you lied to us. It is a great mistake to lie to the *Bratva*, yes?"

Botlhokwa nodded. "Of course, but I did not know Noga had done this thing at the time we spoke before and—"

"And? Yes, and then you found out, but still forgot to mention it to us. You wanted to play both of us off, no? But we find this out. You see, your man, Snake, is not so tough as he thought. It took very little persuading to get him to chatter away like a little schoolgirl."

"What do you want from me?"

"Ah, now you are beginning to see the picture. Very well, I have laid out the broad outlines of our partnership already. Shall I repeat?"

Botlhokwa shook his head. He didn't need to hear them again.

"No? Good. When our people retrieve the minerals, we will move on to the next step. You will be contacted."

The man rose, ground out the stub of his cigar on the antique desk's polished surface, and walked to the door.

"You have some rubbish out here that will require removing."

The door swung inward, but only as far as Cunningham's foot allowed.

# Chapter Thirty-six

Harvey and Jack finished piling the cones of ersatz orgonite into the back of their truck. They had barely enough room for the load, and in fact, had to stack some of it behind the seat in the cab. They finished securing a tarpaulin over the bed and stepped back to inspect the job.

"The lads did a good job with the cones. That Bondo hardens in a hurry, for a cert."

"Body workers' delight. They need to move the wrecks in and out in a hurry, so they insist the formula have quick hardening characteristics. Smear it on, let it set, sand it, paint it, and out the door."

"Good for us, too, we need to get these bits positioned chop-chop. The money boys will be wanting their pay-back and the buyers are itching to get their hands on this stuff."

"Jack, maybe this isn't the time to question the deal, but don't you get the feeling that this has been a little too easy?"

"Easy? How so?"

"Well, okay, first you connect with the Congo chap and arrange to buy the goods. He says it's a go, and so then we need more money than we can shake a stick at to close the deal. 'Where is it coming from,' I ask. Then, out of the blue, a guy just happens to sit down next to us in the restaurant and he just happens to be interested in advancing us the bloody lolly. Is anybody ever that lucky?"

"So? It happens. Be happy, Harv."

"And then, by Nelly be damned, here comes a buyer who just happens to have heard about the coltan from the money chap. None of this strikes you as a bit jiggy somehow?"

"Money is money. Listen, we've had our ups and downs of late. But the bad luck can't last forever. It's the law of compensation, see? For each drawback, there's a leap forward. And after what…two years in one backwater or another, we stumble on a good deal. This is our leap forward. As soon as we collect the swag, we fly away to where the palm trees sway and lovely brown-skinned ladies wait on a chap hand and foot."

"I still don't like it. This has all been too easy and that Noga person asked too many questions. Let's get this stuff out into the park, mark it up on the GPS thing, and get the bloody hell out of here."

"You worry too much, Harvey. Whoa, who's this?"

The two Boers had left Noga locked in a closet with a dog. It occurred to them that the Toyota had been spotted so they had switched to an old Lada four-wheel drive they'd driven in earlier from South Africa. The left hand drive still caused some difficulties causing the driver to over-steer into the curb and then swerve over into the oncoming lane. They pulled up in front of the shack on the edge of Kazungula late in the afternoon. The two *rooinecks,* the "English" Noga had told them about, stood watching them as they pulled to a stop.

"They've loaded it into their *bakkie.*"

"That's good. They can drive it to the warehouse for us then. Or we may do that job for them."

They stepped down from the SUV and crunched across the gravel toward the other two. The shooter held his rifle down at his side, along his pants leg. There were cars passing by and he did not want it to be seen and produce a call by a concerned citizen to the police. The two men watching their approach saw it, however.

"Here, what's this all about?" the first one said.

"Jack, he's holding a gun."

"I can see that. And I'm holding a mobile phone, Harvey, so we're about Even Steven, I'd say."

The lead Boer took a step forward and swatted the phone to the ground. He moved with remarkable speed for a man of his bulk.

"No phone. Now, please, you will show us the goods you have taken from our boss."

"Goods? You barking mad, chum. We have nobody's goods but our own, thank you very much."

"I told you this was too easy. We've been set up."

"Stay calm, Harvey. Look here, there's been a mistake. You boys have us confused with somebody else."

"No confusion. The Botlhokwa man, Noga, said you are the ones. Let's see what you have here."

While the shooter kept Jack and Harvey at bay, the other stepped up to the truck and slashed the tarpaulin open with his knife.

"What is this?" He reached into the bed of the truck and withdrew a cone-shaped object about the half the size of a traffic warning device. "He has done it to us again," he screamed. He held the cone above his head and then threw it against the shack. It shattered, scattering dust and debris in all directions.

"What are you doing?"

"It's the same stupid *sheis* that Noga person sent us after before. It's...look for yourself. It's rubbish."

Jack and Harvey exchanged looks. Harvey gave Jack a wink and turned to the two men.

"Here now, that's valuable stuff you're tossing about. That's orgonite. It will heal the planet. Haven't you heard about Operation Paradise"

"What?"

"S'truth, those cones have power. You put them down in the proper place on the old *terra firma* and they radiate healing energy. Why, you sure you haven't heard about this? Wait a sec. Now I get it, you're from the United Nations, the Health Organization, right? You're here to stop us. Well listen, Mr.

UN obstructionist, you may stop us this time, but there are hundreds, no thousands, of us out there and we will overcome." Harvey placed his hand on his heart as he spoke. Jack lowered his chin to his chest and hoped the guys with the beards didn't catch his smile.

The big man, the one holding the knife, looked addled; the other kept glancing over his shoulder at the road. Traffic, for some reason, had slowed and it made him nervous. At that moment, three of the young men who'd help create the cones turned the corner and walked up.

"What is this?" one said as he fingered the ripped edge of the tarpaulin.

""Not to worry, Tailor," Jack said, keeping a straight face, "These gents have us confused with someone else, I think. Or are you from the UN after all?"

""UN? What about the UN? You," the Boer said to the man Jack had called Tailor, "who are you?"

"I am Taolo Rapolasa. My friends and I helped these men prepare the orgonite for placement. We have returned to see if we can offer more help."

"No probs, Tailor, my son. We're good to go as soon as these gents leave."

The two Boers retreated to their vehicle. Whether they believed the "English" or not, a multiple shooting on a busy street did not seem a good idea. And, there was only crap in the truck anyway. They would have to have more words with Noga. This time there would be pain involved.

# Chapter Thirty-seven

Sanderson and Mpitle had managed to assemble an outfit which she thought passable. She did not know what one wore to dinner at the Marina Lodge. Eating out did not happen in her life. Not anymore. Duty kept her in the park, economics kept her in her kitchen. The last time she dined out had been nearly ten years before with her late husband. They had separated earlier, another woman—or was it two, three? It didn't matter any more. And suddenly he called to talk about reconciliation. She'd agreed to talk to him but only in a public place. She would not be reduced to porridge by those brown eyes this time. So, they had met, she determined to resist any talk of his returning, he to inform her he had contracted AIDs and would most probably die in a year. It was a time before the retro virus treatments were generally available.

How could she resist?

She adjusted the scarf Mpitle had loaned her. It had been a present from her boyfriend, David, a nice boy, hard worker, but Mpitle was too young to be thinking of boys, wasn't she? An expensive scarf, if a label that said Dolce and Gabbbna meant what she thought it did. David had found it on the path. Some rich woman's carelessness had been Mpitle's good fortune. She walked into the lobby area searching for Modise. When he didn't appear in ten minutes, she considered turning and leaving. He was a busy man. No doubt he'd received an important call from Gaborone.

"Sanderson, there you are. Where are you going? The restaurant is the other way, come."

She smiled and hoped she did not look so out of place in this expensive tourist hotel. The woman behind the desk smiled at her. What did that mean? Did she look dowdy? She felt dowdy. Or was she laughing at her because she was a simple woman from the village, a square peg in a round hole?

"You are looking very fine, Sanderson. Is that a new dress?"

This situation, she hoped, would soon reveal itself to be a dream, a bad dream. How to answer this question? Oh yes, it is something I just picked up…where? She didn't even know the name of a fancy dress shop. No, it is ten years old and if I move too quickly or, Lord forbid, bend over, I will split every seam in it. She resisted the temptation to laugh. If she started, she knew she would not be able to stop and that could produce more disastrous consequences.

"Thank you," she said.

They found a table with a view of the river and Modise ordered a bottle of wine. He asked her for her preference. She had none. She hadn't drunk wine since that time when her husband had cajoled his way back into her house long enough to die. She smiled and tried to look at ease. This was a big mistake, for sure.

Modise made small talk until their food arrived. Then, while they ate grilled kudu and salad, he told her about the shooting on the Nata road and the suspicion he had that the killers of the constable and truck driver were the same as the ones who'd shot the man in the park.

"I know that constable. He came to the park with Superintendent Mwambe that day. His name is…let me think…Carl something. Oh yes, Carl Kgobela. He…they killed him? Why?"

"We can't be sure. They probably thought he would arrest them. He would have, too. Who the other man was, or why he was killed, I don't know. They found his body in the cab of a *bakkie* belonging to a local big shot. We don't know if there is a connection that way or not."

"The big shot wouldn't be Rra Botlhokwa would it? If so, I am guessing there very definitely is a connection. That man has fingers in everybody's pudding around here. I do not know why he is not in jail." She noticed a flicker in Modise's eyes. Did that mean Botlhokwa will be going to jail? That is news.

"Yes, well, there are all sorts of reasons why he is still around. A new topic, something cheerful."

They asked for their coffees to be served to them out on the terrace. They settled on chairs and watched a boat head upstream against the setting sun.

"So, Sanderson, I know you as the famous game ranger, but I do not know your whole name. Why is that?"

"It is because you have never asked me, Kgabo Modise. That is why. Are you asking me now? And I am not famous."

"People will disagree. Yes, certainly I am asking, but I am embarrassed for having to do it. My social skills are wanting, I think."

"I will not comment on that. I am not known for my ability to charm or converse with any wit either. Perhaps we are the peas in the pod."

"I think you are being too modest. I think you are only out of practice while I have never been any good at this."

"We will never get very far if we spend this evening telling ourselves what dunces we are."

"Sorry. I will be a non-dunce if I can. So, what is your full name? That is where all this started."

"My name is Mpoo Kgopa Sanderson. The people of my village call me Mma Michael. You see, not so hard."

"Kgopa? You are a snail?"

"The naming came from my uncles the one who says he saw a saucy look from me when I was brought home and he thought *kgopa*, snail, would keep me humble. It didn't, I don't believe."

"I will call you Sanderson or Mma Michael. Snail does not suit you. You are much too quick to be thought as one of those."

"Ah, well. I have never eaten one, but in France they eat them and also frogs." She made a face at the thought of a cooked amphibian.

"So I am told. And they think we are strange for eating *phane*. It is a strange world. So much division over so little difference."

"Division? I see. Well, calling me Sanderson is fine. It is how I am known." She wondered if there was any point to this conversation and if Modise would ever get to it.

"They serve very fine food here," he said.

"Yes, they do. They say the Old House has a very fine steak dinner."

"Do they? We should eat there next time."

"There is to be a next time, Modise?"

"Kgabo."

"Kgabo, then. There is to be a next time?"

"I hope so. I mean there is much to discuss about the business in the park, of course, and the cameras, and so on. Oh yes, I think another meeting is needed, truly."

Sanderson smiled. "Oh, I see, indeed the business in the park, illegal entry, surveillance measures. Yes, to be sure, and dinner in an expensive restaurant is the very best place for us to discuss these important topics. With wine and dessert, of course. Modise, what are you about?"

"Kgabo."

"Answer me and then I will decide if you are Christian name friend or a surname friend."

"You are a hard woman, Sanderson. No, I take that back. You are a soft woman in a man's world so you act very tough." Modise paused and contemplated the boat which seemed to have finished whatever it needed to do upstream and now putted back toward the Mowana Lodge. "Very well...I am not good at this. I am a cop twenty-four seven, Mma Michael, and that is mostly what I think about so...but, I find you very ah..."

"Annoying? Pushy? Dowdy? I feel dowdy, you know, sitting here in my ten-year-old dress and pretending I know what I am doing." Where did that outburst come from?

"I was going to say attractive, but had some difficulty getting my tongue around the word. I will go along with the others except dowdy. You are many things, Mma Michael, but dowdy is not one of them."

Sanderson did not know what to say to that. "Are you staying here in the hotel?" she said instead. She already knew he was.

"I have a room here."

"Oh yes?"

# Chapter Thirty-eight

Leo had noticed the PT Cruiser before and thought nothing of it. His as yet undeveloped entryway afforded off-road parking for people sightseeing or visiting one of the mall shops down the road. But PT Cruisers were not that common in Botswana and since the Chrysler Company announced their intention to discontinue the line, not an easy sale either. What were the odds that the identical or a look alike automobile would be parked in the same spot four days in a row? Since the situation with the *Bratva* had pushed its ugly nose into his business, he'd become sensitized, or perhaps paranoid about all sorts of things. He studied the car for a minute. He could not be sure, but he imagined he saw binoculars trained at him or his building. He memorized this number plate, too. He'd hand it to Modise the next time he saw him.

The car reversed and pulled away as Greshenko walked up behind him.

"Shopping for a new automobile, Leo?"

"What? No, just observing. Have you noticed that car parked out on the verge before?"

"Which car? You mean the one that just drove away? No, but then I am not looking that way so very often."

"They pulled off when you showed up. I wonder…would your buddies in the mob be checking up on you, do you think?"

"Oh, yes, I think that is most sure. I am not so sure they would do it that way, though."

"No? How would they?"

"I was talking to the foreman just this minute and he tells me a man approached him with a proposition."

"A man. What sort of man, or rather what sort of proposition?"

"He thinks the man maybe is one of them that works for that fellow we talked to earlier in the year, the Mr. Big, Botlhokwa."

"Why would Botlhokwa want to know what you're up to?"

"Not me he is interested in, you. He thinks Mr. Big wants to squeeze in here somehow, become a stakeholder or something. Your foreman is not so sophisticated in the ways of finance, so he wouldn't know."

"Botlhokwa will be a partner of mine when the Chobe River freezes over. Tell him that."

"I will if he asks, but that is not the point I was making. Botlhokwa is openly bent. The people who are after me work in the darkest of the darkness. They will have someone informing on me and that person, I promise you, will never reveal himself as to the foreman by the Botlhokwa person. And he will not tell either of us about it if they do."

"Why not? I'd pay for the information, they all know that. They're good men."

"Yes, but they are still only men. Men with families, with homes, maybe nothing more than a *rondeval*, but it's theirs and it's a home. They have friends, too, you see?"

"Sorry, no. I'm missing something here, aren't I?"

"Do you remember what I told you about these men? They will make it very clear that if there is any indication they've been compromised, any leak, the man responsible will pay. He will die, his family will die, and his home will disappear. They do not recruit with money, Leo. They do it with terror."

"Bastards. So what about the guy in the PT Cruiser at the gate?"

"I am guessing that is a separate operation, maybe by the same people, maybe not. We are building a casino, yes?"

"Yes, so?"

"Who or what sorts of people are interested in casinos, any casino, and large amounts of money, and the chance to wash, you know…"

"Launder?"

"Exactly, launder other cash from less overt enterprises."

"They are going to attempt to muscle into my, into our, casino?"

"Your guess. Me, I am certain of it."

"So what do we do?"

"Shut the door with some muscle of our own, I think."

"And that would be…?"

Greshenko shrugged and stared off in space. "Perhaps our friend Modise will have an idea."

Kgabo Modise was otherwise occupied at that particular moment.

◇◇◇

As soon as the two goons in the SUV left, Jack and Harvey thanked Taolo Rapolasa and his friends, gave each a one hundred *pula* note, and told them to stay out of sight.

"For you own good, lads. Some people don't understand our calling, right?"

The men nodded, grinned their thanks, and disappeared around the corner. Jack and Harvey climbed into the truck after repairing the tarp as best they could, and wheeled away from their rented shack. It was not quite dark enough to attempt an entrance into the park, so they drove over to the police station and parked in its lot.

"Safest place in town," Jack said, and popped open a can of Saint Louis.

"Until we're spotted. Those two guys were slow, but whoever hired them won't be. They'll be after us in a heartbeat as soon as they hear what we did."

"Easy, Harvey, you go on too much. First, they have to report in. I'm thinking they won't do that right away, at least not until they come up with a story that will pass muster, and one they both can remember. No easy task, that. Then they will stall about a bit hoping for something to fall out of the sky and into their laps. If they have a brain bigger than a pea, they will mull on it, the go search out our friend Tailor—"

"It's Taolo, not Tailor."

"Really? Whatever. And they will pump him. He won't take to the rough stuff so he will tell them that we stuffed the cones with coltan, and then they'll come running after us."

"You think they will go after Taolo now?"

"Nah, not right off. They're a bit too short in the smarts for that. Pig stupid, they are. But I reckon their boss will bloody well suggest it and then…well that won't be 'til tomorrow sometime, and by then the swag will be scattered all over the park and anybody who wants it pays for it through their honker. Relax."

"We'll need to put the GPS in a safe place like insurance. Life insurance."

"Right-o and I know just the spot."

"Where?"

"I'm announcing to any and all that it is tucked away on Sududu Island right smack in the middle of the all the elephants and crocodiles."

"I don't know, Jack. Elephants can be dangerous. You walk into a herd of those jumbos and if they're in a mood, look out. You're not afraid of elephants?"

"Actually, I am, but it don't matter, Harv. It only matters that they are. So, we tell them that's where the dingus is. Genius, right?"

"I don't know, Jack. It's bloody risky. I'll be glad when this is over."

"Be happy. You're about to become a very poncey rich man."

"Get stuffed, Jack."

# Chapter Thirty-nine

Sanderson awoke to the sound of pots clattering on the range in the next room, Mpitle making the porridge, no doubt. She rolled over to go back to sleep, then jerked upright. What time was it? She would be late for work. She slid out of bed, wrapped up in her worn but still serviceable Chinese robe, and moved to the next room.

"So, Mma, you were very late coming in last night. What were you up to with Mr. Modise, the famous police detective?"

"Up to? I am up to nothing. We had dinner. We chatted about his work. We—"

"Oh, his work. I am sure of that. Tell the truth, Momma, what did Mr. Monkey do?"

"Monkey? Where is that coming from?"

"His name is Kgabo, monkey. Did you make some monkey business last night? You can tell me."

"You will watch your mouth young lady, or I will take that spoon you are holding in your hand and give you what you deserve."

"Then, since you don't answer me a yes or a no, it must be a yes. Michael, you hear? Momma is having monkey business last night."

Sanderson reached for the spoon in her daughter's hand. Mptle pirouetted away with a laugh and danced to the door.

"I am off to school. You must hurry with your breakfast or you will be late for your job. Michael, you tell her."

Sanderson turned to her son who, it seemed, felt stronger this day and was sitting up in a chair by his bed.

"Tell me what?"

"Your daughter is teasing, Mma. Be at peace with that. There is little enough laughter in this house."

"No, it is just that we are so busy."

"No, thank you, Mma, it is not the busyness, it is because of me. I lie here day after day. I cannot get better, I cannot die and finish this journey. It drags you all down."

"That is too harsh, Michael. It is what it is."

"No, that is not so. I do not want to argue with you, but you have had too much of this dying going on in your house. First my father, now me."

Sanderson spooned her breakfast into a bowl and sat across from her son.

"Do not speak like that anymore."

"I will try not to make you sad, Mma, but you know it is the truth. So, no monkey business, how was your date?"

"Date? Is that what it was? I don't know. It has been so long since I did anything like that." She pulled her robe closer. She could smell the coffee, but had not poured a cup yet. She would let it cool.

"Michael, you are old enough. Tell me. Was I right?"

"Right? How do you mean?"

"Right to leave you and Mpitle and go out with Kgabo Modise? It felt so strange."

"Mma you have cared about us so much. You need to find some happiness. Mpitle is almost grown. Soon she will be away at university, or married, or both. I am…well, I am not going anywhere except to either heaven or hell. Not soon, I'm afraid, but there is nothing that anyone can do for me. You must find a life, Mma. If this Modise is serious or even if he is only Mpitle's 'monkey business,' it doesn't matter. You must enjoy whatever it turns out to be. You cannot stay at home forever."

Sanderson stood and poured a coffee, her back to Michael. She did not want him to see her tears.

"Ten years of death, Mma. Death, and sacrifice for others, and struggles for you. It is time for you to do for yourself."

She stood staring out the door at the bright red *bakkie* that she and Michael had salvaged the year before. Across the courtyard that defined her village, Rra Kaleke was lighting a fire. People moved about.

They all had lives. She had work.

Work. The cameras. Charles must be wondering what had become of her. He would be looking at the results of the previous night's surveillance. She needed to dress and be on her way.

"Michael, you are right, I am sure, but it doesn't make it any easier for me to do these things."

"No monkey business then?"

"You are as bad as your sister. And as for what happened last night with Kgabo Modise and me, it is none of your business."

"That is the way. Good, my mother launches into the future, her sails set, and a great adventure awaits."

"Be still and eat your food. I am late for work."

◇◇◇

As she expected, Charles had retrieved the tapes from the camera surveillance and was waiting for her.

"You are late, Sanderson. Big night last night, I am thinking."

"Don't you start with me, Charles, or you will find yourself in the park on permanent census duty counting the kudu. I have had all the nonsense I need from my daughter."

He grinned but did not press on with his teasing. The fact that he'd noticed Mpitle's scarf had been in Sanderson's purse, not around her neck, when she had returned the night before, was all he needed to know about her engagement and its late conclusion.

"Yes, well. I have the tapes and have arranged to view them as soon as you are ready."

"Have you had a look?"

"I only made a quick run through. There is not too much footage but there is some activity."

"Well, let's see them then."

They watched as the camera flickered on. A truck, a white *bakkie* like hers, pulled up to the fence and two men alit. They paused, unfastened the fencing, drove the truck through, and refastened it. She watched as the men climbed back into the truck and it pulled away. The time stamp put the activity as occurring at twenty-three-hundred twenty hours. Sanderson did a quick calculation. Military time never worked for her. That would be eleven-twenty o'clock at night. The picture went blank.

In a few seconds, it flashed on again. This time the time stamp read zero four thirty-five. Dawn. The same two men worked at the fence from the inside, repeated in reverse their transit through it, and left. The screen went blank again.

"Did you note the number plate on the vehicle, Charles?"

"I did. Shall I call it in to Superintendent Mwambe?"

Sanderson thought for a moment. What with his apparent complicity in the Takeda business, Mwambe might not be the best option.

"Perhaps another cup of tea. While I think about that. No, I think we will show this to Inspector Modise first."

"Modise? Oh yes, of course, Modise," Charles said, and flashed a mouthful of very white teeth.

"You stop that grinning, Charles, or so help me…"

He tried to stop but failed. She guessed she had it coming, but it was so unfair. Other women went out all the time. They had lovers and friends and…well, all sorts of reasons and no one wasted daylight commenting on them. What made her one date in ten years so special? Because it *was* one date in ten years—of course. Stupid!

"Just bring the tea."

# Chapter Forty

It was still early when Modise drove over to the American's casino. It looked like it would turn out to be a bright sunshiny day. Leo Painter stood waiting for him as he drove up. He looked worried. Well, he should be. His project, like a lamp at night, had attracted some very dangerous insects. Modise climbed out and walked toward the door of the nearly complete office complex.

"Inspector Modise, you are looking very chipper this morning. Life must be treating you nicely."

"It is, Mr. Painter. I have some news for you."

"Good news, I hope. I've enough bad this past week to last me for quite a while."

"Can we sit outside? I don't want to risk even accidental eavesdropping."

Leo led him to his bench, and the two sat admiring the buildings going up before them. At least Leo seemed to be admiring it. Modise had other things on his mind.

"We have a plan for your Mr. Greshenko that should meet the needs of those people who are trying to use him. It is only a temporary relief for him, I am afraid, but it will have to do. What will happen to him with regard to his future is another matter, of course."

"Of course? Well, I guess one day at a time will have to do. What is the plan?"

"Am I correct in saying you have completed installing the devices in your rooms?" Leo nodded. They had. He obviously did not like the idea.

"Very well. As to your hotel, we have enlisted the help of a friendly Arab country who has agreed to use at least some of the devices to feed disinformation to the intelligence gatherers. In fact they thought the opportunity to best one of the super powers would be great fun. They asked if they could do the same to the Americans."

"And you said...?"

"Not this time, later perhaps. You must understand how it is with the smaller nations sometimes. So, one room will be used to do this, the others will be on their own. Frankly, and you cannot quote me, but we don't care what the Russians—we must assume that is who is behind all this maneuvering—what the Russians know or don't know, hear or don't hear. So, that is the set-up here. Now, the more difficult question is what about the Americans in the Mowana Lodge. We cannot allow the American Secretary of State to have her rooms bugged. It is unthinkable, for two reasons at least."

"Only two?"

"For now, yes, two. First, we are very sensitive to them and their position as a world leader."

"And second?"

"Here again, you may not say anything of this to anyone. If you do, you will find yourself back in your Chicago before you can say Jack Robinson."

"I understand. Big deal on the diplomatic scene, right?"

"A very big deal, as you say. And my government is playing the middle man here. There may be meetings between the North Koreans and the Americans in a place you do not need to know, that is if all goes well with the preliminary talks we will moderate out in the Okavango."

"Wow. They're going to make nice to that pipsqueak dictator?"

"Ah, that overstates it, I think. I am not in that end of government so diplomacy is as foreign to me as it is, I think, to you.

But sometimes, we have learned in this part of the world, it is better to accommodate the pipsqueaks than risk them doing something rash. Pipsqueaks crave attention, you see, and our view is it is better to give them some. It is best for all around to try for peace and quiet than rattle the sword. Yes?"

"Okay, not my call. When I was in business, those kinds of egomaniacs were usually shoved under the bus. But it's your game. So what happens with the Mowana Lodge?"

"Here is all you need to know. The American attaché assigned to this sort of thing will arrive here tomorrow and collect the equipment Greshenko has set aside for that project."

"They'll kill Greshenko if that stuff isn't up and running, soon."

"Trust us. It will be, as you say, 'up and running' in plenty of time. Your Greshenko will not risk homicide just yet."

"I never thought of your lot being the devious sort."

"My *lot* is not devious, Mr. Painter. We are careful to protect our country, its reputation for neutrality and fair play. That is all. You should wish this for yours as well, I think."

"Point taken. Okay. For the time being then, we can breathe a little easier. Now, I have another thing for you. For that last several days, there has been a car parked outside the gate area over there with some guy, maybe more than one, watching the place. I have the license number here."

"I will look into it." Modise took the slip of paper Painter handed him and placed it in between the leaves of this notebook.

"I will be in touch if this turns out to be significant."

Sanderson hesitated to call Kgabo Modise. What could she say? She had the information from the incursion into the park, naturally. He would want to hear of that. She wanted to share it, but since the previous night…well, things had changed in their relationship. What should she call him? Should she mention dinner? No, definitely not. This must remain official business. What if he sounded intimate? What if he didn't? She put her cup down and rapped a pencil against the desk top. She stopped when the graphite point snapped and bounced across the surface and onto the floor. She would make the call.

"Modise here." Very business like. Perhaps he hadn't seen her name on the caller ID. Perhaps he didn't have it.

"Modise. Kgabo, um…Sanderson here. We have had a breach of the park fence to report." Perhaps he would like to discuss it at dinner? No at lunch? Heavens above, what was she thinking?

"Ah, Sanderson, I hoped you would call. A bright spot in a dull day. So you had a break-in. Good. I will slip by in an hour or two and we can talk. I can bring sandwiches or something for lunch. We could have a semi-picnic."

"I packed a lunch. I could share."

"Then I will bring something sweet to build it up."

"That would be fine."

She hung up. Something sweet? Her heart rate seemed to be elevated. You are so silly, woman. He is a colleague. No, not quite. Jesus save me, now what? And why didn't she tell him the number of the truck? So slow you are today, woman.

# Chapter Forty-one

Noga spat the blood from his mouth. One of his teeth bounced across the floor. He explored the others still in place. Two moved when he pushed at them with his tongue. Not good. His mouth tasted metallic from so much bleeding. Blood contained iron, didn't it? He ached in a dozen places. They had beaten him for what seemed like hours but was probably no more than ten minutes. It had been enough. Finally he'd convinced them he did not know anything else about the fate of the coltan shipment that he hadn't already told them. Now he sat bound to a chair, his chin on his chest, and waited for what came next. At least now he didn't have to worry about the dog.

He could hear, but not see, the haranguing the two Boers were receiving. Good. They deserved every bad thing that came their way, the bastards. The tall man, who seemed in charge, snarled at them in a mixture of languages. Noga could only make out a word or two.

"You idiots." He understood that part. "What did you do with these men?"

"We looked in their *bakkie* and saw the trash, as we just told you."

"Jan broke one of the things. It was just rocks and sand."

So, one of their names was Jan. The other was who? Dolf, Pieter? They had found the "English" it seemed.

"Как Вы можете быть настолько глупо? "

He didn't know Russian but he was pretty sure that was what he heard and it had something to do with acting stupid. At least he hoped so. Noga wondered if all the people who worked for this man were as dense as these two. No matter. He had his own problems to think about. If he could get out of this alive, he'd head across the border. He had friends in Harare. They could help him get a new start. And he had an idea where the coltan came from in the first place. That knowledge should be worth something. The getting out alive would be the difficult bit. He had no doubt that if they decided they were finished with him, he'd be dead in an instant. What could he do to stay alive?

The man in charge shouted something else at the men, in Afrikaans this time. But there were more Russian words here and there. Russian. Botlhokwa had mentioned something about the Russians, and there was the Russian he'd worked with earlier. He tried to figure out if any of them were connected somehow. He couldn't, but an idea began to come together in his mind, a plan. Perhaps he did have something to offer besides the coltan. In for a penny, in for a pound the English say. He'd never get out of this mess free and clear as it now stood. He needed something to bargain with. So, why not give them Botlhokwa? He would be his bargaining chip. If he had the chance, he'd serve Mr. Big up on a spit. That warthog was probably set to do it to him anyway, so he'd do it to him first.

The two Boers left. Noga waited for what happened next. He didn't believe this man in charge would be the one who pulled the trigger and no one else seemed to be around, so he had some time to think things through.

Botlhokwa. With any luck today Botlhokwa goes down and I go free.

◇◇◇

The two "English" had returned the truck to the leasing agency just after nine when the lot gate opened. The "agency" was actually a used car dealer who had come to realize early on that most of his customers had neither the money nor adequate credit to actually purchase the vehicles they desired. Lease-to-purchase more nearly described the transactions. He accepted the truck back into inventory with some reluctance. The right door panel had acquired a new dent and the wheel wells were crammed with mud and branches. He started to say something but Jack made him an offer that made the dent disappear, so to speak. For cash and anonymity, he would purchase an old Volvo sedan. The cash and car exchanged hands, suitable number plates from a wreck on the back lot were affixed, and the transaction promptly forgotten.

There are several lesser known lodges on the Chobe besides the four, soon to be five, internationally recognized hotels. Jack and Harvey booked into the seediest one just off the main road. Jack called his coltan buyer and they waited. Their need for invisibility rose from the need to avoid the Boers who'd they assumed had taken up the search for them, and the inevitable pressure from the men who'd financed the operation in the first place, and who would want to execute a quick payoff. With interest, of course. But, until Jack and Harvey received their money from the sale of the coltan, they could not pay the lenders. So, they hid out and waited for the call. The lodge had no room service and soon they would have to venture out to eat. But they felt safe enough for the moment.

"We should have stocked up on beer and sandwiches. One of us will have to go for food soon."

"We'll wait a bit, Harv. There's water in that fridge thing there. This place isn't much but it's in pretty good nick and the desk clerk said there would be some snacks in the lobby area noonish. Right now, I am knackered. I'm for grabbing some kip. As soon as we hear from the buyers, we nip out, grab the loot, and fly away."

"Brilliant. That is *if* we hear from the buyers before the others ferret us out."

"Ah, there you go again. We have the GPS, Harvey. They daren't do nothing to us as long as it's under the bushel out on the island."

"But it's not on the island or even under a bushel."

"They won't know that, now will they. Stop worrying. It's tight."

Harvey leaned toward the window and peered out. Several cars had arrived since they checked in and were parked near their Volvo. He didn't like it. Who were these people? What sort of person checked into a hotel in the early morning? People like them, is who. People on the bunk. He didn't like it at all. Too easy, he'd said. And it had been. Something bad was coming their way and he knew it. No sense talking about it though. Jack wouldn't listen.

A PT Cruiser pulled up and two men climbed out. Big men in black suits. What kind of men wore black suits in the heat and humidity of the Chobe. Not from around here, surely.

"Jack, wake up."

"What?"

"There are two big blokes in a sedan just pulled up. They don't look right to me. We may have to pull out in a hurry. Where are the car keys?"

"What are you on about?"

"Come see."

Jack went to the window. Harvey pointed out the car. The two men exited the office and stood at the door. They spoke briefly then and glanced their way.

"Criminy, we're too late, they've got us."

"Who's got us? Those two? Nah, they're inspectors or something. You're as jumpy as a girl on her first go, Harv."

The strangers stared at their door, nodded, and climbed back into their vehicle and left.

"There, you see. What did I tell you. *No mathata*, Harvey."

# Chapter Forty-two

Modise arrived a little after noon. He carried a cake in a box. Sanderson retrieved her battered lunchbox and they settled at her desk. While they ate, Modise ran the number from the pick-up through the motor vehicle registration system. It turned out to be a rental from a company specializing in used, cheap to lease trucks and cars—very popular with border crossers. The names on the forms were probably fake but Modise ran them through Interpol anyway.

"What do you think those men were doing in the park?" Sanderson wanted to talk but did not trust herself to venture anything more than the business at hand.

"You noticed when they entered, there was a load of some sort in the back covered with a tarpaulin."

She had not. She'd been so outraged at the thought of people intruding into the park illegally that she'd concentrated on the men rather than the truck. She nodded anyway.

"Good. And when they left, the bed was empty."

"So, you are saying they were bringing something into the park, not removing something."

Well of course. Why was she babbling away like this? Before last night she could speak to this man almost as an equal. But now…?

"Precisely. The question for us to figure out is, what was the something?"

"I am slow here, Modise. What?"

"If they were smugglers or poachers, the reverse would be the case, would it not? They would have something in the truck bed on the way out, not the way in."

That made sense. But what could that be? "You were telling me about that orgonite business associated with the murder. Could this be more of that? Only this time they were successful? They were in the park for a long time. Perhaps they were placing the orgonite in the park in different places."

"Of course. That is brilliant, Sanderson. You must be right."

Two minutes ago I'm acting like a thirteen-year-old school girl around the star of the football team and now I am suddenly brilliant. "How can we find out? Oh, I can drive about in the park and see if I can find these things, some of them anyway."

"It is a big park, Sanderson. It would be like the needle in the haystack, I am thinking."

"True enough, but it is my park and I have an edge on anyone else who would want to search. I know where you can drive about easily and where not. I am guessing that unless there was a careful plan, these men followed an easy path here and there in their travels in the park."

"Do you have time for that?"

"I will make time this afternoon. It is, after all, a serious intrusion into the park."

Modise wiped some powdered sugar from his lips and dropped the cake wrappings in the bin beside the desk. "You do that. I will ask Mwambe to put out a search for this truck and have it apprehended."

He stood and before she could react, leaned forward and kissed her quickly on the mouth. If she hadn't been sitting, she would have collapsed. She looked out into the corridor to see if anyone had witnessed it. He stood to leave but she grabbed his sleeve, pulled him back down, and returned the kiss. She smiled.

"Do we need another business meeting, Kgabo?"

"I will call you. There are things I must attend to and I might have to fly back to Gaborone later."

"The Old House is very nice if you get there before the truck drivers." She didn't know if the truckers ate early or late or if at all at the Old House. But she liked the early part.

"I will call." This time he made it to the door and out.

Would he?

Sanderson wondered at her behavior. What possessed her to do that? She was becoming a fast woman. What if Mpitle had seen that? Well, so what if she was. No, that was not right either. It is all so confusing.

As she'd promised, she drove out to the park and approached the breach from the inside. Once at the fence she checked to make sure the intruders had fixed it firmly in place. She backed around and drove slowly back along the track, her eyes focused on the ground on either side. Fifty meters from the fence she saw where the truck—she had to assume it was the truck and not some other earlier intruder—had pulled into the bush. She swerved to the right and followed this new path. As the Land Rover edged around a low stand of brush, she saw the first of the cones. The men, it seemed had stopped here. There were a dozen of them in two rough lines corresponding to either side of the vehicle. Smart, she thought. Smart enough not to risk leaving the safety of the truck. They must have pulled the items into the cab from the back through its rear window and then dropped them on the ground out of the doors. She eased open her door and retrieved two of the cones.

She drove on. At one place, she noticed a paint smear where they must have sideswiped a tree branch. In the dark in the bush, that would be easy enough to do. Their path looped back and forth across the more beaten path used by others earlier. She found many more of the orgonite cones. She considered picking them up then decided they posed no harm to the wildlife and collecting them would be a huge waste of time. She made a point, when she could, of driving over some of them. The wheels crushed them into a flat, white pile of dust.

After the better part of three hours, she decided she'd seen enough to report the probable extent of the cones' distribution. These men had worked very hard the night before. She noticed that there did not seem to be a pattern to the drops. Just a dozen cones, more or less, and then a space, then another dozen or so. She didn't pretend to know about the claims made by Operation Paradise but it seemed to her that if there was some energy associated with these devices, they would be laid out in a grid of some sort or at least a geometrical pattern. Not this batch.

Did Andrew Takeda and Mwambe really believe this non-sense? People claimed it could effect great change in the nature of things. The weather, the ecology, even AIDs. That would be a good thing certainly. But such an idea that these ugly lumps of resin and black sand could do something like that was ridiculous.

She headed back to her office. She would give the cones to Modise to examine. Perhaps she would keep one for herself. As a souvenir.

# Chapter Forty-three

Modise called just as the sun set to tell Sanderson some important meeting had been scheduled and he could not meet that night after all. She didn't know whether the feeling she had was one of relief or disappointment. She and Charles Tlalelo finished reloading the cameras and stood in the trees across the road from the gap in the fence. She realized that if many more vehicles tried to pass through, the ruts would soon be too obvious even for a careless crook and a new entrance would be established. Perhaps it already existed. Was there an alternative? And if so, who used it.

"Charles, do we have enough equipment to set up surveillance at another location?"

"Yes, if we can find more of the wireless activators. There are three more cameras and motion detectors for each of them."

"Let us drive slowly along this road. Keep your eyes on the fence, and shout if you see anything that even remotely looks suspicious."

"Do you believe there are still more entrances?"

"It is not a matter of what I believe. It is a matter of what I think possible. That break-in last night could have been only one of many. We must be sure."

They stopped four times to test the fence. Places where it sagged too much, or seemed loose on the post. Three kilometers further west they found a second entryway. A new one it seemed. Only a single set of tire marks coming and going were visible. There may have been more. The light was fading and she couldn't be sure.

"Charles, mark this spot. It will be coming dark when you return. Set up a second camera here. Let's see who else is abusing our hospitality."

Sanderson returned home to her son and daughter and her routine. But something had changed. She had done this every night for so many years and never thought about it. Sometimes she would work late, but always the same work no matter what the hour. But since last night, it seemed so…what?…ordinary, so dull. Last night had been exciting and even dangerous. Now she discovered she had been spoiled for the everyday. Modise had shown her something new and, thereby, made her see her life for what it was. She pursed her lips. He was to blame for this.

But when she pushed through the door. Mpitle looked up from her homework and gave her a wicked look.

"Do not even begin with me, girl."

And then there was Michael's smile and the frustration of the moment evaporated. She carried her cone over to him and placed it beside his bed. Orgonite was probably foolishness but it couldn't hurt. When all hope has been taken from you, you will try anything to bring some back.

"What is that?"

"Good luck."

"It should be safe enough now, Jack. It's nearly dark."

"Can't be too careful, Harv. Have some more cheese crackers. We'll wait a bit longer."

"That car with those two men are back. I swear they look straight at us every time. They know we're here, Jack. We should get out while we can."

"Soon, Harv. When it's dark, we'll relocate to some other digs. That car salesman offered us his back room, for a price, naturally. Maybe we'll take him up on that. What do you think?"

"The people after us will go there, won't they? They saw the number plate."

"Well, let's suppose they did. How do they trace it? I reckon the coppers are on their trail same as they're on ours. So, they can't tap into the police for a vehicle ID. Also, remember, the bloody truck is sitting on the lot nice as you please. They may find it, but won't expect us to still be in it."

"It's a risk."

"Life's a risk. If it ain't why bother to keep on breathing?"

Noga woke. The room had become dark. When had he dropped off? The ropes still cut into his wrists and his wounds screamed for relief. The Boers were back. No luck finding their prey, apparently. He listened to their excuses trying to gauge if their failure had bought him some more time. He didn't know why, but they had not killed him yet so there must be some connection somewhere.

"No, you did not find them. We know. Our other people did."

"Other people? They are more than Hans and me working here? Why is that? We don't need other people."

"No, of course you don't. You geniuses are the aces of criminal efficiency. First you fall for a stupid switch by that man over there."

Noga assumed they must mean him.

"Then you shoot an innocent man in the park for no reason. Then you kill a policeman and another innocent. You go to the men who have our merchandise, and you are talked out of it. And you say you don't need help? I don't know who hired you or why, but I am thinking I might have to find some other line of endeavor for you two."

"But what are these others doing, and why are they in a position to find the man?"

Noga heard a sigh. The tall man was clearly at his rope's end with these two. Now would be a good time to offer an alternative.

"You need to understand only this. We control all ends of every deal that happens. We loaned these two men the money to buy the minerals. When they were successful in wresting it from us in the Congo, we became the buyers. So, either way, we win."

"Then why are we looking for them when you know you will have the stuff eventually anyway?"

The lead voice muttered something that definitely didn't sound like a compliment.

"We do not want to buy it. We will take it and then they will still owe us money. We will have them by the…how do you say?"

"Bollocks," Noga croaked.

"You see, even our guest understands this, yes?"

"I can help you."

"Can you now, and how will you do that? You see how it is? He is scheming to save his life. He thinks he has something we need or want, and his life is worth it. Isn't that so, Mr. Snake?"

"It is. I have much more to offer you than these thick Dutchmen, believe me."

"Oh, I believe that. A baboon has more to offer than these two. But they work for me. You don't. So they live and you will die."

"You'll kill me before you know what I know? That does not sound like the group I thought you must represent. They are professionals."

"And we are not?"

"You said it yourself, booted the park job, killed a constable, lost the coltan, and now police are combing the villages looking for you. If that sounds professional, I'm talking to the wrong people."

"We shall see. What do you know that is worth your life?"

"Untie me, give me a drink, then get these two tree stumps out of my sight and I will tell you."

# Chapter Forty-four

The sun hovered on the horizon and then dipped below it. In the growing darkness, Modise met the American plane at Kasane Airport. A small jet; Modise did not know his airplanes. It could have been a Cessna or a Lear or something French, but as it belonged to the United States government the latter seemed unlikely. Three people ducked out of the plane and wobbled down the stairs that had been dropped for them by a man in uniform. The pilot probably. They spoke for a moment and then walked across the tarmac toward him. This meeting had been the cause of his missing another evening with Sanderson. His mind began to drift, and he forced himself to refocus on the task at hand. He'd already called Painter and he and Greshenko were waiting. The difficulty lay in entering the nearly finished casino without anyone noticing. It would be hard to mistake this crowd for casual tourists.

"Modise," the director general said, "do you know Anna Tarbel? She is the American presence on this undertaking." Modise extended his hand. She did the same, her left hand lightly touching her elbow. Nice. "And this is Jamal Mosawi from Dubai. He will be a participant in this charade as well, the Arab bit." Modise shook his hand as well. He sensed a certain tension between the American and the man from Dubai. Because she was a woman or because she was American? He guessed a little of both and he did not want to know in any case.

Modise walked them across the empty tarmac. The plane would wait for them, or as many of them as necessary, to fly them back to Gaborone that night. Modise had arranged for a delivery van to carry them to the hotel.

"I am sorry about the ride," he said, "but Mr. Painter, who, it turns out, is a very observant gentleman for his age, spotted a suspicious automobile at his gate. We checked the registration and it is a company car belonging to Nexus Aviation. So, I felt it reasonable to assume he is under observation by the people we are concerned about one way or another, and therefore it is necessary we not be seen entering or leaving."

"Very clever, Mr. Modise," Anna Tarbel said. The Arab grunted, whether signaling approval or dismay, he could not tell.

"It will be making several deliveries this night. One to the Mowana Lodge where your room is booked, Ms. Tarbel. Your people are waiting for you there and will help with the…"

Modise paused. How much did the Arab know? The director general touched his knee lightly.

"Other arrangements," he finished. In the darkened van, he thought he caught a frown cross Mosawi's forehead. Need to know? He'd check later. He had the van back up to a covered loading dock and the party alighted and moved quietly into the casino's lobby. The twilight and a very dim view of the hotel allowed them to exit with out being seen.

Painter and Greshenko, both looking ill at ease, greeted them and shook hands as the party was introduced.

"Mr. Painter, I think we have you to thank for this alert." The DG said, and pulled a pen and notebook from inside of his jacket. "We are grateful, of course, to you, Mr. Greshenko. You are doubtless under a lot of stress, I am sure. I am sorry I cannot ease that very much at this time. It is enough to know that whether we proceed this way, or as your former colleagues wished, the stress level would be the same. At least you know that you have done the right thing."

Greshenko did not appear convinced. He'd learned survival on the other side of the fence. On this side, the legal side, he had fewer options. Botswana did not allow private firearms except in certain situations and circumstances. Modise suspected that Painter's friend felt naked and vulnerable. He wouldn't put it past Painter to have remedied the gun situation in his own way. He hoped not, but who could blame him?

The company sat in what would soon be the main gaming room. Greshenko described the installation of the electronic listening devices in the hotel to them. Tarbel asked a series of technical questions that persuaded Modise that if this plan had any chance of working, she was the one to do it.

"Show me the equipment you are to place in the United States' rooms."

Greshenko made an array of items that looked nothing like what Modise had expected. The truth, he didn't know what to expect. His experience with this sort of thing was limited to some of his training years ago at Quantico, and a few raids on houses in the newer area in Phakalane outside Gaborone. The set-up then had been pretty old school. Nothing as sophisticated as these bits and pieces, some no larger than a straight pin.

"That is a microphone?"

The woman looked up and smiled. "Lovely, isn't it? And it can pick up sounds as far away as thirty feet…nine or ten meters. And this," she lifted a small cylinder the diameter of a pencil and shorter than his first knuckle, "is the camera to go with it."

Modise was impressed. "It is amazing. The miniaturization, I mean."

"Yes it is, but Mr. Mosawi will tell you that this is last year's technology."

Mosawi smiled for the first time. This Tarbel was no fool, Modise thought. She just bought him.

"Oh yes, Inspector, now it is even much smaller. But this is very good, very good. Mr. Greshenko, the apparatus in your rooms is similar?"

Greshenko nodded. "Nearly so. Some of it is older but it is all quite good."

"I think," the DG said, "that it would be a good idea to recap for us exactly what you were asked to do, Mr. Greshenko. You told Mr. Painter, who then summarized your understanding of the situation to Modise, who then spoke to me and, well, you see, there is some distance between the beginning of this narrative and its end. It would be tragic if we were to proceed under a misunderstanding."

"Yes, of course." Greshenko looked nervously around the room. He let out a sigh and began. "My former colleagues, if that is what they are, called me to Gaborone. I met with them and they required of me a certain task."

"Excuse me for interrupting, Mr. Greshenko, but do you have any idea...was there any indication which branch of the *Bratva* they represented?"

"It might have been Bout or what is left of his organization, but I think it was this new operator, Oleg Lenka. The man who spoke to me was an old *apparatchik*, you know, from Soviet days."

"Sorry, go on with your story."

"Yes. Well, they threatened to expose me to the Russian and Botswana authorities. That would be you, I suppose, if I did not cooperate."

The DG nodded and indicated Greshenko should continue.

"The task is, or I should say was, to plant listening devices and cameras in the rooms in this hotel where the Arab visitors would be staying as I have just outlined for you. Then I was to use the money they gave me to bribe my way into the Mowana Lodge and perform the same operation in the rooms to be used by the American delegation, particularly the secretary of state. The first part of the job is complete. I have not attempted the second part of the mission, as you know."

"And what of the money? What were you to do with the surplus, assuming there was any?"

"Return it. Of course, they will expect me to skim a little. It is the custom."

"Very well, here is the valise. We calculated what it might have required in bribes and removed that amount. The remainder, minus your skim, you may return to your controller. And good luck with that." The director general thanked Painter and Greshenko and gestured toward the door. "This is the end of the story for you two gentlemen. We will take it from here. It is unwise for you to know any more than you do. Mr. Greshenko, when the set-up has been completed in the Mowana lodge we will let you know so that you can contact…what are we to call those people?"

"*Agents provocateurs,*" Tarbel suggested.

"Too soft, too intellectual, Ms. Tarbel, with respect. They are a threat to the security of this nation and perhaps to the larger world. No, I think something grittier would be more appropriate."

"Hyenas," Modise said.

"Very good, Modise. Precisely. Hyenas scavenge after bigger animals. They pick on the weak and the unwary, and they are also entirely unpleasant. Yes, we will let you know when we are done so you can contact your hyenas."

"Not so fast, Mr. Director General." Leo Painter stood arms akimbo at the door. A man on first name basis with senators, federal judges, and at least one ex-president was not satisfied with the dismissal. "What happens to Yuri? You can't just let him twist in the wind."

"We will do what we can, Mr. Painter. You need to know this much, no more. Ms. Tarbel here will see to the installation of the equipment. It will be up and running by tomorrow, we hope. If so, you may inform your contacts then, Greshenko. It will function perfectly. The listeners, whom we assume in the end will be Russian intelligence, will hear and see all—the arrival of the party, some disingenuous conversation—and so on. Then, within an hour or so, the signal will be jammed."

"Jammed? How jammed? This will bring holy hell down on Yuri's head."

"No, no. They will learn that a leak opened in their system. It appears that your CIA has been dealing with a former associate of Igor Sechin for some time. The information was turned up quite coincidentally."

"You think they will believe that?"

"There is precious little loyalty in the dark side of the Russian intelligence community, it seems. Do not fear, the CIA is, in fact working with this man and the leak will be verified. You, Mr. Greshenko, will be in the clear. What will happen after this, however, I cannot say. They will either discard you, or return for more favors. Unless we can expunge this Lenka organization from the country, you will remain at risk. For what it's worth, I suspect you knew this day would eventually come. It seems it has and that will have to do for now."

With apparent reluctance, Painter and Greshenko left the room. Tarbel reached into her briefcase, removed a scanner, and proceeded to insure that Greshenko had not bugged this room as well. Satisfied he had not, she nodded and Modise and the remaining members of the party sorted the equipment and settled on the operational plan.

Tarbel carrying a suitcase of equipment was "delivered" by van to the Mowana Lodge, the DG and the agent from Dubai to the airport. At midnight, Modise found himself alone in his room at the Marina Lodge, He resisted the temptation to call Sanderson. He poured a night cap, finished it, and turned in.

When his light went out, the men standing in the shadows across the areaway stretched and left. Their replacements would resume the watch in the morning.

# Chapter Forty-five

Rra Botlhokwa tossed and turned in his bed. Scented satin sheets did not produce the expected effect of easing him into unconsciousness. He'd had a bad day. His man Cunningham had been killed in cold blood and it wasn't like he could call the police and report it. Quite the contrary. He had the body taken out to the park through the new entry through the fence he'd ordered placed a few days previously. His men, who'd looked decidedly ill at ease, had dumped Cunningham in the river. The crocodiles and tiger fish would take care of the evidence, or most of it. They'd all heard the whispers but now they must realize the threats by the gangsters from South Africa were real and at this moment Botlhokwa had no answers for them. He could only play along until this nonsense with the attorney general's indictment had been dealt with. He would need to make a call to his contact in Gaborone, the man he referred to as Minister, although he'd not yet served in that capacity.

Losing forty percent of his take would hurt. Still, he had his accounts in the bank in Mauritius and his place in Cape Town. Perhaps he should simply slip away and let them scramble for the leftovers. Perhaps the AG would quash the indictment in exchange for these gangsters. But could he deliver them?

Sleep would not come. He rose and put on a robe. The bottle of single malt and a glass had been set out for him. He shuffled over to the credenza and poured a substantial portion, light on the spritz, and eased out through a pair of French doors to the terrace. The air seemed particularly hot and humid, the night unusually quiet. He sipped his drink and contemplated the options available to him. Standing there in the dim moonlight these thoughts running through his mind, the last thing he expected was the bag thrown over his head and the rough arms around his waist that lifted him in the air. He started to cry out when a sharp pain on his temple and sudden blackness ended it.

He woke up, he couldn't say how much later, lying on a concrete floor, the bag still over his head. He tried to move but his legs and hands were fastened. Duct tape. He shouted only to receive what he assumed was a kick in the stomach. Voices, indistinct, the chirp of a mobile phone. A conversation, he thought he heard his name mentioned. Then silence, the sound of footsteps moving away. Botlhokwa felt the vomit rise in his throat. He dared not throw up in the confines of the bag. He swallowed repeatedly and managed to gain control of his gag reflex. What next?

◇◇◇

Someone tore the sack from his head. The rough burlap scratched his cheek as it pulled away. He stared up into a bright light. He could see nothing except the trouser cuffs and shoes of someone standing in front of him.

"Rra, you are with us, I see. We thought you might have dozed off for a minute."

"Who are you and what do you want? I insist you untie me. Otherwise it will go very hard on you." His voice sounded harsh and ragged from the acid reflux he'd managed to contain earlier. His response only produced laughter. There seemed to be more than one person in the room. Did he recognize one of those laughing?

"Put him in a chair."

He was lifted and plopped down hard in a wooden chair. Botlhokwa did not usually sit in wooden chairs. Cushioned leather, damask, soft.

"What do you want from me? I have already conceded a large share of my earnings to you. You want more? How much more?"

"We have decided we want it all. It appears having you as a partner has become a liability. You are poison, Rra."

"All? That's absurd. Do you think I will work for you for nothing?"

"Work for nothing? No, no of course not. We are replacing you completely, you see?"

"Replace? How? I know too many things and only I can make this group function properly."

"Certainly the first part is correct, unfortunately for you. You do know too much. You might just spill that to the attorney general. Yes? Did that thought cross your mind? I will take a stab and say it did. No matter. Not going to happen. As to the second, we have your replacement."

"My replacement? Who?"

"We have had a wide ranging conversation with your man, Noga. We were going to do you a favor and dispose of him as you asked, but before we could do that we received disturbing news from Gaborone—the indictment, but you know all about that—and then he persuaded us he knew enough about your business to run it until sometime later when we reorganize our affairs in this part of the country."

"Noga told you that? What indictment?" His mind whirled. What had happened? Where were his men? How had they penetrated his grounds? Noga?

"Come, come, do not play the fool with us, Botlhokwa, you know what indictment. And now I suppose you wish to know everything else. Professional courtesy you would say. Ordinarily we wouldn't bother, but tonight we are being kind to you. By the way, your family has been given until nine this morning to clear out of your place in Cape Town. We have need of it. Thank you for signing it over to us."

"I never did anything of the sort."

"Oh, but you did. That and many other papers are even now being collected for your signature."

"I won't sign them"

"No? Well, no matter. I hope your family does not resist. It could become very messy. Your wife has relatives in Swaziland, does she not? She and your daughter will be cared for there, I assume. I cannot make similar arrangements or promises to your mistress, I am afraid. Now, about the indictment and the attorney general. Placing an explosive device in the car park outside the presidential office was a very stupid thing for you to do."

"Bomb! What bomb? What are you—?"

"Your man in Gaborone mentioned to us that you'd called. He said you were under the impression you had enough on him to keep him in line. We assured him that it no longer needed to be the case, and so he mentioned the trouble with the attorney general and so on. Too bad about that."

"I don't know what you're talking about…a bomb?"

"Very foolish of you, Rra. Planting a bomb and trying to assassinate the attorney general. Very foolish."

"I never did any such thing."

"There is a rumor, which your former associate insists must be true, that you ordered the device to be placed in the car park. One man, whom the police know often works for you, has already been arrested in connection with the case. He denies it, of course, but when they search his home and find the blocks of C-4 and detonators, his denial will not be taken too seriously. But you know how that works."

Botlhokwa felt the gorge in his throat rise again. He gulped for air, and fought off his panic.

"Noga?"

"Yes, Rra, I am here."

"Noga, what have you done to me?"

"Following those good Christian principles you rammed down my throat all those years. You know, 'do unto others as they would do unto you.' You were going to have me killed. I just did unto you first."

"You can't kill me."

"No? Well, perhaps not. We will think of something. Are you fond of animals, Rra?"

# Chapter Forty-six

The cameras Charles Tlalelo placed opposite the newest entry through the fence clicked to life just after three-thirty in the morning. They recorded the entry into the park of a battered Volkswagen beetle and a pick-up truck with markings on its doors. Only one man exited the car and managed opening and closing the fence. At four forty-five the car returned alone. The same man managed the mechanics of opening and reclosing. Farther east, nothing would be recorded at the first, original opening.

Minutes before dawn two men approached the Marina Lodge and took up posts to watch the entrance to Kgabo Modise's room. A half hour later two of Superintendant Mwambe's constables arrested them for loitering. Their attempts to call their employer went unanswered. At seven in the morning a fire sprang up in the home of Rra Botlhokwa. It caused no real damage to the main structure but the flames gutted his office destroying all his records and files. Curiously, the filing cabinets, which were labeled fireproof, had been left unlocked and open. Of their contents only ashes remained. The firemen thought they detected the odor of petrol and suspected arson. They reported that finding to the police who said they would investigate.

Rra Botlhokwa could not be located. Calls to his family in Cape Town were not returned. His associate, Mr. Noga, stated he did not know where Botlhokwa could be reached, but noted the last few weeks he'd seemed depressed. Police at the scene noticed that Noga seemed to be in pain and showed indications of severe trauma to his face and neck. He claimed he'd been in a motor accident.

Kgabo Modise heard about an attempted bombing at the president's office complex in Gaborone while at breakfast. The DG called him with the news. As H. E., the President, was traveling abroad at the time he did not appear to be the target. The DG also mentioned that a rumor circulating around the halls at headquarters and probably elsewhere attributed the act to Botlhokwa and an attempt by him to kill the attorney general. The word of his impending indictment had evidently been leaked. The DG did not place much credence on the rumor, however. The AG could not be reached for comment,

The DG also requested Modise to wind up his business in the north, get back to Gabz, and take over the investigation. Modise replied he would need the rest of the day and would return the following morning. The DG said sooner would be better. It was not a suggestion. Modise looked at his watch and began to organize his day. Sanderson, and the Boers, not necessarily in that order. If he could clear those two items from his list he could catch a late flight out to the capital.

◇◇◇

As soon as Noga felt certain his new masters were safely out of sight and the police had taken their investigation into the fire away from the main house, he slipped in through the same French doors Botlhokwa had passed out the night before. He moved silently across to the dining room. He paused, listened, and walked to the heavy mahogany table in the center of the room. No one needed a table this big just to eat dinner. He lifted one end and wrestled it to one side. There was a reason it was so hard to move. He rolled back the Aubusson carpet beneath it and ran his hand across the floor tiles. He found the depression he sought. With the blade of a dinner knife conveniently left on the table, he pried open the lid of the space built in between the floor joists and removed a satchel.

All those hours of spying on his former boss had finally paid off. Botlhokwa had become careless about his secrets lately. Noga knew there could be more money for him if he lingered, a great deal more. He also knew the risks that went with it. His new associates would kill him the instant he ceased being useful. That he knew with certainty, and he had no desire to find out when it might occur. By evening he reckoned he'd be in Harare in possession of Botlhokwa's money, jewelry, and what looked like some negotiable securities. He considered the contents in the bag his severance pay. He replaced the lid, rug, and table, and quietly slipped away.

Two other men, also former employees, saw Noga leave with the satchel and decided they might as well help themselves to whatever might have value remaining in the house that they'd help furnish, as well. Others joined them. Before the police realized what was happening, nearly half of Botlhokwa's belongings had been spirited away.

The police only shrugged. After all, what could they do?

# Chapter Forty-seven

Charles Tlalelo checked both surveillance set-ups on his way to work from his village. This morning he had prepared for this new duty, and had fresh video cassettes on the seat of his government Land Rover. Sanderson had instituted a policy as soon as she was confirmed in her new position that the rangers could drive the vehicles to and from their homes after work and on the way back in to their shift. As there were more rangers than SUVs, a schedule had to be arranged. Charles had one assigned to him this week. He liked this vehicle. It had cup holders and he'd filled both with fresh coffee from one of the lodges before he set out down the road. Coffee, its aroma, and the sweet taste he'd created with three sugars and extra cream made his morning that much brighter.

At the westernmost camera at the newest opening, he alit and walked to the camera set-up. He checked the counter positioned on the camera body. It no longer showed 000. There had been activity at this station the previous night. He swapped out the cassette and drove to the next. The counter on the second camera indicated nothing had moved through the fence at this point. He proceeded to the office and set up the monitor for Sanderson to see the results. Then he finished his restaurant coffee, made tea for Sanderson, and waited.

She arrived twenty minutes later than her usual time. Charles wondered about that. This made two days in a row she had come to work late. It was not his place to comment, but he had no control over his eyebrows, which scaled up his forehead when she breezed into the office.

"Do not give me that look, Charles. It is not what you think. I could not sleep thinking about that rubbish in the park."

"What is your worry? If orgonite is all that the men who believe in it say it is, well, then it will be a good thing. If it is rubbish, as you believe, it cannot hurt. So what is there to worry about? What is it composed of anyway?"

Sanderson placed several of the cone-like objects on her desk and sipped the tea Charles brought her.

"I have no idea. It looks solid enough but when I drove over some of them yesterday, I stopped and looked to see the source of this wonderful power."

"And?"

"There is nothing in them at all. Just sand, and gravel, and bits and bobs of *matlhakala*."

"Then there is nothing to worry about."

"No, I suppose not. Let me pose for you a question, Charles. This is my worry. I know Operation Paradise is not a thing you subscribe to or know about but, if you were putting down these things in the park which are supposed to have such marvelous powers, how would you do it? How would you go about it?"

"How?" Charles stirred his tea and thought. "You are asking me this seriously?"

"Yes. I think it is important, but I don't know why. It is the question that kept me awake and so, I am late this morning."

"I think if I were the one arranging these things, I would put them at certain points or places that I would believe were important, like the river, or a high point, or near something that possibly would affect, somehow, something else. I am not making myself clear, I think."

"No, I understand. I was thinking the same way. Or they would be in a pattern like a grid or a geometrical arrangement. I don't know why I think that, but it struck me that others would, you see?"

"Yes, of course. Are you telling me they were not in any order?"

"None that I could see. It looked like they were just dropped in series out of the truck here and there and all over the place. The only thing that seemed consistent was they were easy to drive up to if someone wanted to collect them later. But they were scattered widely in the park. It makes no sense to me."

"It is a puzzle, surely." Charles refilled their tea cups. "We had another illegal entry last night. This time at the new entrance we found."

"Really? That is interesting. It is a good thing we went searching. Show me the tape."

Jack took the call a little after nine. There'd been no more alarms regarding the strangers in black suits and he and Harvey had even managed to slip out for a meal after dark.

"Here we go, mate. Time to pick up the cash and do our disappearing act."

"You're sure? This isn't a trap?"

"Harvey, Harvey. Your caution is most of the time a very good thing. I tend to be rash, I know, but I've just had a chat with the buyers and I am sure it's the same Johnnies I worked with before. They want the goods. They will pay for the GPS. We will collect the cash, pay our lenders, and cut away. We'll be home free and have Euros to spend in exotic places. Now grab the magic box and keep it out of sight 'til it's time to deliver."

"We haven't made a back-up GPS."

"No need. These are the chaps I spoke to and they want the lot. We get the cash, they get the box."

"Where are we going?"

"Very public place so there can't be any messing about. There's a pull-off opposite the place where they are building that new hotel. It's within view of the police station. We're safe enough, I reckon."

"I'll be glad when this is over."

Kgabo Modise packed and checked out of the lodge. He headed his rental toward the police station. He wanted to see if there had been any news of the two men involved in the shooting. He had just pulled onto the main road when his phone beeped. He pulled off the road to respond, as he'd been trained. Too many wrecks were caused by phoning and texting while driving. And it was the law.

"Modise," Sanderson's voice sounded excited. "You must come right away. There has been another entry into the park, but this one is different."

"Yes? It is important?"

"Very important. Two vehicles went in, only one came out."

"There is still an intruder in the park."

"Yes, a *bakkie* with markings on the doors."

"White?"

"Probably. The night vision does not give color but it looked very light, certainly."

"I must stop and have a talk with Superintendent Mwambe first. Then I will be on my way to your office. By the way, Sanderson, do you have any leave time accrued?"

"What? Leave time? I don't know. I have not used leave for years. What would I do? Why is this important?"

"Just asking. I'll see you soon."

# Chapter Forty-eight

Jack and Harvey drove slowly to their meeting spot. The last thing they needed was to draw the attention of the police.

"Keep that thing out of sight, Harvey. If they push to have a peek, the word is no money, no lookie."

"It's in my pocket with my mobil. If they see a bulge, say, I'll pull out the phone and flip it open like I'm checking for messages. They won't guess the other is in the same pocket."

Jack looked dubious but shrugged. "Just stay cool and collected, chum. We're almost there."

They stepped out of the car and stood away from the road waiting. Moments later, a sedan pulled up behind them and two men climbed out.

"Jaysus, it's the bloody bearded wonders."

Harvey pivoted toward the car. Sure enough, the two lummoxes who'd they'd conned off the stuff before approached. They didn't look happy.

"You gents looking for something?"

"You it is we are looking for and we have found you. You lied to us. Now we are here to collect the goods. You can save yourselves much pain and suffering if you just lead us to it."

"Can't do that, chaps, sorry. We have buyers and they get first go. They should be here at any moment, and I expect they will not take kindly to you mucking about with their deal."

"No buyers are on the way. We are here for them. Buying is not part of the plan. Hand it over."

"No buyers? What's happening here? We have a deal and it stands. No money, no coltan. Simple."

The shorter of the two men removed a nine millimeter pistol from his waist band. He didn't aim it at them, too public, but he made sure they saw it.

"Ease up there, son. No need for that. We can't deliver it even if we wanted to. It's squirreled away. Shoot us and you'll never get it."

"Squirrels put their nuts in a tree. Where is your tree, Englishman?"

"English? Wrong island, pally, and the tree, as you call it, is far away and not readily available, you could say. Now you just ring up your boss, or whoever is calling this dance, and tell them to join us and bring the money."

Harvey heard the pistol being cocked. How far would these two goons take this, he wondered.

"Nobody else will be coming. There is no dancing. Just us. Tell us or somebody will get hurt."

"Okay, okay, listen very carefully. The coltan has been put away in a very safe place. The only way you or anyone else will find it is to pay for the privilege. Got it?"

"By safe you mean…?"

"Okay, I'll give you a taste. Something to tell your next in command. The stuff is scattered all over the game preserve. The only way you can recover it is if we tell you how and where. Now, call your boss."

The man named Jan frowned and made the call. He spoke only long enough to explain what Jack had said. Then he listened, nodding his shaggy head periodically.

"There will be money. Now tell us how you expect us to find this coltan if it is scattered in the park?"

Jack relaxed. "Very sensible of your man. Well, since you asked, and since the money is on the way, it won't hurt to let you in on our secret. We have a GPS device with the location of every drop site registered on it. The money buys the device. You just pay your entry fee and spend an hour or two driving about picking up the cones."

"Cones?"

"Cones, yes, those things you saw before. The stuff is in them, Clever what?"

Jack was babbling. It was a bad habit of his. Harvey had a premonition of impending doom. "Jack, that's probably enough."

"Right you are. Enough said. When the money comes, you get the GPS."

One quick step forward and the gun ended up behind Jack's ear.

"Wrong again, whoever you are. You give us that GPS right now."

"Don't have it here. You think we're daft?"

"Where is it then?"

"We've left it on Sududu Island. Hidden. You want it without paying, go get it."

"You must think we are stupid. Neither one of you knows the first thing about that island and if you did, you'd know that if anybody steps on it for more than a moment, and then only near the shore, the game rangers would be on them in no time. You have not put that thing out there, so tell me where it is."

"Sorry, but a deal is a deal. Money first." Jack did not look quite so confident.

"Search him," the gun holder said. The second man patted jack down, then punched him very hard in the stomach.

He doubled over and retched. "I don't have it. I told you already…safe place."

"Me either," Harvey said, and hoped he wouldn't be searched. Hoped in vain. The man stepped forward.

"Empty your pockets."

Harvey did so as slowly as possible, making sure the men saw each item as he removed it. The searcher inspected each item and then laid it on a wall next to the car. He made a particular show of removing the phone, wagging it about so it caught the light.

"This is all I've got."

"Put all that on the wall with the rest."

Harvey stepped to the wall, his back to the speaker. With the best bit of sleight of hand he could muster, he slipped the

GPS out and placed it with the items on the wall. Without a glance at the wall or its display, the man stepped forward and patted him down.

"Nothing more."

"Look at the stuff on the wall."

"I saw him empty the pockets. There's nothing."

"Check anyway."

Harvey's heart sank. The game was up. The man walked to the wall and stared at the items. Keys, wallet, coins, the cell phone, and something else.

"So, what is this?" He leaned closed and read the label. "Garmin etrex H GPS. It is the tracking device." He reached out to pick it up and at that moment it disappeared in a gray blur. The monkey, who'd evidently been attracted by the earlier flicker from the phone, had sailed out of the trees, scampered across the wall, and snatched the largest of the items in the collection.

"Chrissake, stop him."

The man holding the gun spun and snapped off three shots at the monkey who had by then attained the tree limbs and was moving rapidly away. Had the shooter used the rifle which he had secured behind the seat, he might possibly have brought the monkey down, but with a nine millimeter pistol fired at a moving target at a distance of fifteen meters and growing...not going to happen.

"You idiot, you can't shoot a gun here."

"What am I to do? The monkey took the thing and is getting away."

"They will have a backup, yes?" The taller Boer swung back and started at Jack.

"No, sorry, no time to make one."

"We are stupid, you think?"

Harvey began to laugh. "No, we're the stupid ones. That monkey just ran off with a half million Euros we expected to make and we still owe half of that to some of your people, I'm guessing. We couldn't find the muck without it if we wanted to. We're all done for now."

# Chapter Forty-nine

Gun shots are a rarity in Kasane. Heads turned. Some hearers unfamiliar with the sound assumed one of the huge tractor-trailers passing along the main highway to the ferry must have backfired. Others flinched. How to react? At that precise moment Modise had completed his call to Sanderson and laid his phone down on the seat beside him. He lifted his foot from the brake pedal and started wheeling from the curb to the road. Certain that the shots originated from somewhere close by and in front of him, he punched the accelerator. The car jerked forward. As it happened he didn't have far to travel. At the next slight bend in the road he spotted the four men, two he recognized from Sanderson's video tape of the incursion into the park. The other two could very well be the Boers the local police had been searching for. One of them still held a pistol up in the air and gesticulated at the fourth man.

He pulled up behind the sedan and, keeping his door between him and the shooter, he stepped out.

"Police," he shouted and flashed his ID. "Drop the gun and put your hands on your head."

Modise had been issued a hand gun. DIS officers and special units were usually armed. Ordinarily, like most police personnel, he did not carry it except in those rare circumstances which might warrant the use of deadly force. Traveling to the police station to confer with Superintendent Mwambe probably did not qualify as such an occasion. But so much had happened in the last few days he had clipped his to his belt. The man holding the pistol turned and took aim.

"Jan," his companion yelled, "don't be a fool. Not to shoot. It's a police."

"Kill one of them, kill two of them. What is the difference to us now?" He fired at Modise. The bullet missed by millimeters. Modise felt a tug on the fabric of his jacket. The car door window exploded into a thousand pieces. Modise felt his hands and face sting as some of the shards flew up and away. He ducked behind the panel. All of his experience with the government issued Glock had been on the gunnery range and at targets. Modise had never shot at a man. He jerked his pistol free. This would be a first.

In the cinema, he thought irrelevantly, this scene would be shown in super slow motion with people moving as if underwater. In reality he knew if he did not do something and quickly he had only seconds to live. He heard shouting, the pop, pop from the other pistol. The car rocked. By now the man opposite, whose face he noticed for the first time was fiery red, had realized he would not get his target through the door and advanced on an angle toward the car. In the adrenalin rush of the moment neither he nor Modise heard the hee-haw, hee-haw of police sirens.

Not only had everyone in the area heard and reacted to the gun shots, Superintendent Mwambe had as well. He had no doubts as to what they were and what they meant. He quickly marshaled three cars and six constables, two of whom were armed. They were on the road and on the way to the shooting scene in what seemed seconds. The police vehicles screeched up to the scene and all seven men tumbled out. Modise stood and sighted down the barrel of his gun. This was not target practice. The shooter spun, aimed at the nearest police vehicle and squeezed off a single round. A dozen shots from Modise and the police marksmen followed and the shooter dropped in his tracks.

Modise climbed out from behind his car and exhaled. He realized he hadn't taken a breath since the first shot had been fired in his direction. He checked status of the remaining three men. The two he'd recognized from the tape were backing away, hoping to slip off in the confusion, he supposed.

"Stop those two," he said and pointed in their direction. Three constables stepped over and blocked their escape. One of them seemed to be laughing. From relief or hysteria? Modise wondered what anyone could find amusing in this situation.

The police established a cordon around the area and attempted to wave bystanders on their way. An ambulance arrived and attendants gathered up the bleeding but apparently still living shooter. The remaining three were taken into custody and placed in cars to be transported back to the police station. Slowly the area returned to normal. Mwambe strolled over to Modise and handed him a handkerchief.

"You will need this. Your face looks terrible but I think it is not so bad. You should have someone look at those cuts, though." Modise thanked him and mopped at his face and hands and made a face at the blood on the cloth. "Now I think we need to go back to my office and have a conversation about these events, Modise."

"Yes, we should. Your people probably saved my life, I think, Superintendent."

"Perhaps yes. Who can say? But it is not something we need to waste time speaking about. It is what we do. We are all policemen, are we not?"

"We are, Superintendent. We are indeed."

Modise took one more look around the area. He realized he still held his gun in his hand. He cleared the breech, ejected the clip, and returned it to his holster. He would not need it any more this day, he hoped.

"Okay, Superintendent, let's go."

# Chapter Fifty

A constable with paramedic training cleaned up Modise's cuts and applied some disinfectant. Mwambe watched with a satisfied look on his face. Modise wondered if he would gloat over his success at apprehending four criminals and saving his life.

"You were very brave, Modise," he said after the constable had excused himself and left.

"How is that?"

"If you had not confronted those men, I do not know what might have happened. I think we might have arrived to find three corpses."

Modise shrugged. Was this true or did Mwambe have something else in mind?

"We found a high powered rifle and sniper attachments in the Boers' automobile. I am almost sure the ballistics will show these two were responsible for the killing in the park and the shooting of Sergeant Kgobela and the other man, him certainly"

"That will tie up some loose ends. Will the shooter live do you think?"

"It is in the hands of God. We will save the government some money in care, incarceration, and trials if he dies. Perhaps he will make a contribution to our national economy by doing so."

"Maybe. I hope he lives long enough to tell us who he works for. I do not believe he and his partner came up here from South Africa to start this sort of trouble on their own."

"If he doesn't, we still have the other one. So, what do we do with the two white men who were party to this fiasco?"

"I don't know. All we have on them at the moment is a successful but illegal entry into the park. It seems they were planting that orgonite rubbish. Oh, I am sorry, Mwambe. I forgot you are a believer in that business. I will concede it would be nice if it were true, but…"

"Never mind that now. We cannot link them to anything else in the area. It would be nice to know what they were doing with the two killers. If we question them on the reasons they ended up in that shooting spree, they will surely lie. Is there any real reason to hold them?"

"Your colleague, Sanderson, will be unhappy if we let them go, but no, I don't see any reason to clutter up the jails with them. We have bigger problems on the horizon to concern us I'm afraid. Sweat them a while. If they don't tell us what they were up to with the two South Africans, cut them loose."

Mwambe snorted at the mention of Sanderson's name. Modise let it go.

"I will interrogate them with some hard words and then release them tomorrow with the strong insistence they leave the country at once. Perhaps they will have greater luck across the border in Zimbabwe with Uncle Bob, but I doubt it."

Modise nodded and considered how best to broach the business of the *Bratva's* appearance in the area. Mwambe shuffled some papers on his desk and held one up as if to read.

"We had a fire at the home of Rra Botlhokwa. It seems suspicious. Also, we cannot locate either him or any member of his family. Can you offer any suggestions as to this?"

"Suspicious? How so?"

"Besides the evidence of petrol which points to arson, his office was completely gutted including his filing cabinets. They should have been locked if he was away, but they were open and every piece of paper in the place was burned. Also, his computer had been disassembled and its hard drive removed."

"Someone wished him erased, it would seem."

"Precisely. And his man Noga has dropped out of sight as well. We think he left the country."

"Really? It is a thought or confirmed? Sanderson will want to know."

"A source at the border said he was seen passing through the crossing into Zimbabwe this morning. I am guessing he has relatives or at least friends there."

"Okay, that will have to do for now. I assume your source is generally reliable. Well, I do not know if this is connected or not, but there have been some serious developments in the last several days that could be related to all this."

Modise filled the superintendent in on the bugging at the hotels, the involvement of the intelligence community, and the threats made to Greshenko and Painter. He couldn't be sure just how much he ought to tell the superintendent, what would be his "need to know" level. He kept it simple and vague. He could fill in the details later if he needed to.

"What do you wish us to do?" Mwambe did not seem eager to be involved in international intrigue.

"For now, nothing. Leave it to us. The less you know the better. This is merely a heads-up because the American and his colleague may behave strangely for a while."

"You mean the Russian, Greshenko. What do we do about him?"

"We will keep a close eye on him. The future? Who knows? People with associations to criminal organizations are hard to trust no matter how they protest they have reformed. For now, we just watch and wait."

Mwambe nodded agreement. Whether he agreed with the plan or not, Modise could not say.

"As part of the surveillance and so on, there may be some clandestine meetings set up in the park which will require you and your constables to facilitate. Our concern is with the press which will be dogging the American Secretary of State during her visit. If our negotiations go well, she will meet with the North Koreans at a designated camp site in Savuti, or some similar venue. We cannot say for sure just now."

"This is all too deep for me, Modise. I am a policeman, not a secret agent."

"No need. If this comes to pass, you will only be asked to stall the press at the gate into the park. Check IDs or something until she is well away. The lady will presumably be on a safari drive. That's what they will say, but she will be headed elsewhere. The press must not follow. That is all."

"Fine, I can see to that. What is the serious thing you mentioned before, or was that it?"

"Ah. There has been an incident in Gaborone." Modise paused wondering how much detail Mwambe needed or could handle.

"This is about the unexploded bomb in the car park?"

Bad news travels fast. Modise should not have been surprised that Mwambe had heard of the bomb. Botswana may comprise an area as large as France, but its people remained close knit. Old tribal loyalties and social connections kept people better informed than the press.

"Yes. The rumor has it that it was ordered by your missing Botlhokwa because he wanted to punish the attorney general for an impending criminal indictment. The director general does not believe what they are saying. Something else, something bigger and nastier is coming at us, I am afraid. We are looking at the beginning moves by some very bad people."

Modise outlined the facts at hand that indicated the *Bratva* would be coming into the country and north to the Chobe.

"I knew that building a gambling casino up here was a bad idea," Mwambe said. Modise tended to agree. The temptation to convert this paradise into a little Las Vegas would be too hard to resist by operators who profited from human weakness and indulgence.

"I have never met your Botlhokwa. Have you a description of him I can see?"

"Yes certainly. You wish to look for him?"

"I cannot be sure, but I think I may have found him. I must check at Sanderson's newest tapes and inspect the park first. Then I will know."

# Chapter Fifty-one

"You see, Modise? There must be someone still in the park. The *bakkie* did not come out, only that broken down bush buggy."

"I see. And you are sure this truck did not exit the park later, say after it opened. It is very close to dawn when the car exits. Could not the truck have been doing something—"

"Doing what?"

"Perhaps more orgonite, who knows."

"It is a possibility, I guess." Sanderson looked chagrinned. Modise had punctured her balloon.

"Mind you, I think your theory is correct, but we must consider all of the alternatives. Okay, let us say it is not more orgonite." He twisted around in his chair and studied the cones on the table top beside him. "This is a sample of what you found out there?"

"Yes. It is scattered all over the park and in no identifiable pattern. It looks like those men just stopped here and there and dropped a few of these things off, and then moved on a few hundred meters in a different direction and did it again."

"We could make something of that or we can assume that the whole notion is silly, so why expect anything sensible to show up in distribution patterns or anything else?"

"We can't, I guess. Still, if I were in charge of the business, I would be thinking, 'how can I get the most effectiveness from my things,' you see?"

"I do. I wish I had time to dig into this further, but there are more urgent matters that must be addressed, I am afraid."

"There are other things I do not know about?"

Modise nodded and reran the tape. "I cannot be sure, but the markings on that truck look like the same ones on the truck driven by the man who was shot on the Nata road."

"It couldn't be a coincidence, could it?"

"Not likely. By the way, you can rest easier now. The man Noga, the one who threatened you, has fled the country. It is doubtful he will return anytime soon."

"That is a big relief. You're sure?" Modise smiled and nodded. "So what are we to make of this?"

"The only way to find out is to go and see for ourselves. Can you find the trail they made in the park?"

"It will be easier if we go into the park the way they did." Modise stood and gestured toward the door.

Sanderson picked up her equipment, including her rifle, and led him outside to her Land Rover.

It took only fifteen minutes more or less to reach the newer opening. Sanderson let Modise undo the straps holding the fence in place and redo them after she'd driven through. They drove carefully through the forested area of the park and then out into the relatively open area defined as bush country.

"We are looking for the truck first. Once we have found it, we will see if there is anything or anybody else to discover. Will you have difficulty following the trail?"

Sanderson shook her head. The SUV bounced over the dusty ground. Sanderson scanned ahead and to the sides. Then she accelerated a little.

"You see something?" Modise squinted at the ground ahead trying to make out what trail Sanderson followed. He couldn't see anything. No tire marks, no footprints, nothing.

"Look up," she said. "There." She pointed through the wind screen at the sky ahead of them. "*Manong*. They have come to feed. Your truck will be close by, I think."

Sure enough, Modise saw the vultures circling immediately ahead. Vultures meant death. That meant the man, or men, associated with the truck were somewhere up ahead and either dead or dying.

"Can we go faster?"

Sanderson stepped down hard on the gas pedal and the truck shot forward, lurched through a ditch and swerved over a stretch of loose sand. Modise's head smacked the overhead first, then the roof pillars.

"Not that fast."

Sanderson grinned and slowed. "Just there," she said, and pointed to a bush that stood as high as their vehicle. She wheeled around it and leaned on the car horn. It blared loud enough to scatter the hyenas that were tearing at the carcass on the ground. She pulled to a stop just short of the body. Modise started to step out.

"Wait," she said her tone sharp and insistent. She unsheathed her rifle, loaded it and unlatched her own door. "Now." She stepped out onto the ground. Modise followed suit. He patted the gun at his side. Might he need it? He hoped not. One shooting a day was more than enough.

Sanderson waved and shouted and the hyenas retreated still further. "It is one man only."

"So it seems. Who knows, we may find another later. That is very interesting."

"A dead man is interesting? You have strange interests, Modise. But then you are a policeman so that would explain it."

"It is interesting from an investigative point. He has no head. Well, almost no head."

"Yes, so? The hyenas have beat us to him."

"You miss my point. You are the animal expert. Would not they first tear into the soft parts? The head is a tough nut to crack. Sorry, bad joke—not intended."

"Yes, that is so."

"But they did not. The head is nearly gone. Now, if a man is first shot in his head with the right sort of bullet, it will create the sort of conditions that might make an attack on it by animals easy, yes?"

"Yes. So you think this man is shot first?"

"Yes. So it would seem."

Modise bent and scrutinized the corpse. "It is Rra Botlhokwa, I think."

Sanderson looked at what was left of the man—the hyenas had been both hungry and efficient. Not much remained of the recognizable portion of the man. "If you say so, but how can you tell from this mess?"

"Your hyenas do not like finger food, I think."

"What? No, I suppose daintiness is not something they are famous for. So what?"

"It was a pun, Sanderson, another bad joke. Look at the hands. They are intact. There is a ring on the left one. It is what they call a pinky ring. Apparently whoever brought Botlhokwa here did no believe removing it worth the trouble. Because your hyenas do not like finger food, the hands are still intact." He bent closer to inspect the ring, consulted a scrap of paper in his hand, and straightened up. "It is Botlhokwa's ring and it is fitting so snugly I must assume it is his hand and, therefore, the rest of this, such as it is, must also be the man himself."

"If he was as bad as they say, I will have a sick pack of hyenas this day." She turned and surveyed the area close by. The hyenas suddenly bolted away.

"Oh, oh. Modise, into the truck, now."

"Wait, I want to check this body and then—"

"Modise, get into the truck now!"

Modise looked up irritated. That was when he saw the lions. He couldn't recall how he got into the truck. Only that he had and had slammed the door closed and locked it before Sanderson had even moved. But then she knew about the animals.

"What do we do now?"

She put the truck in gear and drove over the body, being careful to straddle it. She braked when it lay directly beneath them. She stared for a moment at the pride of lions and reached for her radio.

"Now, we call for help."

# Chapter Fifty-two

Modise had lived his entire life in Botswana, but like many who grew up in tight communities in the south, this was as close to a pride of lions as he'd ever come. He watched as they shifted their positions. It was as if they were consulting one another. Which shall be the appetizer, which the entrée? Sanderson or Modise? He didn't see a male. Where was the boss? He twisted in his seat and glanced out the rear window. The hyenas had returned. They milled about waiting for the lions to make a move, he guessed. Sanderson chattered away on the radio.

"Sanderson, we have to do something."

"We are doing something. We are protecting this body until we can remove it. I have called my rangers and your police. I am not sure Superintendent Mwambe was so pleased to hear from me, though. He sounded more positive when I said you were here. So, help is on the way."

Two of the lions began a slow advance on the Land Rover. Sanderson tapped the horn button and they shied away.

"Won't that make them angry?"

"Probably, but if we do not keep them back, they will come here and try to pull that Botlhokwa out from under the truck. Then we are done."

"But we are parked over him. Isn't that enough? I thought the lions did not bother vehicles this big."

"They don't, as a rule, but most times there isn't any food for them underneath, either. Lions are almost always hungry,

Modise. We are keeping them from a meal." She tapped the horn again. The lions did not respond quite as quickly this time as they had before. "You are not afraid, are you?"

Modise shrugged. In fact, he was.

"Modise, you are so strange. You can stare at a man with a gun who shoots at you and nearly kills you but you sit here in this nice safe auto and are afraid of those animals?"

"Aren't you?"

"If they were shooting at me, I might be."

"What if they try to drag Botlhokwa out from under the car?"

"That would be too bad. This old Land Rover is high from the ground. They might push us over."

"They could do that?" Now he really was frightened.

"I have seen a large and very hungry pride of lions pull down a medium sized elephant. If they wanted to, they could."

As she spoke, the pride started to shuffle forward. Tapping the horn only deterred one smaller lion. Sanderson slid the hatch back on the roof, grabbed her rifle, and stood on the seat, her head and shoulders exposed.

"Are you going to shoot them?" Modise almost hoped she was.

"No, that would be silly." She squeezed off two shots. The lions wheeled and returned to their original spot. She slumped back in the seat. "Let us hope help comes soon."

"That seemed to work. The gun, I mean."

"Yes, but at a small price, I am thinking."

"Price? What price?"

"Those cats, they are not stupid, you know. They do not like the guns and will stay back, but they also saw the roof has a hole in it. If they decide to circle this vehicle they can get on top of the roof. Even with your help with that pop gun of yours, I can't shoot them all that fast."

Modise swallowed. "The roof hatch, it will hold, won't it?"

Sanderson bobbed her head from side to side. "I hope so. But they can be very strong and if they can slip their claws into the gap, well…Why did you ask me about leave time?"

"What? Leave time? Sanderson, we are under attack by a pack of—"

"Pride. It is called a pride."

"A pride of lions, then. By your own admission they could rip open the roof like a can of sardines and have us for dinner, and you want to discuss leave time? Why don't we just drive the hell out of here?"

"You would lose your body. If we leave now, there will be nothing left in an hour. What the lions don't eat, the hyenas will. How will you complete your investigation? You wish to know who killed this man. You need his body, I think. So we will wait for rescue. And you are the person who asks about leave time, remember?"

Modise turned and tried to read Sanderson's face. Was she having him on? A horn sounded off to one side. He looked up and saw two more Land Rovers bouncing over the rough terrain toward them. Sanderson spoke rapidly into the microphone.

"Modise, roll down your window and fold that rearview mirror back."

She already had her window down and the mirror on her side folded. He followed suit. He was sure the lions took note of his exposed arm. He rolled the window up and nearly snagged his sleeve in it. The two other vehicles pulled up on either side, their fenders nearly scraping.

"Now they cannot reach under and get our friend."

"Good. But neither can we."

"Patience, Modise." Sanderson rolled down her window again. "Hello, Charles. This is nice. Old Nathan has two new cubs, it seems."

Charles Tlalelo, sitting in the adjacent SUV waved a greeting to Modise. "Just two? I thought the driver from the Safari Lodge said he saw three."

"Who's Nathan?" Modise's head swam. How could these people be so calm?

"Nathan is the male who rules this pride. He must be snoozing somewhere."

The lions, who had been contemplating this new and more complex arrangement that prevented them from gaining the food they wanted, stood as one and edged back into the bush. To have another consultation, Modise imagined. The hyenas lingered. An ambulance and two police vehicles drove in. The lions had had enough, wheeled and strolled off. How far was anyone's guess. The hyenas gave up their vigil as well and trotted away. Sanderson directed the ambulance to back up until its rear bumper touched hers. Then she pulled forward. She stopped when her vehicle formed a rough cross with the other three. The body, now exposed in its center, but screened from the animals, could be collected. She was certain with so many vehicles moving in and the noise, neither the lions nor the hyenas posed a threat, but the police and the ambulance personnel would not know that. Better safe than sorry.

The attendants cautiously opened the rear doors of the ambulance. Pictures were taken and Botlhokwa, or what was left of him, deposited in the van. Doors slammed. The group caravanned out of the park and to on police headquarters.

"So, what is this about my leave time?"

# Chapter Fifty-three

It took the better part of two hours to sort out the events of the day. Sanderson listened, occasionally standing to refill their cups. Modise told her as much as he could about his urgent recall to the capital.

"That is why you asked about leave? You imagined I might follow you?"

"I only hoped." He drummed his fingers and fidgeted in his chair. "You see I am not very smooth in these matters, the asking and so on."

"Kgabo Modise, yes, you are very *not smooth*, you are sandpaper. You know I cannot leave a teenaged daughter and a dying son and flounce off to Gaborone with you. What would I be doing while you are out chasing international crooks? You should not even ask."

"I'm...you are right. It was out of line. For a moment when we spoke on the phone, I had this picture of us together and it...well, the complications did not appear in the picture, I guess you could say."

She smiled at him and laid her hand on his. "Modise, I will tell you this, if the complications did not exist, I would go to Gaborone with you, for sure."

Modise shifted in his chair and drained his cup. The tea had gone cold. "I do not know how long it will take to investigate the bombing attempt. It will be complex and involve other agencies probably...but I promise you this, I will be back here, and soon."

"You are so sure?"

"There are two big reasons I am guaranteed a return to the Chobe. That American's casino is a bright light that will surely attract all the crooked moths in the area. They will be flying here trying to take him over and perhaps the other lodges as well."

"And the second reason?"

"You are here, Sanderson. That is enough."

She felt the heat climb up her neck and on to her face. "What is that? I am just a woman past her time with children and holding down a job. That cannot be such a wonderful thing that the famous detective from Gaborone is coming to Kasane."

"No, you are right. This detective must be crazy. But he will come anyway."

Modise looked at his watch. He had just enough time to meet his flight. He would have to hurry. He grabbed his bags and headed to the door, then turned.

"What shall I call you? I do not find it so easy to use your Christian name."

"Call me the Lion Queen."

"No, that is appropriate, certainly, but...no."

"Then just call me Sanderson and I will call you Modise. And that will be the way it will be until there is significant change in our circumstances."

He waved and left.

"Mr. Painter, we found this with some other things." Painter's foreman stood in the office door holding an oblong object that had evidently seen some hard use.

"What is it?" He reached forward and took the item from the rough calloused hands of his worker and read the markings on its front, Garmin etrex H GPS. "It's a GPS tracking device, I think. Where did you find it?"

"That monkey took Sammi's keys and this time we chased it. Sammi cannot lose his keys, so he threw a stick at him and the monkey drops the keys. At the foot of this tree are many things the little thief has taken. This was one of them. What is that thing used for?'

"Hunters, fishermen, reporters and hikers, like that, use them to mark places they've been so they can find the spot again if they want to. Fishermen especially like to return to their special fishing holes."

"A person wishing to hide something might use this to find it later, yes?"

"Could be. Plot for a book I expect."

"Maybe it is a treasure map."

Leo tossed the device into a drawer and shoved it closed. "What're the chances?"

It had been two weeks since Modise returned to Gaborone. Sanderson had had a dozen calls from him already. So much attention.

She left Michael sitting up in a chair. His fever had subsided and he seemed stronger. Perhaps this pneumonia is finished. Perhaps the orgonite cone worked after all…no, it could not be. She was a modern woman…still, who can know what the Lord God is thinking. If He wants it to be this or that, it will be. She moved the cone closer to his chair.

She stopped at her office only long enough to be told that Superintendent Mwambe needed to speak to her urgently. The Land Rover backed into the area reserved for visitors and she walked into police headquarters. She'd been summoned. What did the Baboon want with her now?

Mwambe waited for her in his office. He did not get up when she entered. Typical. She sat, without waiting for an invitation. Two could play the game of rude behavior.

"Sanderson, sit. I have some news that I thought I should tell you personally." He leaned back in his chair, folded his hands across his stomach, but said nothing.

"And that would be?" Really this was so silly, this man-woman business Mwambe and his cohorts played.

"It is in the matter of the death of Rra Botlhokwa. The official report is here." He leaned forward and shoved a sheet of paper across the desk to her. She was to read it, it seemed. She lifted it from the surface and fished her reading glasses. They were missing one stem. She'd been meaning to find a new pair at the store but…she read.

"What is this? Superintendent Mwambe you are not seriously saying this. You have suicide on the brain. First it is the poor Congolese man is murdered and you say suicide, and now this?"

"Sanderson, it is the way the finding is being made. We—"

"It is foolishness. Botlhokwa was murdered."

"The report says—"

"It says nothing that makes sense. What sort of man is it who decides to kill himself, then drives into the park in his pajamas and lets the predators eat him?"

"He shot himself in the head. The animals were secondary."

"He shoots? This again? Where is your gun for this shooting, Superintendent?"

"The report will read that he did this. There will be no mention of a gun. It is implied, you see."

"No one will believe this. It is nonsense."

"Everyone will believe this and you will be the one to make sure they do."

"I? I will spread this rubbish about? I do not think so. I am a game ranger and I tell you, Superintendent, the evidence is clear. There were two vehicles entering the park that night, only one comes out. The body was only partially devoured. That means it is lying out there for some time before the animals found it. That means our Botlhokwa was deposited in the park dead or nearly so by someone else. That is the truth. Suicide!"

"Mma Michael, we have our differences. I doubt we will ever sort them out. Personally, I don't have any great desire to do so, but, and this is important, understand please this version of the events in the Chobe Game Park comes from the highest level, not me. For the purposes of future investigations and other circumstances about which your friend Modise has recently spoken to you, I believe, you will report this to any who ask, as a tragic suicide of one of Kasane's leading citizens. You do understand those particular circumstances?"

"The Russian gangsters, you mean?" Sanderson let that sink in. "Modise says this?"

"He does. The director of the DIS does as well, you see?"

"Then it must be so."

# Chapter Fifty-four

Andrew Takeda had to be the luckiest man alive. He appeared at his arraignment certain he would spend an important part of his life behind bars. He'd been fired from his position as game ranger, but that had been expected. But this?

He'd immediately recognized the magistrate assigned to his hearing and within an hour he had been sentenced to a year in jail, but to be released daily to perform an unspecified amount of public service. Specifically, he was to spend whatever time it took to locate the orgonite presumably dumped in the park, and under the supervision of Superintendant Mwambe of the Police Department, deal with it in an appropriate manner.

Sanderson was appalled.

Early morning mist lifted from the forest floor. Sunlight streamed through the canopy and the morning songs and sounds eased aside the night stillness. *Patriarche* moved cautiously down the hillside toward his former feeding grounds. He passed the body of the man whom he had hit with his stick. He paused and stared, curious, at the crumpled body. The forest creatures had already found it and begun the recycling nature requires of all that it creates. He huffed for his group to follow and moved down to the area where the men had started digging. The men were gone. Nothing remained of their recent presence but some tents that were already beginning to sag from their guy ropes, and a pile of miscellaneous items including the remains of two of *Patriarche's* group and a dying infant left in its cage.

The sound of an approaching vehicle caused the troop to scatter back into the forest. They watched in silence as the truck pulled off the track and into the trees. The man driving stepped out and scanned the sky, then pulled some branches out of the nearby underbrush and covered the back of the truck.

Noga had used some of Botlhokwa's Euros to move through Zambia to Rwanda and thence, southward to this spot. He knew there would be coltan but not exactly where. That Englishman, Jack, talked too much for his own good. The Congolese general, it seemed, had been killed by gorillas. That story sounded like nonsense to him. None of the late warlord's soldiers would admit to knowing anything. They would mutter *Meurtrières gorilles* and turn away whether in shame or fear, he could not say. Finally he approached a fighter, a young man, old beyond his years, and for a few American cigarettes and dollars, received the approximate location of the mine. Now, it was his. He would need some help from locals to exploit it and finding some he could trust would not be easy, but he now stood at the entrance of the mine staring at more wealth than he'd ever imagined. He would clean up the site. He would make it disappear. He did not want anyone else to stumble on his find before he could start it up again.

He spent the next three hours removing all the evidence of there ever having been an encampment. He covered the mine adit with branches. If anyone did a fly-over, he'd see nothing. All this he did under the curious gaze of some dozen pairs of sad brown eyes.

The troop had remained remarkably quiet while the man moved about the camp site. Each time he pulled down a tent and shoved its tattered remnants out of sight in the underbrush, the gorillas nearby drifted back, only to shuffle back to their vantage point when he retreated. Nothing more would have happened were it not for what he did next. Gorillas may be gentle and pacific but their memory, while no match for that of humans, still functions at a very high level, and the earlier attack on them by this thing's troop remained fresh in their minds. So, when the man approached the cage holding the infant and kicked it, *Patriarche* reacted.

He huffed to his troop. And then, moving with remarkable speed, he closed the distance between him and the human. He did not have his stick. He didn't need it. It was not a weapon. His bulk slammed into the man and knocked him flat. Before he could respond, *Patriarche* did what he would have done to any challenger. He leapt up and landed heavy footed on the man's chest. This he repeated several times. Then, certain of his victory, he stood on his vanquished enemy and pounded his chest. The troop joined him.

*Patriarche* surveyed the area. The infant, head lolling to one side, looked out of his cage toward him with crusted eyes. *Patriarche* banged his large fist on the top of the cage. The infant only blinked at the noise and violent shaking. Finally, the top caved in and the old gorilla gently lifted the baby out. He was dead before another female could be found to adopt him.

*Patriarche* signaled for the troop to gather and together they pushed, shoved, and carried all the detritus, the remains of their relatives to the mouth of the mine and let them fall into its depths. They dragged the man to the mine opening and shoved him in as well. They paused. *Patriarch* bellowed and pounded his chest, the others followed suit. Then they turned and melted into the trees and brush. Almost as an afterthought, *Partiarche* stepped back to the mine and returned the branches that the man had used to cover the entrance. He blinked at the foliage, turned his gaze to survey the area. Within days the jungle would have swallowed up any remaining evidence it had ever existed. They would be safe enough for the time being, but as long as someone knew about the coltan and the mine, it could not last.

The men would return.

# Glossary

Setswana is a Bantu language, as is Zulu and many other dialects spoken in sub-Saharan Africa.

The stem is Tswana
+ Ba…the people of. . .(Batswana)
+ Bo…the country of…(Botswana)
+ Mo…a person of…(Motswana)
+ Se…the language of…(Setswana)

## Some Phrases and Words that Appear Variously in the Text:

*Bakkie* = Afrikaans' word for pickup truck

*Bas* = boss

*Botlhokwa* = important, big

*Cohiba* = a fine cigar from Cuba. Highly appreciated by those who smoke them.

Crazy Bob = a disrespectful appellation for Robert Mugabe of Zimbabwe. More commonly referred to as "Uncle Bob" in the same context.

DIS = Directorate of Intelligence and Security

*Ditshukudu…dinaka* = Rhino horns

*Dipheri* = hyenas

*Dumela*…hello + *Mma, Rra* = ma'am, sir

*Fausse minéraux* = French, fake minerals, look alike for coltan

Gabz = a contraction for Gabarone. Whereas Gabarone is pronounced with the G as a guttural ch, as in *loch*, the contraction has a hard G.

H. E. = abbreviation for His Excellency as in: H. E., the President

DG = abbreviation for Director General

*Kaffir* = when applied to black people in southern Africa it is the derogatory equivalent of nigger

*Kak* = South Africa slang, crap

*Ke teng* = I am well

*Kgabo* = monkey

*Kgobela* = heap

*Kgopa* = snail

*Le kae* = *how are you?*

*Manong* = vultures

*Matlhakala* = trash

*Mma* = Mrs., a title of respect for a woman

*Modisa* =escort, herder

*Makoro*= dugout canoe

*Moloi* = witch doctor

*Motsholela* = manure

*Motsheganong* = May

NGO = Non Government Organization (usually a non-profit)

*No mathata* = no problem, no worries

*Noga* = snake

*Ntle* = beautiful, fair, pretty

Panel beaters = auto body shop

*Pectopah* = restaurant spelled with Russian characters looks like this to a non Russian.

*Phane* = fried or cooked caterpillars, considered a delicacy

*Pula* (literally, rain) = the currency of Botswana and *Thebe* = (shield) coins.

*Rondeval* = a circular house fashioned from mud bricks with a thatch roof, traditional dwelling of the Tswana

*Rapolasa* = farmer

*Reseturente* = restaurant

*Rra* (pronounced rah) = Mr. or sir (with respect)

*Rooineck* = Afrikaner derogatory term for an English speaking South African. Literally, redneck

*Taolo* = commandment

*Tlalelo* = trouble

*Tshwene* = baboon

## Some Other Notes:

People are often called by the names of their first born with the appropriate title, i.e., Mma Julie or Rra Robert.

The following has been lifted from Botswana's official web site:

> *The Republic of Botswana is situated in Southern Africa, nestled between South Africa, Namibia, Zimbabwe and Zambia.*

*The country is democratically ruled, boasts a growing economy and a stable political environment.*

*Botswana has some of Africa's last great wildernesses including the famous Okavango Swamps and the Kalahari Desert.*

*Botswana is the largest exporter of gemstone diamonds in the world as well as a large beef exporter to the European Union.*

People have asked about the likelihood of a gorilla attack on humans as they are generally viewed as peaceful and non aggressive. I refer them to: http://news.mongabay.com/2007/1205-gorillas.html

To receive a free catalog of Poisoned Pen Press titles, please contact us in one of the following ways:

Phone: 1-800-421-3976
Facsimile: 1-480-949-1707
Email: info@poisonedpenpress.com
Website: www.poisonedpenpress.com

Poisoned Pen Press
6962 E. First Ave. Ste. 103
Scottsdale, AZ 85251